Shadow Mountain

Center Point
Large Print

Also by Dane Coolidge and available from Center Point Large Print:

The Desert Trail
The Fighting Fool
Jess Roundtree, Texas Ranger

Shadow Mountain

DANE COOLIDGE

CENTER POINT LARGE PRINT
THORNDIKE, MAINE

This Center Point Large Print edition
is published in the year 2024 by arrangement with
Golden West Inc.

Copyright © 1919 by W. J. Watt & Company.

All rights reserved.

First US edition: Doubleday and Company, Inc.

The text of this Large Print edition is unabridged.
In other aspects, this book may vary
from the original edition.
Printed in the United States of America
on permanent paper sourced using
environmentally responsible foresting methods.
Set in 16-point Times New Roman type.

ISBN: 979-8-89164-369-7

The Library of Congress has cataloged this record
under Library of Congress Control Number: 2024943155

CHAPTER I

THE LAST OF TEN THOUSAND

Under the rim of Shadow Mountain, embraced like a pearl of great price by the curve of Bonanza Point and the mined-out slope of Gold Hill, the deserted city of Keno lay brooding and silent in the sun. A dry, gusty wind, swooping down through the northern pass, slammed the great iron fire-doors that hung creaking from the stone bank building, caught up a cloud of sand and dirt and, whirling it down past empty stores and assay offices, deposited it in the doorways of gambling houses and dance halls, long since abandoned to the rats. An old man, pottering about among the ruins, gathered up some broken boards and hobbled off; and once more Keno, the greatest gold camp the West has ever seen, sank back to silence and dreams.

A round of shots wakened the echoes of Shadow Mountain; a lonely miner came down the trail from Gold Hill, where in the old days the Paymaster had turned out its million a month; and then, far out across the floor of the desert on the road that led in from the railroad, there appeared an arrow-point of dust. It grew to a racing streak of white, the distant purring of the motor gave way to a deep-voiced thunder and as the powerful car glided swiftly up the street the doors of old houses opened unexpectedly and the last of ten thousand looked out.

There were old men and cripples, left stranded by the exodus; and prospectors who had moved into the vacant houses along with the other desert rats; but out on the gallery of the old Huff mansion—where the creepers still clung to the lattice—there was a flutter of white and a girl came out with a kitten in her arms. In the days of gold—when ten thousand men, the choice spirits of two hemispheres, had tramped down this same deserted street—the house of Colonel Huff, the discoverer of the Paymaster, had been the social center of Keno. And so it was still, for the Widow Huff remained; but across the front of the hospitable gallery where the Colonel had entertained the town, a cheap cloth sign announced meals fifty cents and Virginia, his daughter, was the waiter. She stood by the sign, still high-headed and patrician, and when the driver of the car saw her he came to a sudden stop. He was long and gaunt, with deep lines around his mouth from bucking the wind and dust and after a moment's hesitation he threw on his brake and leapt out.

"Did you want something?" she asked and, glancing warily about, he nodded and came up the steps.

"Yes," he said, still eying her doubtfully, "what's the chance for something to eat?"

"Why, good," she answered with a suspicion of a smile. "Or—well, come in; I'll speak to Mother."

She showed him into the spacious dining room, where the Colonel had once presided in state, and hurried into the kitchen. The young man gazed after her, looked swiftly about the room and backed away towards the door; then his strong jaw closed down, he smiled grimly to himself and sat down unbidden at a table. The table was mahogany and, in a case against the wall, there was a scant display of cut glass; but the linen was worn thin and the expensive velvet carpet had been ruined by hob-nailed boots. Heavy workingmen's dishes lay on the tables, the plating was worn from the knives, and the last echoing ghost of vanished gentility was dispelled by a voice from the kitchen. It was the Widow Huff, once the first lady of Keno, but now a boarding-house cook.

"What—a dinner now? At half-past three? And with this wind fairly driving me crazy? Well, I can't *hire* anybody to keep such hours for *me* and—"

There was a murmur of low-voiced protest as Virginia pleaded his cause and then, as the Widow burst out anew, the young man pushed back his chair. His blue eyes, half hidden beneath bulging brows, turned a steely, fighting gray, his wind-blown hair fairly bristled; and as he listened to the last of the Widow's remarks his lower lip was thrust up scornfully.

"You danged old heifer," he muttered and then the kitchen door flew open. The baleful look which he had intended for the Widow was surprised on his face by Virginia and after a startled moment she closed the door behind her.

"Why—Wiley Holman!" she cried accusingly and a challenge leapt into his eyes.

"Well?" he demanded and gazed at her sullenly as she scanned him from head to foot.

"I knew it," she burst out. "I'd know that stubborn look anywhere! You double up your lip like your father. Honest John!" she added sarcastically and brushed some crumbs from the table.

"Yes—Honest John!" he retorted. "And you don't need to say it like that, either. He's my father—I know him—and I'll tell you right now he never cheated a man in his life."

"Well, he did!" she flared back, her eyes dark with anger, "and I'll bet—I'll bet if my father was here he'd—he'd prove it to your face!"

She ended in a sob and as he saw the tears starting the son of Honest John relented.

"Aw, Virginia," he pleaded, "what's the use of always fighting? He's gone now, so let's be friends. I was just going by when I saw you on

8

the gallery, and I thought—well, let's you and I be friends."

"What? After old Honest John robbed Papa of the Paymaster, and then hounded him to his death on the desert?"

"He did nothing of the kind—he never robbed anybody! And as for hounding your father to his death, the Old Man never even knew about it. He was down on the ranch, and when they told him the news—"

"Yes, that's you," she railed, stifling back her sobs, "you can always prove an alibi. But you'd better drift, Mr. Holman; because if Mother knows you're here—"

"Well, what?" he demanded, truculently.

"She'll fill you full of buckshot."

"Pah!" he scoffed and snapped his fingers in the air, after which he lapsed into silence.

"Well, she will," she asserted, after waiting for him to speak, but Wiley only grunted.

"Wait till I get that dinner," he said at last and slumped down into a chair. He muttered to himself, gazing dubiously towards the kitchen, and turned impatiently to look at some specimens in a case against the wall. They were the usual chunks of high-grade gold ore, but he examined one piece with great care.

"Where'd you get this?" he asked, holding up a piece of white rock, and she sighed and brushed away her tears.

"Over on the dump," she answered wearily. "That's all Paymaster ore. Don't you think you'd better go?"

"Never ran away yet," he answered briefly and balanced the rock in his hand. "Pretty heavy," he observed, "I'll bet it would assay. Have you got very much on the dump?"

"What—*that?*" she cried, snatching the specimen away from him and bursting into a nervous laugh. "That assay? Well, you are a greenie—it's nothing but barren white quartz!"

"Oh, it is, eh?" he rejoined and gazed at her hectoringly. "You seem to know a whole lot about mineral."

"Yes, I do," she boasted. "Death Valley Charley teaches me. I've learned how to pan, and everything. But that rock there—that's the barren quartz that the Paymaster ran into when the values went out of the ore. Old Charley knows all about it."

"Yes, they all do," he observed and as his lip went up her eyes dilated suddenly in a panic.

"Oh, you went to that school—I forgot all about it—where they study about the mines! Are you in the mining business now?"

"Why, yes," he acknowledged, "but that doesn't make much difference. I find I can learn something from most everybody."

"Well, of course, then," she stammered, "I shouldn't have said that; but the whole Paymaster dump is covered with that heavy quartz, and everybody knows it's barren. Are you just looking around or—"

She hesitated politely and as he reached for another specimen she noticed a ring on his finger. It was of massive gold and, set in clutching claws, there were three stupendous diamonds. Not imitation stones nor small, off-colored diamonds, but brilliants of the very first water, clear as dew, yet holding in their hearts the faintest suggestion of blue.

"Oh!" she gasped, and as he did not seem to notice, she drew her skirts away with a flourish. "I'm surprised," she mocked, "that you condescend to speak to us—of course you own your own mines!"

"Nope," he replied, shrugging his shoulders at her sarcasm, "I'm nothing but a prospector, yet. And you don't need to be so surprised."

"No!" she retorted, giving way to swift resentment. "I guess I don't—when you consider how you got your money. Here's Mother out cooking for you, and I'm the waiter; and you're traveling around in racing cars with thousand-dollar rings on your hands. But if old Honest John hadn't sold all his stock while he was advising my father to hold on—"

"He did not!"

"Yes, he did! He did, too! And now, after Father has been lost in Death Valley, and we have come down to this, your father writes over and offers to buy our stock for just the same as nothing. That's *my* ring you're wearing, and the money that paid for it—"

"Oh, all right then," he sneered, stripping off the ring and handing it abruptly over to her, "if it's your ring, take it! But don't you say my father—"

"Well, he did," she declared, "and you can keep your old ring! It won't bring back my father—now!"

"No, it won't," he agreed, "but while we're about it I just want to tell you something. My father went broke, buying back Paymaster stock from friends he'd advised to go in—and he's got the stock to prove it—and when he heard that the Colonel was dead he decided to buy in your mother's. He mortgaged his cows to raise the money for her and then that old terror—I don't care if she is your mother—she slapped him in the face by refusing it. Well, he didn't like to say anything, but you can tell her from me she don't have to cook unless she wants to! She can sell—or buy—a hundred thousand shares of Paymaster any day she says the word; and if that isn't honest I don't know what is! I ask you, now; isn't that fair?"

"What, at ten cents a share? When it used to sell for forty dollars! He's just trying to get control of the mine. And as for offering to buy or sell, that's perfectly ludicrous, because he knows we haven't any money!"

"Well, what *do* you want?" he demanded irritably, and then he thrust up his lip. "I know," he said, "you want your own way! All right, I'll never trouble you again. You can keep right on guarding that hole-in-the-ground until you dry up and blow away across the desert. And as for that old she-devil—"

He paused at a sudden slam from the kitchen, and Virginia's eyes grew big; but as he rose to face the Widow Huff he slipped the white rock into his pocket.

CHAPTER II
THE SHOTGUN WIDOW

The Widow Huff was burdened with a tray and her eye sought wildly for Virginia but when she glimpsed Wiley moving swiftly towards the door she set down his dinner with a bang. The disrespectful epithet which he had applied to her had been lost in the clatter of plates, but the moment the Widow came into the room she sensed the hair-trigger atmosphere.

"Here!" she ordered, taking command on the instant. "Come back here, young man, and pay me for this dinner! And Virginia Huff, you go out into the kitchen—how many times do I have to speak to you?"

Virginia started and stopped, her resentful eyes on Wiley, a thin smile parting her lips.

"He said—" she began, and then Wiley strode back and slapped down a dollar on the table.

"Yes, and I meant it, too," he answered fiercely. "There's your pay—and you can keep your mine."

"Why, certainly," responded the Widow without knowing what she was talking about, "and now you eat that dinner!"

She pointed a finger to the tray of food and looked Wiley Holman in the eye. He wavered, gazing from her to the smiling Virginia, and then he drew up his chair.

"I'll go you," he said and showed his teeth in a grin. "You can't hurt my feelings that way."

He lifted the T-bone steak from the platter and transferred it swiftly to his plate and then, as he fell to eating ravenously, the Widow condescended to smile.

"When I go to the trouble of cooking a man a steak," she announced with the suggestion of a swagger, "I expect him to stay and eat it."

"All right," mumbled Wiley, and glancing fleeringly at Virginia, he went ahead with his meal.

The Widow looked over her shoulder at her daughter and then back at the stranger, but as she was about to inquire into the cause of their quarrel she spied his diamond ring. She approached him closer under pretext of pouring out some water and then she sank down into a chair.

"That is a very fine ring," she stated briefly. "Worth fifteen hundred dollars at the least. Haven't I seen you somewhere, before?"

"Very likely," returned Wiley, not venturing to look up, "my business takes me everywhere."

"I thought I recognized you," went on the Widow ingratiatingly; "you're a mining man, aren't you, Mister—er—"

"Wiley," he answered, and at this bold piece of effrontery Virginia caught her breath.

"Ah, yes, I remember you now," said the Widow. "You knew my husband, of course—Colonel Huff? He passed away on the twentieth of July; but there was a time, not so many years ago, that I wore a few diamonds myself." She fixed her restless eyes on his ring and heaved a discontented sigh. "Virginia," she directed, "run out into the kitchen and clean up that skillet and all. I declare, you do less and less every day—are you a married man, Mr. Wiley?"

Without awaiting the answer to this portentous question, Virginia flung out into the kitchen and, left alone, the Widow drew nearer and her manner became suddenly confidential.

"I'd like to talk with you," she began, "about my husband's mine. Of course you've heard of the famous Paymaster—that's the mill right over east of town—but there are very few men that know what I do about the reasons why that mine was shut down. It was commonly reported that Colonel Huff was trying to get possession of the property, but the truth of the matter is he was deceived by old John Holman and finally left holding the sack. You see, it was this way. My husband and John Holman had always been lifelong friends, but Colonel Huff was naturally generous while Holman thought of nothing but money. Well, my husband discovered the Paymaster—he was led to it by an Indian that he had saved from being killed by the soldiers—but, not having any money, he went to John Holman and they developed the mine together. It turned out very rich and such a rush you never saw—this valley was full of tents for miles—but it was so far from the railroad—seventy-four miles to Vegas—that the work was very expensive. The Company was reorganized and Mr. Blount, the banker, was given a third of the promotion stock. Then the five hundred thousand shares of treasury stock was put on the market in order to build the new mill; and when the railroad came in there was such a crazy speculation that everybody lost track of the transfers. My husband, of course, was generous to a fault and accustomed to living like a gentleman—and he invested very heavily in real estate, too—but this Mr. Blount was always out for his interest and Honest John would skin a dead flea."

"Honest John!" challenged Wiley, looking up from his eating with an ugly glint in his eye, but the Widow was far away.

"Yes, Honest John Holman," she sneered, without noticing his resentment. "They called him Honest John. Did you ever know one of these 'Honest John' fellows yet that wasn't a thorough-paced scoundrel? Well, old John Holman he threw in with Blount to deprive Colonel Huff of his profits and, with these street certificates everywhere and no one recording their transfers, the Colonel was naturally deceived into thinking that the selling was from the outside. But all the time, while they were selling their stock and hammering down the price of Paymaster, they were telling the Colonel that it was only temporary and he ought to support the market. So he bought in what he could, though it wasn't much, as he was interested in other properties, and then when the crash came he was left without anything and Blount and Holman were rich. The great panic came on and Blount foreclosed on everything, and then Mr. Huff fell out with John Holman and they closed the Paymaster down. That was ten years ago and, with the litigation and all, the stock went down to nothing. The whole camp went dead and all the folks moved away—but have you ever been through the mine? Well, I want you to go—that ground has hardly been scratched!"

Wiley Holman glanced up doubtfully from under his heavy eyebrows and the Widow became voluble in her protests.

"No, sir," she exclaimed, "I certainly ought to know, because the Colonel was Superintendent; and when he had been drinking—the town was awful, that way—he would tell me all about the mine. And that was his phrase—he used it always: 'That ground has hardly been scratched!' But when he fell out with old John Holman he—well, there was an explosion underground and the glory-hole stope caved in. They cleaned it out afterwards and hunted around, but all the rich ore was gone; but I'm just as certain as I'm sitting here this minute the Colonel knew where there was more! He never would admit it—he was peculiar, that way, he never would discuss his business before a woman. But he wouldn't deny it, and when he had been drinking—well, I know it's there, that's all!"

She paused for her effect but Mr. Wiley, the mining man, was singularly unimpressed. He continued eating in moody silence and the Widow tried the question direct.

"Well, what do you think about it?" she demanded bluffly. "Would you like to consider the property?"

"No, I don't think so," he answered impersonally. "I'm on my way up north."

"Well, when you come back, then. Since my husband is gone I'm so sick and tired of it all I'll consider any offer—for cash."

"Nope," he responded, "I'm out for something different." Then to stem the tide of her impending protest, he broke his studious silence. "I'm looking for molybdenum," he went on quickly, "and some of these other rare metals that are in demand on account of the war. Ever find any vanadium or manganese around here? No, I guess they're all further north."

He returned to his meal and the Widow surveyed him appraisingly with her bold, inquisitive eyes.

She was a big, strapping woman, and handsome in a way; but the corners of her mouth were drawn down sharply in a sulky, lawless pout.

"Aw, tell me the truth," she burst out at last. "What have you got against the property?"

A somber glow came into his eyes as he opened his lips to speak, and then he veiled his smouldering hate behind a crafty smile.

"The parties that I represent," he said deliberately, "are looking for a *mine*. But the man that puts his money into the Paymaster property is simply buying a lawsuit."

"What do you mean?" demanded the Widow, rousing up indignantly in response to this sudden thrust.

"I mean, no matter how rich the Paymaster may be—and I hear the whole district is worked out—I wouldn't even go up the hill to look at it until you showed me the title was good."

The Widow sat and glowered as she meditated a fitting response and then she rose to her feet.

"Well, all right, then," she sulked, "if you don't want to consider it—but you're missing the chance of your life."

"Very likely," he muttered and reached for his hat. "Much obliged for cooking my dinner."

He started for the door, but she flew swiftly after him and snatched him back into the room.

"Now here!" she cried, "I want you to listen to me—I've got tired of this everlasting waiting. I waited around for ten years on the Colonel, to settle this matter up, and now that he's gone I'm going to settle it myself and get out of the cussed country. Maybe I don't own the mine, but I own a good part of it—I've got two hundred thousand shares of stock—and I could sell it tomorrow for twenty thousand dollars, so you don't need to turn up your nose. There must be something there after all these years, to bring an offer of ten cents a share; but I wouldn't take that money if it was the last act of my life—I just hate that Honest John Holman! He cheated my husband out of everything he had—and yet he did it in such a deceitful way that the Colonel would never believe it. I've called him a coward a thousand times for tolerating such an outrage for an instant, and now that he's gone I'm going to show Honest John that he can't put it over *me!*"

She shook her head until her heavy black hair flew out like Medusa's locks and then Wiley laughed provokingly.

"All right," he said, "but you can't rope me in on your feuds. If you want to give me an option on your stock in the company for five or ten cents a share I may take a look at your mine. But I'll tell you one thing—you'll sign an agreement first to leave the country and never come back. I'm a business man, working for business people, and these shotgun methods don't go."

"Well, I'll do it!" exclaimed the Widow, passing

by his numerous insults in a sudden mad grab at release. "Just draw up your paper and I'll sign it in a minute—but I want ten cents a share!"

"Ten cents or ten dollars—it makes no difference to me. You can put it as high as you like—but if it's too high, my principals won't take it. I can't stop to inspect it now, because I'm due up north, but I'll tell you what I'll do. You give me an option on all your stock, with a written permission to take possession, and if the other two big owners will do as much I'll come back and consider the mine. But get this straight—the first time you butt in, this option and agreement is off!"

"What do you mean—butt in?" demanded the Widow truculently, and then she bit her lip. "Well, never mind," she said, "just draw up your papers. I'll show you I'm business myself."

"Huh!" he grunted and, whipping out a fountain pen, he sat down and wrote rapidly at a table. "There," he said tearing the leaf from his notebook and putting it into her hands, "just read that over and if you want to sign it we'll close the deal, right here."

The Widow took the paper and, turning it to the light, began a labored perusal.

"Memorandum of agreement," she muttered, squinting her eyes at his handwriting, "hmm, I'll have to go and get my glasses. 'For and in consideration of the sum of ten dollars—to me in hand paid by M. R. Wiley,' and so forth—oh well, I guess it's all right, just show me where to sign."

"No," he said, "let me read it to you—you ought to know what you're signing."

"No, just show me where to sign," protested the Widow petulantly, "and where it says ten cents a share."

"Well, it says that here," answered Wiley, putting his finger on the place, "but I'm going to read it to you—it wouldn't be legal otherwise."

He wiped the beaded sweat from his brow and glanced towards the kitchen door. In this desperate game which he was framing on the Widow the luck had all come his way, but as he cleared his throat and commenced to read Virginia came bounding in. She was carrying a kitten, but when she saw the paper between them she dropped it on the floor.

"Virginia!" cried her mother, "go and hunt my glasses. They're somewhere in my bedroom."

"All right," she responded, but when she came back she glanced inquiringly at the paper.

"You can go now," announced the Widow, adjusting her glasses, but Virginia threw up her head.

"Do you know who that is?" she demanded brusquely, pointing an accusing finger at Wiley.

"Why—er—no," returned the Widow, now absorbed in the agreement.

"Well, all right," she said after a hasty perusal, "but where's that sum of ten dollars? Now you hush, Virginia, and go—into—the—*kitchen!* Now, it says right here—oh, where is that place? Oh yes, 'the receipt whereof is hereby acknowledged'! *Virginia!*"

She stamped her foot, but Virginia's blood was up and she made a grab at the paper.

"Now, *listen!*" she screamed, stopping her mother in her rush. "That man there is Wiley Holman! Yes—Holman! Old Honest John's son! What's this you're going to sign?"

She backed away, her eyes fixed on the agreement, while the Widow stood astounded.

"Wiley *Holman!*" she shrieked, "why, you limb of Satan, you said your name was Wiley!"

"It is," returned Wiley with one eye on the door, "the rest of my name is Holman."

"But you signed it on this paper—you wrote it right there! Oh, I'll have the law on you for this!"

She clutched at the paper and as Virginia gave it to her mother she turned an accusing glance upon Wiley.

"Yes, that's just like you, Mr. M. R. Wiley," she observed with scathing sarcasm. "You were just that way when you were a kid here in Keno—always trying to get the advantage of somebody. But if I'd thought you had the nerve—" She glanced at the paper and gasped and Wiley showed his teeth in a grin.

"Well, she crowded me to it," he answered with a swagger. "I'm strictly business—I'll sign up anybody. You can just keep that paper," he nodded to the Widow, "and send it to me by mail."

He winked at Virginia and slipped swiftly out the door as the Widow made a rush for her gun. She came out after him, brandishing a double-barreled shotgun, just as he cranked up his machine to start.

"I'll show you!" she yelled, jerking her gun to her shoulder. "I'll learn you to get funny with *me!*"

She pulled the trigger, but Wiley was watching her and he ducked down behind the radiator.

Clank, went the hammer and with a wail of rage the Widow snapped the other barrel.

"You, Virginia!" she cried in a terrible voice, "have you been monkeying with my shotgun?"

The answer was lost in a series of explosions that awoke every echo in Keno, and Wiley Holman leapt into his machine. He jerked off his brake and stepped on the foot throttle but as he roared off up the street he waved a grimy hand at Virginia.

CHAPTER III
THE SHADOW

The old, settled quiet returned to sleepy Keno—the quiet of the desert and of empty, noiseless houses stretching in long, sunburned rows down the canyon. The black lava patch, laid across the gray rhyolite flank of Shadow Mountain like the shade of an angry cloud, still frowned down upon the town like a portent of storms to come. But the sky was hot and gleaming and no storms came; nor did Wiley Holman return, though the Widow waited for him patiently. After all his boldness, his unbelievable effrontery in trying to steal her Paymaster stock, he had gone on laughing to seek other adventures and left her with the mine on her hands. But he would come back, she knew it; and with her gun loaded with buckshot she watched from the shelter of the gallery.

Yet the days went by and then the weeks and at last the Widow, with a sigh of vexation, put up her gun and retired within. Now that the episode was over she felt vaguely regretful that he had failed, after all, in his purpose. If he had procured his option, under cover of her blindness, and obtained her quit-claim to the mine, she would at least have had the satisfaction of obtaining her own terms—and she would have the twenty thousand to spend. It was maddening, disgusting, when she thought it over, that he had turned out to be Holman's son, and she never quite forgave Virginia for dinning the fact into her ears. For what you don't know will never hurt you, and she had lost her last chance to sell. When she went back into the house she went back into the kitchen, and there she would have to stay. Either that or take Honest John's money.

But he wanted the property—the Widow knew it—else why had he sent his son? All the wise-acres in Keno agreed with the Widow that Honest John had designs on her property and Death Valley Charley, who had jumped half the claims in the district, began once more to carry his gun. It was by virtue of that, more than of assessment work done or of any other legal right, that Charley held title to his claims; and until Wiley had come through town and attempted to bond the Paymaster he had feared no one but Stiff Neck George. Stiff Neck George had been Blount's gunman on the momentous occasion when they had tried to jump the Paymaster— and the Widow Huff had put him to flight with one blast from her trusty shotgun. But now that big interests were sending in their experts and mining was picking up everywhere Stiff Neck George might forget that humiliating defeat, so Death Valley Charley put on his six-shooter.

He was a little, stooping man, burned chocolate

brown by the sun and with eyes half blinded by the glare, and as the Widow gave up her fruitless vigil, Death Valley Charley took her place. But he was not alone, for through all the weary weeks Virginia had been watching her mother. She had slipped in and out, now lingering on the gallery, now listening through the doorway, expectant but at the same time afraid. She knew Wiley Holman much better than her mother, and she knew that he would come back. He was patient, that was all, more patient than an Indian, and he had his eye on their mine. For ten years and more Colonel Huff, and now the Widow, had held physical possession of the Paymaster. Every great iron-bound door was locked and padlocked and the Huff family held the keys, but in all those ten years Holman had never come near it and Blount had merely seized it on a labor lien. The very title to the mine was shrouded in mystery, for no one could locate the shares, and to openly lay claim to it and produce a majority of the stock would be equivalent to a confession of treachery. All that anyone knew surely was that some one of the three original owners—or some unsuspected party outside—had bought in and sequestered the almost valueless stock and was patiently biding his time. Since the Huffs did not own the stock themselves they knew for a certainty that it was held by either Holman or Blount.

As Virginia sat on the gallery, listening subconsciously for the drumming of Wiley's racing motor up the road, she ran over in her mind the circumstances of his visit; and she could explain them all but one. Why, after failing of his mission, and narrowly escaping her mother's gun, had he waved his hand and smiled so gayly as he thundered away up the street? Had he other schemes more subtle; or was he simply reckless, regarding even this adventure as a joke? As a boy he had been both—a crafty schemer and reckless doer—but now he was grown to a man. And if the lines about his mouth were any criterion he would soon be coming back to carry out by stealth what he failed to accomplish by assault. So she, too, waited patiently, to foil his machinations and uphold the honor of the Huffs.

In the good old days it had never been forgotten that the Huffs belonged to the Virginia quality, while the Holmans came from Maine; hence the Colonel's relations with Honest John Holman had at first been strictly business. John Holman was a Northerner, with no social graces and abstemious to a fault, but when his commercial honor upon a certain occasion had saved the Colonel from bankruptcy he had cast the traditions of the South to the winds and taken Honest John as his friend. "My friend," he called him and neither his wife nor his enemies could shake the Colonel's faith in his partner. Then, after years of mutual trust, the panic had come on, and the crash in Paymaster stock; and as their fortunes went tumbling and ugly rumors filled the air they had broken their friendship completely. Yet so great was his love for his old-time friend that he had never openly accused him; and Honest John Holman, after months of somber silence, had moved away and started a cow ranch. But it was a question of honesty between the two men and their children had never forgotten. Ten years had passed since they had been boy and girl together, but the moment they met the old quarrel flashed up again and now the feud was on.

A boisterous blast of wind, whirling dust and papers down the street, announced the beginning of another sandstorm; and Death Valley Charley, who had been sitting outside the gate, came muttering up the steps. Behind him trotted Heine, his worshipful little dog, and as Virginia's pet cat suddenly arched its back, Death Valley took Heine in his arms.

"Can't you hear 'em?" he asked tiptoeing rapidly up to Virginia. "It's them big guns, over in Europe. It's them forty-two-centimeter howitzers and the French seventy-fives in the trenches along the Somme."

"Do you think so?" murmured Virginia, smoothing down her cat's back, "it sounds like blasting to me."

"No—big guns!" repeated Charley, regarding her intently through his wavering, sun-blinded eyes, and then he burst into a laugh. "You can hear 'em, can't you, Heine?" he cried to his dog, and Heine squirmed ecstatically and sneezed. "Hah, that's my little dog—you're so confectionate! Now get down on the floor, and don't you go near that cat."

He put down the dog and advanced closer to Virginia.

"He's coming!" he whispered. "I can hear him, plain—jurrr, jurrr; hud, hud, hud, hud, hud!"

"Who's coming?" demanded Virginia, looking swiftly up the road.

"Why—him! The man you're waiting for. Can't you hear him! Hrrrr—rud! He's coming to grab you and take you away in his auto!"

"Oh, Charley!" exclaimed Virginia, not entirely displeased, "and where will you go then?"

"I'll go to Death Valley," he answered mysteriously. "There's lots of gold over there. I came back one time and they says to me: 'Charley, where've you been for such a long time?' 'In Death Valley,' I says, 'in the Funeral Range. Working in the Coffin mine, on the graveyard shift.' Hah, hah; they can't get nothing out of me. I know where there's gold—in the Ube-Hebes; it's a place where nobody goes. I saw your father there, the last time I went through, and he sent word to you not to worry. 'But for Christ's sake,' he says, 'don't tell my wife I'm here—I'm tired of her devilish chatter!'"

"Charley!" reproved Virginia, and as he subsided into mutterings, she looked about with shocked eyes. "You talk too much," she said at last. "Didn't I tell you not to say that again? Because if Mother hears it she'll drive you out of the house, and then what will Heine do?"

"Heine! Come here, sir!" commanded Charley abruptly, and slapped him until he yelped. "Well, now," he warned as Heine slunk away, "you look out or you lose your house."

"I guess you'd better go now," said Virginia discreetly, and continued her vigil alone. Death Valley was harmless, but when he began hearing things there was no telling where he would stop. The next minute he would be seeing things, and then getting messages, and then looking through mountains with radium. He was harmless, of course, but when there was a sandstorm—well, some people thought he was crazy. And there was a sandstorm coming up. It was blowing in from the north and rushing clouds of dirt down the street; and along in the night, when it had gained its full force, the sand and gravel would fly. She rose to go in, but just at that moment she heard a low drumming up the street. It increased to a bubbling, a drumming, a thunder, and like the spirit of the rough north wind Wiley Holman went racing through the town. His hat was off and as he drifted by his hair thrashed wildly in his eyes, yet he glanced up in passing and it seemed to Virginia that he gave her a roguish smile. Then in a series of explosions that brought the Widow running he dashed on and whirled out across the desert.

"Oh, that devil!" she raged, brandishing her heavy shotgun at the disappearing cloud of dust. "He's just making that hubbub to mock me! He'll be coming back—I know it, the scoundrel—but you wait, he won't fool me again!"

She stood on the gallery while the food scorched in the kitchen and watched the boring arrow of dust, but it swept on and on across the boundless desert until at last it was lost in the storm. "Oh, he'll be back!" she screamed to the gathering neighbors. "I know him, he's after my mine. But he'd better watch out! If he ever goes near it, I'll shoot him, you mark my word!"

"No, he won't," said Virginia, but when they were all gone she came back and gazed down the road.

CHAPTER IV
THE GHOST-MAN

As the sun paled to nothing in the yellow murk of dust, a high cloud of sand overleapt the northern peaks and came sifting down the slopes of Shadow Mountain. The gusts of wind began to wail in boding fury and then the storm struck the town. Dirt and papers flew before it; tin cans leapt forth from holes and alleys; and sticks and small stones, sucked up in the vortex, joined in on the devil's dance. Ancient signs creaked and groaned and threatened to leave their moorings, old houses gave up shingles and loose boards, and up the street on the deserted bank building, the fire-doors banged like cannon. Then the night came on and the streets of Keno were empty, except for the flying dirt.

But it is nights such as this that move some men to greater daring and as Wiley Holman, far out on the desert, felt the rush and surge of wind he struck a swift circle and, turning back towards Keno, he bored his way into the teeth of the storm. The gravel from the road slashed and slatted against his radiator and his machine trembled before the buffets of the gale, but it was just such a night as he needed for his purpose and he ran with his lights switched off. If the Widow Huff, by any chance, should glance out across the plain she might notice their gleam and divine his purpose, which was to inspect the Paymaster mine. As a stockholder and part owner it was, of course, his right to enter the premises at will, but the Widow had placed her own personal mandate above the laws of the land, and it was better, and safer, to avoid all discussion by visiting the property after dark.

Up the long slope of the valley the white racer moved slowly, shuddering and thundering as it took the first hill, and as the outlying houses leaped up from the darkness, Wiley muffled his panting exhaust. In the sheltered valley, under the lee of Shadow Mountain, the violence of the wind was checked and some casual citizen, out looking at the stars, might hear him above the storm. He turned off the main road and, following up a side street, glided quietly into the shelter of a barn, and five minutes later, with his prospector's pick and ore-sacks, he toiled up the trail to the mine.

The Paymaster Mine lay on the slope of Gold Hill, directly overlooking the town—first the huge, dismantled mill; then the white slide of the waste dump; and then, up the gulch, the looming gallows-frame of the hoist and the dim bulk of abandoned houses. The mine had made the town, and the town had clustered near it in the broad oval of the valley below; but in its day the Paymaster had been a community by itself, with offices and bunk-houses and stores. Now all was deserted and in the pale light of the moon it seemed the mere ghost of a mine. A loose strip of zinc on the corrugated-iron mill drummed and shuddered in a menacing undertone and at uncertain intervals some door inside smote its frame with a resounding bang. Straining timbers creaked and groaned, the wind mourned like a disembodied spirit, and as Wiley Holman jumped at a sudden sound he turned and glanced nervously behind him.

It was not a shadow but the passing of a shadow that caught his roving eye and as he stripped off his wind-goggles and looked again he felt by instinct for his six-shooter. But it was not on his hip. He had taken his pick instead, and for the first time he felt a thrill of fear—not fear for his life nor of anything tangible, but that old, primordial fear of the night that only a gun can banish. He picked up a rock and walked back down the trail; but nothing leapt forth at him— even the shadow was gone, and he threw the rock petulantly away. It was the wind, and the noises, and the blinders on his goggles; but now that the great fear was born he jumped at every sound. He had been out before on worse nights than this— what was it, then, that he feared? With his back against a rock he stared about and listened until at last his nerve returned; then he went boldly to the dump, where the white quartz lay the thickest, and began to dig a hole with his pick.

Deep as he could dig there was nothing but the white waste and he paced off the width of the pile; then very systematically he moved across the slope, grabbing handfuls of fine dirt at measured intervals and throwing them into an ore-sack. There was something about Virginia's piece of "barren quartz" that had appealed to his prospector's eye and even in the excitement of meeting the Widow he had not forgotten to sequester it. But a piece of rock from a girl's case of specimens is a far call from "ore in place" and he had come back that night to look the mine over and collect an average sample from the dump. There were hundreds of tons of that rock on the dump and it certainly was his right, as a part owner in the property, to sample it and have it assayed.

Back and forth across the slide, now buffeted by the wind, now pelted by loosened stones, he continued his methodical test and then as he knelt to dig out a hole a great rock came bounding past. It came out of the darkness and went smashing down the hillside like some terrific engine of destruction and before he had more than scrambled from its path a second boulder was upon him. He dodged it by a hair's breadth and fell flat on his face, just as a stream of loose stone which the first flying rock had dislodged sent him rolling and tumbling down the slope in an avalanche of flying debris. For a minute he lay breathless while the waste rattled past him, and then he looked up the hill. No movement of his had started those great boulders. They had been launched by someone from above, and as he raised his head cautiously he beheld a gaunt figure standing outlined against the sky. It stood like a gibbet, its head to one side, a pistol in its hand; but as Wiley moved the man crouched and drew back as if he feared to be seen.

Who he was Wiley did not know, nor could he divine his animus in thus attempting to take his life, but, being caught in the open without his gun, he played safe and lay quiet where he had fallen. The wind howled along the ridges and trailed off into silence and, looking around, Wiley caught the wink of a lantern as it came across the flat from town. The crash of the boulders as they bounded down the dump and then on through the brush below had undoubtedly aroused some inquisitive citizen, who was coming over to investigate. Wiley rose up quickly, for he did not wish to be discovered, but as he started towards the trail he met the ghost-man, creeping forward with his pistol ready to shoot.

At times like this a man acts by instinct, and Wiley Holman dropped to the ground; then with the swiftness of an Indian he bellied off down the hill, looking back after every lightning move. The man was a murderer, a cold-blooded assassin; and, thinking him injured, he had been stealing up to his hiding-place to give him the *coup de grace.* Wiley rolled into a gulch and peered over the bank, his eyes starting out of his head with fear; and then, as the lantern began to bob below him, he turned and crept up the hill. Two trails led towards the mine, one on either side of the dump, and as the wind swept down with a sudden gust of fury, he ran up the farther trail. Once over the hill he could avoid both his pursuers and, cutting a wide circle, slip back to his machine and escape. The wind died to nothing as he neared the summit and he turned and looked back down the trail. Something moved—it was the man, his head twisted over his shoulder, his gun still held at a ready, creeping waspishly up the path.

Wiley turned and fled, sick with rage at his own impotence, but as he whipped over the dump the earth opened up before him and he slipped and stopped on the brink of a chasm. It was the caved-in stope, the old glory-hole of the Paymaster, and it cut off his last escape. A sudden sinking of the heart, a feeling of fate being against him, came over him as he slunk along the bank; and then, as a path opened up before him, he took the steep slope at a bound. Further on in the darkness he saw the roof of the mill and the broken hummocks of the dump; beyond lay the other trail and the open country and his car—

and the six-shooter—beyond! His feet seemed to fly as he dashed across the level and breasted a sudden ascent and then on its summit as the wind snatched him back someone struck him in full flight. "God!" he cried, and fought himself free but the other clutched him again.

"Run!" she begged, and he knew it was Virginia, but he was in a panic for fear of what was behind.

"No!" he cried, catching her roughly in his arms and starting the other way, "there's a crazy man back there and—"

"No—no—no!" she clamored, bringing him to a halt with her struggles. "The other way—can't you hear what I'm saying to you—" And then Wiley saw the Widow.

She was standing on the dump with her shotgun raised and pointed, and he hurled Virginia to one side.

"Don't shoot!" he yelled, but as he ducked and started to run, the Widow's gun spoke out. A blow like that of a club struck his leg from under him and he fell to the ground in a heap, but even in his pain he remembered the presence which had followed with its head on one side.

"You danged fool!" he cursed as the Widow ran up to him. "Keep that cartridge, whatever you do. There's a crazy man after me and—"

"I see him!" shrieked the Widow, making a dash for the bank with her gun at her hip for the shot. "You git, you dastard!" she shrilled into the darkness and once more the old shotgun roared forth.

"Oh, Mother!" wept Virginia, throwing her arms about Wiley, and attempting to raise him up. "Oh, look what you've done—it's Wiley Holman—and now I hope you're satisfied!"

"You bet I'm satisfied!" answered the Widow, exultingly. "That other fellow was Stiff Neck George!"

CHAPTER V
A LOAD OF BUCKSHOT

Since he had turned back, far out on the desert, and braved the storm to inspect the Paymaster Mine, Wiley Holman had met nothing but disaster; but as he lay on the ground with one leg full of buckshot he blamed it all on the Widow. Without warning or justification, without even giving him a chance, she had sneaked up and potted him like a rabbit; and now, as men came running to witness his shame, she gloried in her badness.

"Aha-ah!" she jeered, coming back to stand over him and Wiley reached for a stone.

"You old she-cat," he burst out, "you say another word to me and I'll bounce this rock off your head!"

He groaned and dropped the rock to take his leg in both hands, and then Virginia rushed to the rescue.

"How badly are you hurt?" she asked, kneeling down beside him, but he jerked ungraciously away.

"Go away and leave me alone!" he shouted to the world at large and the Widow took the hint to withdraw. Then in a series of frenzied curses

Wiley stripped off his puttee and felt of his injured leg. It was wet with blood and two shot-holes in his shin-bone were giving him the most exquisite pain; the rest were just flesh-wounds where the buckshot had pierced his leggings and imbedded themselves in the muscles. He looked them over hastily by the light of a flashing lantern and then he rose up from the ground.

"Gimme that gun for a crutch!" he demanded of the Widow; and Mrs. Huff, who had been surveying her work with awe, passed over the shotgun in silence. "All right, now," he went on, turning to Death Valley Charley, who had been patiently holding his lantern, "just show me the trail and I'll get out of camp before some crazy dastard ups and kills me."

"That was Stiff Neck George," observed Charley mysteriously. "He's guarding the Paymaster for Blount."

"Who—that fellow that was after me?" burst out Wiley in a passion as he hobbled off down the trail. "What the hell was he trying to do? The whole rotten mine isn't worth stealing from anybody. What's the matter with you people—are you crazy?"

"Well, that's all right!" returned the Widow from the darkness. "You can't sneak in and jump *my* mine!"

"*Your* mine, you old tarrier!" yelled Wiley furiously. "You'd better go to town and look it up. The whole danged works is mine—I bought it in for taxes!"

"You—what?" cried the Widow, brushing Virginia and Charley aside and halting him in the trail. "You bought the Paymaster for *taxes!*"

"Yes, for taxes," answered Wiley, "and got stung at that! Gimme eighty-three dollars and forty-one cents and you can have it back, with costs. But now listen, you old battle-ax; I've taken enough off of you. You went up on my property when I was making an inspection of it and made an attempt on my life; and if I hear a peep out of you, from this time on, I'll go down and swear out a warrant."

"I didn't aim to kill you," defended the Widow, weakly. "I just tried to shoot you in the leg."

"Well, you did it," returned Wiley, and, pushing her aside, he limped on down the trail. The Widow followed meekly, talking in low tones with her daughter, and at last Virginia came up beside him.

"Take him right to our house," she said to Charley, "and I'll nurse him until he gets well."

"No, you take me to the Holman house!" directed Wiley, obstinately. "I guess we've got a house of our own."

"Well, suit yourself," she murmured, and fell back to the rear while Wiley went hobbling on. At every step he jabbed the muzzle of the shotgun vindictively into the ground, but as he reached the flat and met a posse of citizens, he submitted to being carried on a door. The first pain had passed and a deadly numbness seemed to take the place of its bite; but as he moved his stiffened muscles, which were beginning to ache and throb, he realized that he was badly hurt. With a leg like that he could not drive out across the desert, seventy-four long miles to Vegas; nor would he, on the other hand, find the best of accommodations in the deserted house of his father. It had been a great home in its day, but that day was past, and the water connections too, and somebody must be handy to wait on him.

"Say," he said, turning to Death Valley Charley, "have you got a house here in town? Well, take me to it and I'll pay you well, and for anything else that you do."

"It won't cost you nothing," answered Charley quickly. "I used to know your father."

"Well, you knew a good man then," replied Wiley grimly, but Death Valley did not respond. The Widow Huff was listening behind; and besides, he had his doubts.

"I'll run on ahead," said Charley noncommittally, and when Wiley arrived a canvas cot was waiting for him, fully equipped except for the sheets. Virginia came in later with a pair on her arm, and after a look at Charley's greasy blankets Wiley allowed her to spread them on the bed. Then, as Death Valley laid a grimy paw on his leg and began to pick out the shot Wiley jerked away and asked Virginia impatiently if she didn't have a little carbolic.

"Aw, he'll be all right," protested Charley cheerfully, as Virginia pushed him aside; "them buckshot won't hurt him much, nohow. Jest put on some pine pitch and a chew of tobacco and he'll fall off to sleep like a child."

He stood blinking helplessly as Virginia heated some water and poured in a teaspoonful of carbolic, then as she bathed the wounds and picked out the last shot, Charley placed a disc on his phonograph.

"Does he want some music?" he inquired of Heine, who was sitting up and begging, but Virginia put down her foot. "No, Charley," she said with a forbidding frown, "you go ask Mother for a needle and thread."

"He's kind of crazy to-night," she whispered to Wiley, when Death Valley was safely out of sight, "you'd better come over to the house."

"Huh, I guess we're all crazy," answered Wiley, laughing shortly. "I can stand it—but how does he act?"

"Oh, he hears things—and gets messages—and talks about Death Valley. He got lost over there, three years ago last August, and the heat kind of cooked his brains. He heard your automobile, when you came back to-night—that's why Mother and all the rest of them went over to the mine to get you. I'm sorry she shot you up."

"Well, don't you care," he said reassuringly. "But she sure overplayed her hand."

"Yes, she did," acknowledged Virginia, trying not to quarrel with her patient, "but, of course, she didn't know about that tax sale."

"Well, she knows it now," he answered pointedly, and when Charley came back they were silent. Virginia bandaged up his wound and slipped away and then Wiley lay back and sighed. There had been a time when he and Virginia had been friends, but now the fat was in the fire. It was her fighting mother, of course, and their quarrel about the Paymaster; but behind it all there was the old question between their fathers, and he knew that his father was right. He had not rigged the stock market, he had not cheated Colonel Huff, and he had not tried to get back the mine. That was a scheme of his own, put on foot on his own initiative—and brought to nothing by the Widow. He had hoped to win over Virginia and effect a reconciliation, but that hole in his leg told him all too well that the Widow could never be fooled. And, since she could not be placated, nor bought off, nor bluffed, there was nothing to do but quit. The world was large and there were other Virginias, as well as other Paymasters—only it seemed such a futile waste. He sighed again and then Death Valley Charley burst out into a cackling laugh.

"I heard you," he said, "I heard you coming—away up there in the pass. Chuh, chuh, chuh, chud, chud, chud, chud; and I told Virginny you was coming."

"Yes, I heard about it," answered Wiley sourly, "and then you told the Widow."

"Oh, no, I didn't!" exulted Charley. "She'd've killed you, sure as shooting. I just told Virginny, that's all."

"Oh!" observed Wiley, and lay so still that Charley regarded him intently. His eyes were blue and staring like a newborn babe's, but behind their look of childlike innocence there lurked a crafty smile.

"I told her," went on Charley, "that you was coming to git her and take her away in your auto. She's a nice girl, Virginny, and never rode in one of them things—I never thought you'd try to steal her mine."

"I did not!" denied Wiley, but Death Valley only smiled and waved the matter aside.

"Never mind," he said, "they're all crazy, anyhow. They get that way every north wind. I'm here to take care of them—the Colonel asked me to, and keep people from stealing his mine. It's electricity that does it—it's about us everywhere—and that's what makes 'em crazy; but electricity is my servant; I bend it to my will; that's how I come to hear you. I heard you coming back, away out on the desert, and I knowed your heart wasn't right. You was coming back to rob the Colonel of his mine; and the Colonel, he saved my life once. He ain't dead, you know, he's over across Death Valley in them mountains they call the Ube-Hebes. Yes, I was lost on the desert and he followed my tracks and found me, running wild through the sand-hills; and then Virginia and Mrs. Huff, they looked after me until my health returned."

"You can hear pretty well, then," suggested Wiley diplomatically. "You must know everything that goes on."

"It's the electricity!" declared Charley. "It's about us everywhere, and that's what makes them crazy. All these desert rats are crazy, it's the electric storms that does it—Nevada is a great state for winds. But when they comes a sandstorm, and Mrs. Huff she wraps up her head, I feel the power coming on. I can hear far away and then I can hear close—I make the electricity my slave. But the rest, they go crazy; they have headaches and megrims, and Mrs. Huff she always wants to fight; but I'm here to take care of 'em—the Colonel asked me to, so you keep away from that mine."

"Oh, sure," responded Wiley, "I won't bother the mine. As soon as I'm well I'll go home."

"No, you stay," returned Charley, becoming suddenly confidential. "I'll show you a mountain of gold. It's over across Death Valley, in the

Ube-Hebes; the Colonel is over there now."

"Is that so?" inquired Wiley, and Charley looked at him strangely, as if dazed.

"Aw, no; of course not!" he burst out angrily. "I forgot—the Colonel is dead. You Heine; come over here, sir."

Heine crept up unwillingly and Charley slapped him. "Now—shut up!" he admonished and went off into crazy mutterings.

"What's that?" he cried, rousing up suddenly to listen, and a savage look replaced the blank stare. "Can't you hear him?" he asked. "It's Stiff Neck George—he's coming up the alley to kill you. Here, take my gun; and when he opens the door you fill him full of holes!"

Wiley listened intently, then he reached for the heavy pistol and sat up, watching the door. The wind soughed and howled and rattled at the windows, over which Charley had stretched heavy blankets, and it seemed to his startled imagination that someone was groping at the door. The memory of the skulking form that had followed him rose up with the distinctness of a vision and at a knock on the door he cocked his pistol and beckoned Death Valley to one side.

"Come in!" he called, but as the door swung open it was Virginia who stood facing his gun.

"O—oh!" she screamed, and then she flushed angrily as Charley began to laugh.

"Well, laugh then, you fool," she said to Wiley,

"and when you're through, just look at this that we found!"

She held up the ore-bag that Wiley had lost and strode dramatically in. "Look at that!" she cried, and strewing the white quartz on the table she pointed her finger in his face. "You stole my specimen!" she cried accusingly. "That's why you came back for more. But you give it back to me—I want it this minute. I see you're honest—like your father!"

She spat it out venomously, more venomously than was needful, for he was already fumbling for the rock; and when he gave it back he smiled over-scornfully and his lower lip mounted up.

"All right," he said, "you don't have to holler for it. You're getting to be just like your mother."

"I'm not!" she denied, but after looking at him a minute she burst into tears and fled.

CHAPTER VI
ALL CRAZY

The wind was still blowing when Wiley was awakened by the cold of the October morning. In the house all was dark, on account of the blankets which Death Valley had nailed over the windows, but outside he could hear the thump of an axe and the whining yelp of a dog. Then Charley came in, his arms full of wood, and lit a roaring fire in the stove. Wiley dozed off again, for his leg had pained him and kept him awake half the night, and when he woke up it was to the strains of music and the mournful howls of Heine.

"Ah, you are so confectionate!" exclaimed Charley in honeyed tones and laughed and patted him on the back. "Don't you like the fiddle, Heine? Well, listen to this now; the sweetest song of all."

He stopped the rasping phonograph to put on another record and when Heine heard "Listen to the Mocking-bird" he barked and leapt with joy. Wiley listened for a while, then he stirred in bed and at last he tried to get up; but his leg was very stiff and old Charley was oblivious, so he sank back and waited impatiently. Heine sat upon the floor before the largest of three phonographs, which ground out the Mocking-bird with variations; and each time he heard the whistled notes of the bird he rolled his eyes on Charley with a soulful, beseeching glance. The evening before, when his master had cuffed him, Wiley had considered Heine badly abused; but now as the concert promised to drag on indefinitely he was forced to amend his opinion.

"Say," he spoke up at last, in a pause between records, "what's the chance of getting something to eat?"

"Yes, there's plenty," answered Charley, and went on with his frolic until Wiley rose up in disgust. He had heated some water, besides tearing down a blanket and letting the daylight in, when there came a hurried knock at the door and the Widow appeared with his breakfast. She avoided his eyes, but her manner was ingratiating and she supplied the conversation herself.

"Good morning!" she smiled,—"Charley, stop that awful racket and let Heine go out for his scraps. Well, I brought you your breakfast—Virginia isn't feeling very well—and I hope you're going to be all right. No, get right back into bed and I'll prop you up with pillows; Charley's got a hundred or so. I declare, it's a question which can grab the most; old Charley or Stiff Neck George. Every time anyone moves out—and sometimes when they don't—you'll see those two ghouls hanging around; and the minute they're gone, well, you never saw anything like it, the way they will fight for the loot. Charley's got a whole room filled up with bedding, and stoves and tables and chairs; and George—he's vicious—he takes nearly everything and piles it up down in his warehouse. It isn't his, of course, but—"

"He hauls it off in a wheelbarrow," broke in Charley, virtuously. "He don't care what he does. They was a widow woman here whose daughter got sick and she had to go out for a week, and when she came back—"

"Yes, her whole house was looted—he carried off even her sewing-machine!"

"And a deep line of wheelbarrow tracks," added Charley, unctuously, "leading from her house right down to his. She nailed up all her windows before she went, but he—"

"Yes, he broke in," supplied the Widow. "He's a desperate character and everybody is afraid of him, so he can do whatever he pleases; but you bet your life he can't run it over me—I filled him up with buckshot twice. Oh—that is—er—did you ever hear how he got his head twisted? Well, go right ahead now and eat up your toast. I asked him one time—that was before we'd had our trouble—what was the cause of his head being to one side. He looks, you know, for all the world like he was watching for a good kick from behind; but he tried to appear pathetic and told me a long story about saving a mother and her child in a flood. And when it was all over, according to him, he fell down in a faint in the mud; but the best accounts I get say he was dead drunk in the gutter and woke up with his head on one side."

She ended with a sniff and Wiley glanced at Charley, but he was staring blankly away.

"I don't like that man," spoke up Charley at last, "he kicked my dog, one time."

"And he bootlegs something awful," added the Widow, desperately, for fear that the chatter would lag. "There doesn't a day go by but some drunken Piute comes whooping up the road, and that bunch of Shooshonnies—"

"Yes, he sells to the bucks," observed Death Valley, slyly. "They're no good—they get drunk and tell. But you can trust the squaws—I had one here yesterday—"

"You what?" shrieked the Widow, and Charley looked up startled, then rose and whistled to his dog.

"Go lay down!" he commanded and slapped him till he yelped, after which he slipped fearfully away.

"The very idea!" exclaimed the Widow frigidly and then she glanced at Wiley.

"Mr. Holman," she began, "I came out here to talk business—there's nothing round-the-corner about me. Now what about this tax sale, and what does Blount mean by allowing you to buy it in for nothing?"

"Well, I don't know," answered Wiley. "He refused to pay the taxes, so I bought in the property myself."

"Yes, but what does he *mean?*"

The Widow's voice rose to the old quarrelsome, nagging pitch, and Wiley winced as if he had been stabbed.

"You'll have to ask *him,* Mrs. Huff, to find out for sure; but to a man with one leg it looks like this. Whatever you can say about him, Samuel J. is a business man, and I think he decided that, as a business investment, the Paymaster wasn't worth eighty-three, forty-one. Otherwise he would have bought it himself."

"Unless, of course," added the Widow scornfully, "there was some understanding between you."

"Oh, yes, sure," returned Wiley, and went on with his eating with a wearied, enduring sigh.

"Well, I declare," exclaimed the Widow, after thinking it over, "sometimes I get so discouraged with the whole darned business you could buy me out for a cent!"

She waited for a response, but Wiley showed no interest, so she went on with her general complaint.

"First, it was the Colonel, with his gambling and drinking and inviting the whole town to his house; and then your father, or whoever it was, started all this stock market fuss; and from that time it's gone from bad to worse until I haven't a dollar to my name. I was brought up to be a lady—and so was Virginia—and now we're keeping a restaurant!"

Wiley pulled down his lip in masterful silence and set the breakfast tray aside. It was nothing to him what the Widow Huff suffered—she had brought it all on herself. And whenever she was ready to write to his father she could receive her ten cents a share. That would keep her as a lady for several years to come, if she had as many shares as she claimed; but there was nothing to his mind so flat, stale and unprofitable as a further discussion of the Paymaster. Indeed, with one leg wound up in a bandage, it might easily prove disastrous. So he looked away and, after a minute, the Widow again took up her plaint.

"Of course," she said, "I'm not a business woman, and I may have made some mistakes; but it doesn't seem right that Virginia's future should be ruined, just because of this foolish family quarrel. The Colonel is dead now and doesn't have to be considered; so—well, after thinking it over, and all the rest of it, I think I'll accept your offer."

"Which offer?" demanded Wiley, suddenly startled from his ennui, and the Widow regarded him sternly.

"Why, your offer to buy my stock—that paper you drew up for me. Here it is, and I'm willing to sign it."

She drew out the paper and Wiley read it silently, then rolled it into a ball and chucked it into the corner.

"No," he said, "that offer doesn't hold. I didn't know you then."

"Well, you know me now!" she flashed back resentfully, "and you'd better come through with that money. I've taken enough off of you and your father without standing for any more of your gall. Now you write me out a check for twenty thousand dollars and here's my two hundred thousand shares. I know you're robbing me but I simply can't endure it—I can't stay here a single day longer!"

She burst into angry tears as he shook his head and regarded her with steady eyes.

"No," he said, "you can't do business that way. I haven't got twenty thousand dollars."

"But—you offered it to me! You wrote out this paper and put it right under my eyes—"

"No," he said, "I never offered you twenty thousand—I offered to take an option at that price. I wanted to see that mine, and I wanted to see it peaceably, and I thought I could do it that way; but that piece of paper simply gave me the option of buying the stock if I wanted to."

"Well, you wanted to buy the stock—you were

crazy to get hold of it—and now, when I'm willing, you won't take it!"

"No, that's right," agreed Wiley, leaning back against his pillow. "And now, what are you going to do about it?"

"I'm going to kill you!" shrieked the Widow in a frenzy. "I'm going to *make* you take it! I declare, it seems like every single soul is against me—and me a poor helpless woman!"

She sank back in a chair and began to sob hysterically and Wiley looked about for the old shotgun. It was far too short, but it had served once as a crutch, and in a pinch it must serve him again. Keno was no place for him, he saw that very plainly, and it was better to risk the long drive across the desert than to stay with this weeping virago. If she didn't kill him then she would kill him later, and he was powerless to strike back in defense. She would take advantage of every immunity of her sex to obtain her own way in the end. He located the gun—it was down behind his bed where he had dropped it when they helped him in—but as he was fishing it up the door burst open and Virginia stood looking at her mother. Behind her appeared Death Valley Charley, his eyes blinking fearfully; but at sight of the Widow he ducked around the corner while Virginia came resolutely in.

"Oh, Mother!" she burst out in a pleading, reproachful voice, "can't you see that Wiley is sick? Well, what's the use of creating a scene when it's likely to make him worse?"

"I don't care!" wailed the Widow. "I hope he dies. I wish I'd killed him—I do!"

"You do not!" returned Virginia, and shook her reprovingly. "I declare, I wonder what poor Father would think if he heard how we'd treated a guest. Now you go back to the house and don't you come out again until Mr. Holman sends for you."

"You shut up!" burst out the Widow, pushing her brusquely aside. "I guess I know what I'm about. But I'll fool you," she cried, whirling about on Wiley as she started towards the door. "I'll sell my stock to Blount!"

She paused for the effect but Wiley did not answer and she returned to pursue her advantage.

"I know you!" she announced. "You and old Honest John—you're trying to steal my mine. But I'm going to fool you, I'm going right down to Vegas and sell every share to Blount!"

"Well, go to it," returned Wiley after a long, defiant silence, "and I hope you stick him a-plenty!"

"Why, what's the matter?" inquired the Widow, brushing Virginia away again and swaggering up to his bed. "I thought you and Blount were good friends."

"Yeh, guess again," replied Wiley grimly. "I'll tell him the mine shows up fine."

"Well, it does!" she asserted. "The Colonel said it wasn't scratched. And didn't you steal that piece of quartz from Virginia? Oh, you gave it back, eh? Well, how did it assay? I know you found *something* pretty good!"

"How could I give it back, if I'd had it assayed?" asked Wiley with compelling calm.

"Well what *did* you come back for?" demanded the Widow, triumphantly. "You must have figured to win somewhere."

"Yes, I did," sighed Wiley, "but I was badly mistaken. All I want now is to get out of town."

"Well, how about your father? That offer he made me! Has he backed out on that, too?"

"No, he hasn't," answered Wiley, "my father keeps his word. You can get your money any time."

"Well, of all the crazy crooked deals," the Widow began to rave, and then Wiley grabbed for the shotgun.

"It may be crazy!" he shouted savagely, "but believe me, it isn't crooked. My father never did a crooked thing in his life, and you know it as well as I do; and if it wasn't that you're such a crook yourself—"

"Wiley Holman!" raged the Widow, but he rose up on his crutch and shouldered his way out the door.

"You're crazy!" he yelled, "the whole danged town's crazy. All except old Charley and me."

He jerked his head and winked at Charley as he hobbled towards the street and Death Valley nodded gravely. There was a long, hateful silence; then the great motor roared out and the white racer rushed away across the desert.

"Well, I don't care!" declared the Widow as she gazed after his dust and when the stage went out that day it took a lady passenger to Vegas.

CHAPTER VII
BETWEEN FRIENDS

The madness of the Widow and Old Charley and Stiff Neck George was no mystery to Wiley Holman—it was the same form of mania which he encountered everywhere when he went to see men who owned mines. If he offered them a million for a ten-foot hole they would refuse it and demand ten million more, and if he offered them nothing they immediately scented a conspiracy to starve them out and gain possession of their mine. It was the illusion of hidden wealth, of buried treasure, which keeps half the mines in the West closed down and half of the rest in litigation; except that in Keno it seemed to be associated with gun-plays and a marked tendency towards homicide. So, upon his return from a short stay in the hospital he came up the main street silently, then stepped on the throttle and went through town a-smoking. But the Widow was out waiting for him in the middle of the road and, rather than run her down, he threw on both brakes and stopped.

"Well, what now?" he inquired, frowning at the odor of heated rubber. "What's your particular grievance this trip?" He regarded her coldly, then bowed to Virginia and waved a friendly hand at

Charley. "Hello, there, Death Valley," he called out jovially, as the Widow choked with a rush of words, "what's the news from the Funeral Range?"

"Now, here!" exclaimed the Widow, advancing from the dust cloud, and glancing into the machine. "I want you to bring back that gun!"

"I'm sorry, Mrs. Huff," he replied with finality, "but you'll have to get along without it. I turned it over to the sheriff, along with three buckshot and an affidavit regarding the shooting—"

"What, you great, big coward!" stormed the Widow in a fury. "Did you run and complain to the sheriff?"

"No, I walked," said Wiley, "and on one leg at that. But I might as well warn you that next time you make a gun-play you're likely to break into jail."

"You're a coward!" she taunted. "You're standing in with Blount to beat me out of my mine. First you sneak off with my gun, so I can't protect my rights, and then Stiff Neck George comes up and jumps the Paymaster!"

"The hell!" burst out Wiley, rising up in his seat and looking across at the mine.

"Yes, the hell," she returned, "and he's warned off all comers and is holding the mine for Blount!"

"For Blount!" he echoed and, seeing him roused at last, the Widow became subtly provocative.

"For Samuel J. Blount," she repeated impressively. "He—he's got all my stock on a loan."

"Oh!" observed Wiley, and as she raved on with her story he rubbed his chin in deep thought.

"Yes, I went down to see him and he wouldn't buy it, so I left it as collateral on a loan. And then he came out here and looked over the mine again and told Stiff Neck George to stand guard. They're fixing to pump out the water."

"Oho!" exclaimed Wiley, and his eyes began to kindle as he realized what Blount had done. Then reaching for the pistol that lay handy beside his leg, he leapt out with waspish quickness, only to stop short as he hurt his lame foot.

"Go on!" hissed the Widow, advancing to his shoulder and pointing the way up the trail. "He stays right there by the dump. The mine is yours; go put him off—I would, if I had my gun."

"Aw, pfooey!" he exclaimed, suddenly turning back and clamoring into his seat. "I've got one game leg already. Let 'im have the doggoned mine."

"What? Are you going to back out? Well, you are a good one—and it stands in your name, this minute!"

"Yes, and it isn't worth—that!" he said with conviction, and snapped his finger in the air. "He can have it. You can tell Blount, the next time you see him, he can buy in that tax title for the costs."

He paused and muttered angrily, gazing off towards the dump where crooked-necked George stood guard, and then he hopped out to crank up.

"Want a ride?" he asked, as he saw Virginia watching him and she hesitated and shook her head. "Come on," he smiled, casting aside his black mood, "let's take a little spin—just down on the desert and back. What's going on—getting ready to move?"

He gazed with alarm at a pile of packing boxes that the Widow had marshaled on the gallery and then he looked back at Virginia. She was attired in a gown that had been very chic in the fall of nineteen ten, but, though it was scant for these bouffant days, she was the old Virginia still— slim and strong and dainty, and highbred in every line, with dark eyes that mirrored passing thoughts. She was the Virginia he had played with when Keno was booming and his own sisters had been there for company; and now after ten years he remembered the time when he had asked her, in vain, for a kiss.

"I've got something to tell you," he said at last and Virginia stepped into the racer.

"Virginia!" reminded the Widow, and then at a glance she turned round and flung into the house. There were times and occasions when she had found it safer not to press her maternal authority too far, and the look that she received was first notice from Virginia that such an occasion had arrived. The motor began to thunder, Wiley threw in the clutch, and with a speed that was startling, they whipped a sudden circle and went bubbling away down the road.

It stretched on endlessly, this road across the desert, as straight as a surveyor's line, and as they cleared the rough gulches and glided down into its immensity Virginia glanced at the desert and sighed.

"Pretty big," he suggested and as she nodded slowly he raised his eyes to the hills. "I don't know," he went on, "whether you'll like Los Angeles. You'll get lonely for this, sometimes."

"Yes, but not for that"—she jerked a thumb back at Keno—"that place is pretty small. What's left, of course; but it seems to me sometimes they're all of them lame, halt and blind. Always quarreling and backbiting and jumping each other's claims—but—what do you think of the Paymaster?"

She shot the question at him and it occurred suddenly to Wiley that perhaps she had a programme, too.

"Well, I'll tell you," he began, deftly changing his ground, "I'm in Dutch on that, all around. When I came home full of buckshot and the Old Man heard about it I got my orders to come back and apologize. Well, I'll do that—to you—and you can tell your mother I'm sure sorry I went up on that dump."

He grinned and motioned to his injured foot, but Virginia was in no mood for a joke.

"That's all right," she said, "and I accept your apology—though I don't know exactly what it's for. But I asked your opinion of the Paymaster."

"Oh, yes," he replied and then he began to temporize. "You'd better tell me what you want it for, first."

"What? Do you have one opinion for one set of people and another for somebody else? I thought!"—She paused and the hot blood leapt to her cheeks as she saw where her temper had led her. "Well," she explained, "I've got a few shares of stock."

She said it quietly and the suggestion of scolding gave way to a chastened appeal. She remembered—and he sensed it—that winged shaft which he had flung back when she had said he was honest, like his father. He had told her then she was becoming like her mother, and Virginia could never endure that.

"Ah, I see," he answered and went on hurriedly with a new note of friendliness in his voice. "Well, I'll tell you, Virginia, if it will be any accommodation to you I'll take over that stock myself. But—well, I hate to advise you—because—how many shares have you got?"

"Oh, several thousand," she responded casually. "They were given to me by Father—and by different men that I've helped. Mr. Masters, you know, that I took care of for a while, he gave me all he had when he died. But I don't want to sell them—I know there's no market, because Blount wouldn't give Mother anything—but if he should happen to strike something—"

She glanced across at him swiftly but Wiley's face was grim.

"Yes, *him* find anything!" he jeered. "That fat-headed old tub! He knows about as much about mining as a hog does about the precession of the equinox. No; miracles may happen but, short of that, he'll never get back a cent!"

"No, but Wiley," she protested, "you know as well as I do that the Paymaster isn't worked out. Now what's to prevent my stock becoming valuable sometime when they open it up?"

"What's to prevent?" he repeated. "Well, I'll tell you what. If Blount makes a strike he'll close that mine down and send the company through bankruptcy. Then he'll buy the mine back on a judgment and you'll be left without a cent."

"But what about you?" she suggested shrewdly. "Will you let him serve *you* like that?"

"Don't you think it!" he answered. "I know him too well—my money is somewhere else."

"But if you should buy the mine?"

"Well—" he stirred uneasily and then shot his machine ahead—"I haven't bought it yet."

"No, but you offered to, and I don't see why—"

"Do you want to sell your stock?" he asked

abruptly and she flushed and shook her head. "Well!" he said and without further comment he slowed down and swung about.

"Oh, dear," she sighed, as they started back and he turned upon her swiftly.

"Do you know why I wouldn't have that mine," he inquired, "if you'd hand it to me as a gift? It's because of this everlasting fight. I own it, right now, if anybody does, and I've never been down the shaft. Now suppose I'd go over there and shoot it out with George and get possession of my mine. First Blount would come up with some other hired man-killer and I'd have a bout with him; and then your respected mother—"

"Now you hush up!" she chided and he closed down his jaw like a steel-trap. She watched him covertly, then her eyes began to blink and she turned her head away. The desert rushed by them, worlds of waxy green creosote bushes and white, gnarly clumps of salt bush; and straight ahead, frowning down on the forgotten city, rose the black cloud-shadow of Shadow Mountain.

"Oh, turn off here!" she cried, impulsively as they came to a fork in the road and, plowing up the sand, he skidded around a curve and struck off up the Death Valley road. They came together at the edge of the town—the long, straight road to the south, and the road-trail that led west into the silence. There were no tracks in it now but the flat hoof-prints of burros and the wire-twined wheel-marks of desert buckboards; even the road was half obliterated by the swoop of the winds which had torn up the hard-packed dirt, yet the going was good and as the racer purred on Virginia settled back in her seat.

"I can't believe it," she said at last, "that we're going to leave here, forever. This is the road that Father took when he left home that last time—have you ever been over into Death Valley? It's a great, big sink, all white with salt and borax; and at the upper end, where he went across, there are miles and miles of sand-hills. He's buried out there somewhere, and the hills have covered him—but oh, it's so awful lonesome!"

She turned away again and as her head went down Wiley stared straight ahead and blinked. He had known the Colonel and loved him well, and his father had loved him, too; but that rift had come between them and until it was healed he could never be a friend of Virginia's. She distrusted him in everything—in his silence and in his speech, his laughter and his anger, in his evasions and when he talked straight—it was better to say nothing now. He had intended to help her, to offer her money or any assistance he could give; but her heart was turned against him and the most he could hope for was to get back to Keno without a quarrel. The divide was far ahead, where the road struck the pass and swung over and down into the Great Valley; and, glancing up at the sun, he turned around slowly and rumbled back into town. Shadow Mountain rose before them; it towered above the valley like a brooding image of hate but as he smiled farewell at the sad-eyed Virginia something moved him to take her hand.

"Good-by," he said, "you'll be gone when I come back. But if you get into trouble—let me know."

He gave her hand a squeeze and Virginia looked at him sharply, then she let her dark lashes droop.

"I'm in trouble now," she said at last. "What good did it do to tell you?"

He winced and shrugged his shoulders, then gazed at her again with a challenge in his eyes.

"If you'd trust *me* more," he said very slowly, "perhaps I'd trust *you* more. What is it you want me to do?"

"I want you to answer me—yes or no. Shall I keep my stock, or sell it?"

"You keep it," he answered, and avoided her eye until she climbed out and entered the house.

CHAPTER VIII
THE TIP

"Well?" inquired the Widow as her daughter came back from her ride with Wiley Holman; but Virginia was not giving out confidences. At last, and by a trick, she had surprised the truth from Wiley and he had told her to keep her stock. For weeks, for months, he had told her and everybody else that the Paymaster was not worth having; but when she had drooped her lashes and asked him for his opinion he had told her not to sell. Not hesitatingly nor doubtfully, or with any crafty intent; but honestly, as a friend, perhaps as a lover—and then he had looked away. He knew, of course, how his past actions must appear in the light of this later advice; but he had told her the truth and gone. The question was: What should she do?

Virginia returned to her room and locked the door while her mother stormed around outside and at last she came to a decision. What Wiley had told her had been said in strictest confidence and it would not be fair to pass it on; but if he advised her not to sell he had a reason for his advice, and that reason was not far to find. It was in that white stone that he had stolen from her collection, and in the white quartz he had gathered from the dump. He claimed, of course, that he had not had her specimen assayed; but why, then, had he come back for more? And why had he been so careful to tell her and everyone that he would not take the Paymaster as a gift? As a matter of fact, he owned it that minute by virtue of his delinquent tax sale, and his goings and comings had been nicely timed to enable him to keep track of his property. He was shrewd, that was all, but now she could read him; for he had spoken, for once, from his heart.

The mail that night bore a sample of white quartz to a custom assayer in Vegas, but Virginia guarded her secret well. She had gained it by wiles that were not absolutely straight-forward, in that she had squeezed Wiley's hand in return, and since by so doing she had compromised with her conscience she placated it by withholding the great news. If she told her mother she would create a scene with Blount and demand the return of her stock; and the secret would get out and everybody would be buying stock and Wiley would blame it on her. No, everything must be kept dark and she mailed her sample when even the postmistress was gone. Perhaps Wiley was right in his extreme subterfuges and in always covering up his hand, but she would show him that there were others just as smart. She would take a leaf from his book and play a lone hand, too; only now, of course, she could not leave town.

"Virginia!" scolded the Widow, when for the hundredth time she had discovered her dawdling at her packing. "If you don't get up and come and help me this minute I'll unpack and let you go alone."

"Well, let's both unpack," said Virginia thoughtfully, and the Widow sat down with a crash.

"I knew it!" she cried. "Ever since that Wiley Holman—"

"Now, you hush up!" returned Virginia, flushing angrily. "You don't know what you're talking about!"

"Well, if I don't know I can guess; but I never thought a Huff—"

"Oh, you make me tired!" exclaimed Virginia, spitefully. "I'm staying here to watch that mine."

"That—mine!" The Widow repeated it slowly and her eyes opened up big with triumph. "Virginia, do you mean to say you got the best of that whipper-snapper and—"

"No, nothing of the kind! No! Can't you hear me? Oh, Mother, you'd drive a person crazy!"

"I—see!" observed the Widow and stood nodding her head as Virginia went on with her protests. "Oh, my Lord!" she burst out, "and I put up all my stock for a measly eight hundred dollars! That scoundrelly Blount—I saw it in his eye the minute I mentioned my stock! He's tricked me, the rascal; but I'll fool him yet—I'll pay him back and get my stock!"

"You'll pay him back? Why, you've spent half the money to redeem your jewels and the diamonds!"

"Well, I'll pawn them again. Oh, it makes me wild to think how that rascal has tricked me!"

"But, Mother," protested Virginia, "*he* hasn't done any work yet. They haven't made any strike at the mine. Why not let it go until they pump out the water and really find some ore? And besides, how could Wiley know anything about it? He's never been down the shaft."

"But—why you told me yourself—"

"I never told you anything!" burst out Virginia tearfully. "You just jump at everything like a flea. And now you'll tell everybody, and Wiley'll say I did it, and—"

"Virginia Huff!" cried her mother, dramatically, "are you in love with that—thief?"

"He is not! No, I am not! Oh, I wish you'd quit talking to me—I tell you he never told me *anything!*"

"Well, for goodness sake!" exclaimed the Widow pityingly, and stalked off to think it over.

"You, Charley!" she exclaimed as she found Death Valley on the gallery pretending to nail up a box, "you leave those things alone. Well, that's all right; we've changed our minds and now we're going to stay."

"That's good," replied Charley, laying his hammer aside, "I've been telling 'em so for days. It's coming everywhere; all the old camps are opening up, but Keno will beat them all."

"Yes, that's right," assented the Widow absently, and as she bustled away to begin her unpacking, Death Valley looked at Heine and leered.

"Didn't I tell you!" he crowed and, scuttling back to get his six-shooter, he went out and began re-locating claims. That was the beginning. The real rush came later when the pumps began to throb in the Paymaster. A stream of water like a sheet of silver flowed down the side of the dump and as if its touch had brought forth men from the desert sands, the old-timers came drifting in. Once more the vacant sidewalks resounded to the thud of sturdy hob-nailed boots; and along with the locaters came pumpmen and miners to sound the flooded depths of the Paymaster.

It was a great mine, a famous mine, the richest in all the West; within twenty months it had produced twelve million dollars and the lower levels had never been touched. But what was twelve million to what it would turn out when they located the hidden ore-body? On its record alone the Paymaster was a world-beater, but the ground had barely been scratched. Even Samuel

Blount, who was cold as a stone and had sold out the entire town, even he had caught the contagion; and he was talking large on the bank corner when Holman came back through town.

Wiley drove in from the north, his face burned by sun and wind and his machine weighed down with sacks of samples, but when he saw the crowd, and Blount in the middle of it, he threw on his brakes with a jerk.

"Hello!" he hailed. "What's all the excitement? Has the Paymaster made a strike?"

All eyes turned to Blount, who stepped down ponderously and waddled out to the auto. He was a very heavy man, with his mouth on one side and a mild, deceiving smile; and as he shook hands perfunctorily he glanced uneasily at Wiley, for he had heard about the tax sale.

"Why, no," he replied, "no strike as yet. How's everything with you, Mr. Holman?"

"Fine and dandy, I guess," returned Wiley civilly. "Where did all these men jump up from?"

"Oh, they just dropped in, or stopped over in passing. Do you still take an interest in mines?"

"Well, yes," responded Wiley. "I'm a mining engineer, and so naturally I do take quite an interest. And by the way, Mr. Blount, did it ever occur to you that the Paymaster has been sold for taxes? Oh, that's all right, that's all right; I didn't know whether you'd heard about it—do you recognize my title to the mine?"

"Well," began Blount, and then he smiled appeasingly, "I didn't just know where to reach you. Of course, according to law, you do hold the title; but I suppose you know that the stockholders of the company have five years in which to buy back the mine. Yes, that is the law; but I thought under the circumstances—the mine lying idle and all—you might be willing to waive your strict rights in the interests of, well, harmony."

"I get you," answered Wiley, glancing at the staring onlookers, "and of course these gentlemen are our witnesses. You acknowledge my title, and that every bit of your work is being done on another man's ground; but, of course, if you make a strike I won't put any obstacles in your way. I'm for harmony, Mr. Blount, as big as a wolf; but there's one thing I want to ask you. Did you or did you not employ this Stiff Neck George to act as guard on the mine? Because two months ago, after I'd bought in the Paymaster for taxes, I went over to inspect the ground and Stiff Neck George—"

"Oh, no! Oh dear, no!" protested Blount vigorously. "He was acting for himself. I heard about his actions, but I had nothing to do with them—I never even knew about it till lately."

"But was he in your employ at the time of the shooting, and did you tell him to drive off all comers? Because—"

"No! My dear boy, of course not! But come

over to my office; I want to talk with you, Wiley."

The banker beamed upon him affectionately and, shaking out a white handkerchief, wiped the sudden sweat from his brow; and then Wiley leapt to the ground.

"All right," he said, "but let's go and see the mine first."

He strapped on his pistol and waited expectantly and at last Blount breathed heavily and assented. Nothing more was said as they went across the flat and toiled up the trail to the mine. Wiley walked behind and as they mounted to the shaft-house his eyes wandered restlessly about; until, at the toolshed, they suddenly focussed and a half-crouching man stepped out. He was tall and gnarly and the point of his chin rested stiffly on the slope of his shoulder. It was Stiff Neck George and he kept a crook in his elbow as he glanced from Blount to Wiley.

"How's this?" demanded Wiley, putting Blount between him and George, "what's this man doing up here?"

"Why, that's George," faltered Blount, "George Norcross, you know. He works for me around the mine."

"Oh, he does, eh?" observed Wiley, in the cold tones of an examining lawyer. "How long has he been in your employ?"

"Oh, since we opened up—that's all—just

temporarily. This gentleman is all right, George; you can go."

Stiff Neck George stood silent, his sunken eyes on Wiley, his sunburned lips parted in a grin, and then he turned and spat.

"Eh, heh; hiding!" he chuckled and, stung by the taunt, Wiley stepped out into the open. His gun was pulled forward, his jaws set hard, and he looked the hired man-killer in the eye.

"Don't you think it," he said, "I know you too well. You're afraid to fight in the day-time; you dirty, sneaking murderer!"

He waited, poised, but George only laughed silently, though his poisonous eyes began to gleam.

"What are you doing on my ground?" demanded Wiley, advancing threateningly with his pistol raised. "Don't you know I own this mine?"

"No," snarled Stiff Neck George, coming suddenly to a crouch, "and, furthermore, I don't give a damn!"

"Now, now, George," broke in Blount, "let's not have any words. Mr. Holman holds the title to this claim."

"Heh—Holman!" mocked George, "Honest John's boy—eh?" He laughed insultingly and spat against the wind and Wiley's lip curled up scornfully.

"Yes—Honest John," he repeated evenly. "And

it's a wonder to me you don't take a few lessons and learn to spit clear of your chin."

"You shut up!" snapped George as venomous as a rattlesnake. "Your damned old father was a thief!"

"You're a liar!" yelled Wiley and, swinging his pistol like a club, he made a rush at the startled gunman. His eyes were flashing with a wild, reckless fury and as Stiff Neck George dodged and broke to run he leapt in and placed a fierce kick. "Now you git, you old dastard!" he shouted hoarsely and as George went down he grabbed him by the trousers and sent him sprawling down the dump. Sand, rocks and waste went avalanching after him, and a loose boulder thundered in his wake, until, at the bottom George scrambled to his feet and stood motionless, looking back. His head sank lower as he saw Wiley watching him and he slunk down closer to the ground, then with the swiftness of a panther that has marked down its prey he turned and skulked away.

"That's bad business, Wiley," protested Blount half-heartedly and Wiley nodded assent.

"Yes," he said, "he's dangerous now. I should have killed the dastard."

CHAPTER IX

A PEACE TALK

While his blood was pounding and his heart was high, Wiley Holman went down into his mine. He rode down on the bucket, deftly balanced on the rim and fending off the wall with one hand, and when he came up he was smiling. Not smiling with his lips, but far back in his eyes, like a man who has found something good. Perhaps Blount surprised the look before it had fled for he beamed upon Wiley benevolently.

"Well, Wiley, my boy," he began confidentially as he drew him off to one side, "I'm glad to see you're pleased. The gold is there—I find that everyone thinks so—all we need now is a little co-operation. That's all we need now—peace. We should lay aside all personal feelings and old animosities and join hands to make the Paymaster a success."

"That's right, that's right," agreed Wiley cheerfully, "there's nobody believes in peace more than I do. But all the same," he went on almost savagely, "you've got to get rid of old George. I'm for peace, you understand, but if I find him here again—well, I'll have to take over the property. He's nothing but a professional murderer."

"Yes, I know," explained Blount, "he's a dangerous man—but I don't like to let an old man starve. He's got a right to live the same as any of us, and, since he can't work—well, I gave him a job as watchman."

"Well, all right," grumbled Wiley, "if you want to be charitable; but I suppose you know that, under the law, you're responsible for the acts of your agents?"

"That's all right, that's all right," burst out Blount impatiently, "I'll never hire him again. He refused to obey my orders and—"

"*And* he tried to kill me!" broke in Wiley angrily, but Blount had thrown up both hands.

"Oh, now, Wiley," he protested, "why can't we be reasonable? Why can't we get together on this?"

"We can," returned Wiley, "but you've got to show me that you're not trying to jump my claim."

"Oh, you know," exclaimed Blount, "as well as I do that a tax sale is never binding. The owners of the property are given five years' time—"

"It is binding," corrected Wiley, "until the property is bought back—and I happen to be holding the deed. Now, here's the point—what authority have you got for coming in here and working this property?"

"Well, you may as well know," replied Blount shortly, "that I own a majority of the stock."

"Aha!" burst out Wiley. "I was listening for that. So you're the Honest John?"

"What do you mean?" demanded Blount and, seeing the anger in his eyes, he hastened to head off the storm. "No, now listen to me, Wiley; it's not the way you think. I knew your father well, and I always found him the soul of honor; but I never liked to say anything, because Colonel Huff was my partner, too. So, when this trouble arose, I tried to remain neutral, without joining sides with either. It pained me very much to have people make remarks reflecting upon the honesty of your father, but as the confidant of both it was hardly in good taste for me to give out what I knew. So I let the matter go, hoping that time would heal the breach; but now that the Colonel is dead—"

"Aha!" breathed Wiley and Blount nodded his head lugubriously.

"Yes," he said, "that is the way it was. Your father was absolutely honest."

"Well, but who sold the stock, and then bought it back—and put all the blame on my father?"

"I can't tell you," answered Blount. "I never speak evil of the dead—but the Colonel was a very poor business man."

"Yes, he was," agreed Wiley, and then, after a silence: "How did it happen that you got all his stock?"

"Well, on mortgages and notes; and now as

collateral on a loan that I made his widow. I own a clean majority of the stock."

"Oh, you do, eh?" observed Wiley and rubbed his jaw thoughtfully while Blount looked mildly on. "Well, what are you going to do?"

"Why, I'd like to buy back that tax deed," answered Blount amiably, "and get control of my property."

"Oh," said Wiley, and looked down the valley with eyes that squinted shrewdly at the sun. "All right," he agreed, "just to show you that I'm a sport, I'll give you a quit-claim deed right now for the sum of one hundred dollars."

"You will?" challenged Blount, reaching tremulously for his fountain pen and then he paused at a thought. "Very well," he said, but as he filled out the form he stopped and gazed uneasily at Wiley. Here was a mining engineer selling a possessory right to the Paymaster for the sum of one hundred dollars; while he, a banker, was spending a hundred dollars a day in what had proved so far to be dead work. "Er—I haven't any money with me," he suggested at length. "Perhaps—well, perhaps you could wait?"

"Sure!" replied Wiley, rising up from where he was seated, "I'll wait for anything, except my supper. Where's the best place to eat in town, now?"

"Why, at Mrs. Huff's," returned Blount in surprise. "But about this quit-claim, perhaps a check would do as well?"

"What, are the Huffs still here?" exclaimed Wiley, starting off. "Why, I thought—"

"No, they decided to stay," answered Blount, following after him. "But now, Wiley, about this quit-claim?"

"Well, gimme your check! Or keep it, I don't care—I came away without my breakfast this morning."

He strode off down the trail and Blount pulled up short and stood gazing after him blankly, then he shouted to him frantically and hurried down the slope to where Wiley was waiting impatiently.

"Here, just sign this," he panted. "I'll write you out a check. But what's the matter, Wiley—didn't the mine show up as expected?"

Wiley muttered unintelligibly as he signed the quit-claim which he retained until he had looked over the check. Then he folded up the check and kissed it surreptitiously before he stored it away in his pocketbook.

"Why, yes," he said, "it shows up fine. I'll see you later, down at the house."

Blount sat down suddenly, but as Wiley clattered off he shouted a warning after him.

"Oh, Wiley, please don't mention that matter I spoke of!"

"What matter?" yelled back Wiley and at

another disquieting thought Blount jumped up and came galloping after him.

"The matter of the Colonel," he panted in his ear, "and here's another thing, Wiley. You know Mrs. Huff—she's absolutely impossible and—well, she's been making me quite a little trouble. Now as a personal favor, please don't lend her any money or help her to get back her stock; because if you do—"

"I won't!" promised Wiley, holding up his right hand. "But say, don't stop me—I'm starving."

He ran down the trail, limping slightly on his game leg, and Blount sat down on a rock.

"Well, I'll be bound!" he puffed and gazed at the quit-claim ruefully.

The tables were all set when Wiley re-entered the dining-room from which he had retreated once before in such haste, and Virginia was there and waiting, though her smile was a trifle uncertain. A great deal of water had flowed down the gulch since he had advised her to keep her stock, but the assayer at Vegas was worse than negligent—he had not reported on the piece of white rock. Therefore she hardly knew, being still in the dark as to his motives in giving the advice, whether to greet Wiley as her savior or to receive him coldly, as a Judas. If the white quartz was full of gold that her father had overlooked—say fine gold, that would not show in the pan—then Wiley was indeed her friend; but if the quartz was barren and he had purposely deceived her in order to boom his own mine—she smiled with her lips and asked him rather faintly if he wanted his supper at once.

But if Virginia was still a Huff, remembering past treacheries and living in the expectancy of more, the Widow cast aside all petty heart-burnings in her joy at the humiliation of Stiff Neck George. Leaving Virginia in the kitchen, to fry Wiley's steak, she rushed into the dining-room with her eyes ablaze and all but shook his hand.

"Well, well," she exulted, "I'll have to take it back—you certainly did boot him good. I said you were a coward but I was watching you through my spy-glass and I nearly died a-laughing. You just walked right up to him—and you were cursing him scandalous, I could tell by the look on your face—and then all at once you made a jump and gave him that awful kick. Oh, ho, ho; you know I've always said he looked like a man that was watching for a swift kick from behind; and now—after waiting all these years—oh, ho ho—you gave him what was coming to him!"

The Widow sat down and held her sides with laughter and Wiley's grim features, that had remained set and watchful, slowly relaxed to a flattered grin. He had indeed stood up to Stiff Neck George and booted him down the dump, so that the score of that night when he had been hunted like a rabbit was more than evened up; for George had sneaked up on an unarmed man and rolled down boulders from above, but he had outfaced him, man to man and gun to gun, and kicked him down the dump to boot. Yes, the Widow might well laugh, for it would be many a long day before Stiff Neck George heard the last of that affair.

"And old Blount," laughed the Widow, "he was right there and saw it—his own hired bully, and all. Say, now Wiley, tell me all about it—what did Blount have to say? Did he tell you it was all a mistake? Yes, that's what he tells everybody, every time he gets into trouble; but he can't make excuses to me. Do you know what he's done? He's tied up all my stock as security for eight hundred dollars! What's eight hundred dollars—I turned it all in to get the best of my diamonds out of pawn. It made me feel so bad, seeing that diamond ring of yours; I just couldn't help getting them out. And now I'm flat and he's holding all my stock for a miserable little eight hundred dollars!"

She ended up strong, but Wiley sensed a touch and his expressions of sympathy were guarded.

"Now, you're a business man," she went on unheedingly. "I'll tell you what I'll do—you lend me the money to get back that stock and I'll sell it all to your father!"

"To my father!" echoed Wiley and then his face

turned grim and he laughed at some hidden joke. "Not much," he said, "I like the Old Man too much. You'd better sell it back to Blount."

"To Blount? Why, hasn't your father been hounding me for months to get his hands on that stock? Well, I'd like to know then what you think you're doing? Have you gone back on your promise, or what?"

"I never made any promise," returned Wiley pacifically. "It was my father that made the offer."

"Oh, fiddlesticks!" exploded the Widow. "Well, what's the difference—you're working hand and glove!"

"Not at all," corrected Wiley, "the Old Man is raising cattle. You can't get him to look at a mine."

"Well, he offered to buy my stock!" exclaimed the Widow, badly flustered. "I'd like to know what this means?"

"It's no use talking," returned Wiley wearily, "I've told you a thousand times. If you send your stock to John Holman at Vegas, he'll give you ten cents a share; but *I* won't give you a cent."

"Do you mean to say," demanded the Widow incredulously, "that you don't want that stock?"

"That's it," assented Wiley. "I've just sold my tax title for a hundred dollars, to Blount."

"Oh, this will drive me mad!" cried the Widow in a frenzy. "Virginia, come in here and help me!"

Virginia came in with the steak slightly scorched and laid his dinner before Wiley. Her eyes were rather wild, for she had been listening through the doorway, but she turned to her mother inquiringly.

"He says he's sold his tax claim," wailed the Widow in despair, "for one hundred dollars—to Blount. And then he turns around and says his father will buy my stock for ten cents a share in cash. But he won't lend me the money to pay my note to Blount and get my Paymaster stock back."

"That's right," nodded Wiley, "you've got it all straight. Now let's quit before we get into a row."

He bent over the steak and, after a meaning look at Virginia, the Widow discreetly withdrew.

"We saw you fighting George," ventured Virginia at last as he seemed almost to ignore her presence. "Weren't you afraid he'd get mad and shoot you?"

"Uh, huh," he grunted, "wasn't I hiding behind Blount? No, I had him whipped from the start. Bad conscience, I reckon; these crooks are all the same—they're afraid to fight in the open."

"But *your* conscience is all right, eh?" suggested Virginia sarcastically, and he glanced up from under his brows.

"Yes," he said, "we've got 'em there, Virginia. Are you still holding onto that stock?"

A swift flood of shame mantled Virginia's brow and then her dark eyes flashed fire.

"Yes, I've got it," she said, "but what's the answer when you sell out your tax claim to Blount?"

"I wonder," he observed and went on with his eating while she paced restlessly to and fro.

"You told me to hold it," she burst out accusingly, "and then you turn around and sell!"

"Well, why don't *you* sell?" he suggested innocently, and she paused and bit her lip. Yes, why not? Why, because there were no buyers—except Wiley Holman and his father! The knowledge of her impotence almost drove her on to further madness, but another voice bade her beware. He had given her his advice, which was not to sell, and—oh, that accursed assayer! If she had his report she could flaunt it in his face or—she caught her breath and smiled.

"No," she said, "you told me not to!"

And Wiley smiled back and patted her hand.

CHAPTER X
THE BEST HEAD IN TOWN

What was Wiley Holman up to? Virginia paced the floor in a very unloverlike mood; and at last she sat down and wrote a scathing letter to the assayer, demanding her assay at once. She also enclosed one dollar in advance to test the sample for gold and silver and then, as an afterthought, she enclosed another bill and told him to test it for copper, lead, and zinc. There was something in that rock—she knew it just as well as she knew that Wiley was in love with her, and this was no time to pinch dollars. For ten years and more they had stuck there in Keno, waiting and waiting for something to happen, but now things had come to such a pass that it was better to know even the worst. For if the mine was barren and Wiley, after all, was only trying in his dumb way to help, then she must pocket her pride and sell him her stock and go away and hide her head. But if the white quartz was rich—well, that would be different; there would be several things to explain.

Yet, if the quartz was barren, why did Wiley offer to buy her stock, and if it was rich, why did he sell his tax deed? And if his father stood ready to pay ten cents a share for two hundred thousand shares of stock why did Wiley refuse to redeem her mother's holdings for a petty eight hundred dollars? He must have the money, for his diamond ring alone was worth well over a thousand dollars; and he had tried repeatedly to get possession of this same stock which he now refused to accept as a gift. Virginia thought it over until her head was in a whirl and at last she stamped her foot. The assay would tell, and if he had been trying to cheat her—she drew her lips to a thin, hard line and looked more than ever like her mother.

The work at the Paymaster went on intermittently, but Blount's early zest was lacking. For eight, yes, ten years he had waited patiently for the moment when he should get control of the mine; but now that he held it, without let or hindrance, somehow his enthusiasm flagged. Perhaps it was the fact that the timbering was expensive and that his gropings for the lost ore body came to nothing; but in the back of his mind Blount's growing distrust dated from the day he had bought Wiley's quit-claim. Wiley had come to the mine full of fury and aggressiveness, as his combat with Stiff Neck George clearly showed; but after he had gone down and inspected the workings he had sold out for one hundred dollars. And Wiley Holman was a mining engineer, with a name for Yankee shrewdness—he must have had a reason.

Blount recalled his men from the drifts where

they had been working and set them to crosscutting for the vein. It was too expensive, restoring all the square-sets and clearing out the fallen rock; and he had learned to his sorrow that Colonel Huff had blown up every heading with dynamite. In that tangle of shattered timbers and caved-in walls the miners made practically no progress, for the ground was treacherous and ten years under water had left the wood soft and slippery. To be sure the hidden chute lay at the breast of some such drift; but to clear them all out, with his limited equipment and no regular engineer in charge, would run up a staggering account. So Blount began to crosscut, and to sink along the contact, but chiefly to cut down expenses.

With the railroad that had tapped the camp torn up and hauled away, every foot of timber, every stick of powder, cost twice as much as it ought. And then there was machinery, and gas and oil for the engine, and valves and spare parts for the pumps, and the board of the men, and overhead expenses—and not a single dollar coming in. Blount sat up late in his office, adding total to total, and at the end he leaned back aghast. At the very inside it was costing him two hundred dollars for every day that he operated the mine. And what was it turning back? Nothing. The mine had been gutted of every pound of ore that it would pay to sack and ship, and unless something was done to locate the lost ore body and give some guarantee of future values, well, the Paymaster would have to shut down. Blount considered it soberly, as a business man should, and then he sent for Wiley Holman.

There were others, of course, to whom he might appeal; but he sent for Wiley first. He was a mining engineer, he had had his eye on the property and—well, he probably knew something about the lost vein. So he sent a wire, and then a man; and at last Holman, M.E., arrived. He came under protest, for he had been showing a mine of his own to some four-buckle experts from the east, and when Blount made his appeal he snorted.

"Well, for the love of Miguel!" he exclaimed, starting up. "Do you think I'm going to help you for nothing? I'm a mining engineer, and the least it will cost you is five hundred dollars for a report. No, I don't think anything; and I don't know anything; and I won't take your mine on shares. I'm through—do you get me? I sold out my entire interest for one hundred dollars, cash. That puts me ahead of the game, up to date; and while I'm lucky I'll quit."

He stamped out of the office—Blount having moved into the bank building where he had formerly officiated as president—and made a break for his machine; but other eyes had marked his arrival in town and Death Valley Charley button-holed him.

"Say," he said, "do you want something good— an option on ten first-class claims? Well, come with me; I'll make you an offer that you can't hardly, possibly refuse."

He led Wiley up an alley, then whisked him around corners and back to his house behind the Widow's.

"Now, listen," he went on, when Wiley was in a chair and he had carefully fastened the door, "I'm going to show you something good."

He reached under his bed and brought out ten sacks of samples which he spread, one by one, on the table.

"Now, you see?" he said. "It's all that white quartz that you was after on the Paymaster dump. I followed the outcrop, on an extension of the Paymaster, and I took up ten, good, opened claims."

"Umm," murmured Wiley, and examined each sample with a careful, appraising eye. "Yes, pretty good, Charley; I suppose you guarantee the title? Well, how much do you want for your claims?"

"Oh, whatever you say," answered Charley modestly, "but I want two hundred dollars down."

"And about a million apiece, I suppose, for the claims? It doesn't cost *me* anything, you know, on an option."

"Eh, heh, heh," laughed Charley indulgently and Heine, who had been looking from face to face, jumped up and barked with delight. "Eh, heh; yes, that's good; but you know me, Mr. Holman—I ain't so crazy as they think. No, I don't talk millions with my mouth full of beans; all I want is five hundred apiece. But I got to have two hundred down."

"Oh," observed Wiley, "that's two dollars for the marriage license and the rest for the wedding journey. Well, if it's as serious as that—" He reached for his check-book and Charley cackled with merriment.

"Yes, yes," he said, "then I *would* be crazy. Do you know what the Colonel told me?

" 'Charley,' he says, 'whatever you do, don't marry no talking woman. She'll drive you crazy, the same as I am; but don't you forget that whiskey.' "

"Oh, sure," exclaimed Wiley, beginning to write out the option, "this money is to buy whiskey for the Colonel!"

"That's it," answered Charley. "He's over across Death Valley—in the Ube-Hebes—but I can't find my burros. They—Heine, come here, sir!" Heine came up cringing and Charley slapped him soundly. "Shut up!" he commanded and as Heine crept away Death Valley began to mutter to himself. "No, of course not; he's dead," he ended ineffectively, and Wiley looked up from his writing.

"Who's dead?" he inquired, but Charley

shook his head and listened through the wall.

"Look out," he said, "I can hear her coming—jest give me that two hundred now."

"Well, here's twenty," replied Wiley, passing over the money, and then there came a knock at the door.

"Come in!" called out Charley and, as he motioned Wiley to be silent, Virginia appeared in the doorway.

"Oh!" she cried, "I didn't know you were here!" But something in the way she fixed her eyes on him convinced Wiley that she had known, all the same.

"Just a matter of business," he explained with a flourish, "I'm considering an option on some of Charley's claims."

"Jest my bum claims!" mumbled Charley as Virginia glanced at him reprovingly. "Jest them ten up north of the Paymaster."

"Oh," she said and drew back towards the door, "well, don't let me break up a trade."

"You'd better sign as a witness," spoke up Wiley imperturbably, and she stepped over and looked at the paper.

"What? All ten of those claims for five hundred apiece? Why, Charley, they may be worth millions!"

"Well, put it down five million, then," suggested Wiley, grimly. "How much do you want for them, Charley?"

"Five hundred dollars apiece," answered Charley promptly, "but they's got to be two hundred down."

"Well?" inquired Wiley as Virginia still regarded him suspiciously, and then he beckoned her outside. "Say, what's the matter?" he asked reproachfully. "Let the old boy make his touch—he wants that two hundred for grub."

"He does not!" she spat back. "I'm ashamed of you, Wiley Holman; taking advantage of a crazy man like that!"

"Well, I don't know," he began in a slow, drawling tone that cut her to the quick, "he may not be as crazy as you think. I've just been offered a half interest in the Paymaster if I'll come out and take charge of it."

"You *have!*" she cried, starting back and staring as he regarded her with steely eyes. "Well, are you going to take it?"

"I don't know," he answered. "Thought I'd better see you first—it might be taking advantage of Blount."

"Of Blount!" she echoed and then she saw his smile and realized that he was making fun of her.

"Yes," went on Wiley, whose feelings had been ruffled, "he may be crazy, too. He sure was looking the part."

"Now don't you laugh at me!" she burst out hotly. "This isn't as funny as you think. What's going to happen to us if you take over that mine?

I declare, you've been standing in with Blount!"

"I knew it," he mocked. "You catch me every time. But what about Charley here—does he get his money or not?" He turned to Death Valley, who was standing in the doorway watching their quarrel with startled eyes. "I guess you're right, Charley," he added, smiling wryly. "It must be something in the air."

"Are you going to take that offer," demanded Virginia, wrathfully, "and rob me and Mother of our mine?"

"Oh, no," he answered, "I turned it down cold. I knew you wouldn't approve."

"You knew nothing of the kind!" she came back sharply, the angry tears starting in her eyes. "And I don't believe he ever made it."

"Well, ask him," suggested Wiley, and went back into the house, whereupon Death Valley closed the door.

"Yes," whispered Charley, "it's in the air—there's electricity everywhere. But what about that option?"

Wiley sat at the table, his eyes big with anger, his jaw set hard against the pain, and then he reached for his pen.

"All right, Charley," he said, "but don't you let 'em kid you—you've got the best business head in town."

CHAPTER XI

A TOUCH

The wrath of a man who is slow to anger cannot lightly be turned aside and, though Virginia drooped her lashes, the son of Honest John brushed past her without a word. She had followed him gratuitously to Death Valley's cabin and seriously questioned his good faith; and then, to fan the flames of his just resentment, she had suggested that he was telling an untruth. He had told her—and it seemed impossible—that Blount had offered him half the Paymaster, on shares; but the following morning, without a word of warning, the Paymaster Mine shut down. The pumps stopped abruptly, all the tools were removed, and as the foreman and miners who had been their boarders rolled up their beds and prepared to depart, the high-headed Virginia buried her face in her hands and retired to her bedroom to weep. And then to cap it all that miserable assayer sent in his belated report.

"Gold—a trace. Silver—blank. Copper—blank. Lead—blank. Zinc—blank."

The heavy white quartz which Wiley had made so much of was as barren as the dirt in the street. It had absolutely no value and—oh, wretched thought—he had offered to buy her stock out of charity! Out of the bigness of his heart—and then she had insulted him and accused him of robbing Death Valley Charley! In the light of this new day Death Valley was a magnate, with his check for two hundred dollars, and Virginia and her mother must either starve on in silence or accept the bounty of the Holmans. It was maddening, unbelievable—and to think what he had suffered from her, before he had finally gone off in a rage. But how sarcastic he had been when she had accused him of robbing Charley, and of standing in with Blount! He had said things then which no woman could forgive; no, not even if she were in the wrong. He had led her on to make unconsidered statements, smiling provokingly all the time; and then, when she had doubted that Blount had offered him the mine, he had said, "Well, ask him!" and shut the door in her face! And now, without asking, the question had been answered, for Blount had closed down the mine in despair and gone back to his bank in Vegas.

The Paymaster was dead, and Keno was dead; and their eight hundred dollars was gone. All the profits from the miners which they had counted upon so confidently had disappeared in a single day; and now her mother would have to pawn her diamonds again in order to get out of town. Virginia paced up and down, debating the situation and seeking some possible escape, but every door was closed. She could not appeal to Wiley, for she knew her stock was worthless, and her hold on his sympathies was broken. He was a Yankee and cold, and his anger was cold—the kind that will not burn itself out. When he had loved her it was different; there was a spark of human kindness to which she could always appeal; but now he was as cold and passionless as a statue; with his jaws shut down like iron. She gave up and went out to see Charley.

Death Valley was celebrating his sudden rise to affluence by a resort to the flowing bowl and when Virginia stepped in she found all three phonographs running and a two-gallon demijohn on the table. Death Valley himself was reposing in an armchair with one leg wrapped up in a white bandage and as she stopped the grinding phonographs and made a grab for the demijohn he held up two fingers reprovingly.

"I'm snake-bit," he croaked. "Don't take away my medicine. Do you want your Uncle Charley to die?"

"Why, Charley!" she cried, "you know you aren't snake-bit! The rattlesnakes are all holed up now."

"Yes—holed up," he nodded; "that's how I got snake-bit. It was fourteen years ago, this month. Didn't you ever hear of my snake-mine—it was one of the marvels of Arizona—a two-foot stratum of snakes. I used to hook 'em out as fast as I needed them and try out the oil to cure rheumatism; but one day I dropped one and he bit me on the leg, and it's been bad that same month ever since. Would you like to see the bite? There's the pattern of a diamond-back just as plain as anything, so I know it must have been a rattler."

He reached resolutely for the demijohn and took a hearty drink whereat Virginia sat down with a sigh.

"I'll tell you something," went on Charley confidentially. "Do you know why a snake shakes its tail? It's generating electricity to shoot in the pisen, and the longer a rattlesnake rattles—"

"Oh, now, Charley," she begged, "can't you see I'm in trouble? Well, stop drinking and listen to what I say. You can help me a lot, if you will."

"Who—me?" demanded Charley, and then he roused himself up and motioned for a dipper of water. "Well, all right," he said, "I hate to kill this whiskey—" He drank in great gulps and made a wry face as he rose up and looked around.

"Where's Heine?" he demanded. "Here Heine, Heine!"

"You drove him under the house," answered Virginia petulantly, "playing all three phonographs at once. Really, it's awful, Charley, and you'd better look out or Mother will give you the bounce."

"Scolding women—talking women," mused

Charley drunkenly. "Well, what do you want me to do?"

"I'm *not* scolding!" denied Virginia, and then as he leered at her she gave way weakly to tears. "Well, I can't help it," she wailed, "*she* scolds me all the time and—she simply drives me to it."

"They'll drive you crazy," murmured Charley philosophically. "There's nothing to do but hide out. But I must save the rest of that whiskey for the Colonel."

He reached for the demijohn and corked it stoutly, after which he turned to Virginia.

"Do you want some money?" he asked more kindly, bringing forth his roll as he spoke. "Well here, Virginny, there's one hundred dollars—it's nothing to your Uncle Charley. No, I got plenty more; and I'm going up the Ube-Hebes just as soon as I find my burros. They must be over to Cottonwood—there's lots of sand over there and Jinny, she's hell for rolling. No, take the money; I got it from Wiley Holman and he's got plenty more."

He dropped it in her lap, but she jumped up hastily and put it back in his hands.

"No, not that money," she said, "but listen to me, Charley; here's what I want you to do. I've got some stock in the Paymaster Mine that Wiley was trying to buy; but now—oh, you saw how he treated me yesterday—he wouldn't take it, if he knew. But Charley, you take it; and the next time you see him—well, try to get ten cents a share. We want to go away, Charley; because the mine is closed down and—"

"Yes, yes, Virginny," spoke up Death Valley, soothingly, "I'll get you the money, right away."

"But don't you tell him!" she warned in a panic, "because—"

"You ought to be ashamed," said Charley reprovingly and went out to hunt up his burros. Virginia lingered about, looking off across the desert at the road down which Wiley had sped, and at last she bowed her head. Those last words of Charley's still rang in her ears and when, towards evening, he started off down the road she watched him out of sight.

It was a long, dry road, this highway to Vegas, but twenty miles out, at Government Wells, there was water, and a good place to camp. Charley stopped there that night, and for three days more, until at last in the distance he saw Wiley's white racer at the tip of a streamer of dust. He went by like the wind but when he spied Charley he slowed down and backed up to his camp.

"Hel-lo there, Old Timer," he hailed in surprise, "what are you doing, away out here?"

"Oh, rambling around," responded Charley airily, waving his hand at the world at large. "It's good for man to be alone, away from them scolding women."

The shadow of a smile passed over Wiley's

bronzed face and then he became suddenly grim.

"Bum scripture, Charley," he said, nodding shortly, "but you may be right, at that. What's the excitement around beautiful Keno?"

"I don't know," lied Charley. "Ain't been in town since you was there, but she was sure booming, then. Say, I've got some stock in that Paymaster Mine that I might let you have, for cash. I'm burnt out on the town—they's too many people in it—I'm going back to the Ube-Hebes."

"Well, take me along, then," suggested Wiley, "and we'll bring back a car-load of that gold. Maybe then I could buy your stock."

"No, you buy it now," went on Charley insistently. "I'm broke and I need the money."

"Oh, you do, eh?" jested Wiley. "Still thinking about that wedding trip? Well, I may need that money myself."

"Eh, heh, heh," laughed Charley, and drawing forth a package he began to untie the strings. "Eh, heh; yes, that's right; I've been watching you young folks for some time. But I'll sell you this stock of mine cheap."

He unrolled a cloth and flashed the certificates hopefully, but Wiley did not even look at them.

"Nope," he said, "no Paymaster for me. I wouldn't accept that stock as a gift."

"But it's rich!" protested Charley, his eyes beginning to get wild. "It's full of silver and gold. I can feel the electricity when I walk over the property—there's millions and millions, right there!"

"Oh, there is, eh?" observed Wiley, and, snatching away the certificates, he ran them rapidly over. "Where'd you get these?" he asked, and Death Valley blinked, though he looked him straight in the eyes.

"Why, I—bought 'em," he faltered, "and—the Colonel gave me some. And—"

"How much do you want for them?" snapped Wiley, and Charley blinked again.

"Ten cents a share," he answered, and Wiley's stern face hardened.

"You take these back," he said, "and tell her I don't want 'em."

"Who—Virginny?" inquired Death Valley, and then he kicked his leg and looked around for Heine.

"Now, here," spoke up Wiley, "don't go to slapping that dog. How much do you want for the bunch?"

"Four hundred dollars!" barked Charley, and stood watchful and expectant as Wiley sat deep in thought.

"All right," he said, and as he wrote out the check Death Valley chuckled and leered at Heine.

CHAPTER XII
THE EXPERT

Like the way of an eagle in the air or the way of a man with a maid, the ways of a mining promoter must be shrouded in mystery and doubt. For when he wants to buy, no man will sell; and when he wants to sell, no man will buy; and when he will neither buy nor sell he is generally suspected of both. Wiley Holman had two fights and a charge of buckshot to prove that he wanted the Paymaster, and the fact that he had refused a half interest for nothing to prove that he did not want it. Also he had sold his tax-title to the property for the sum of one hundred dollars. What then did it signify when he bought Virginia's despised stock for four hundred dollars, cash down? The man who could answer that could explain the way of a man with a maid.

Samuel J. Blount made the claim—and he had his pile to prove it—that he could think a little closer than most men. A little closer, and a little farther; but the Paymaster had been his downfall. He had played the long game to get possession of the mine, only to find he had bought a white elephant. Every day that he held it he had thrown good money after bad and he sent out a search party for Wiley Holman. Wiley had refused half the mine, but that only proved that half of the mine did not appeal to him—perhaps he would take it all. Samuel J. had been a student for a good many years in the school of predatory business and he had learned the rules of the game. He knew that the buyer always decried the goods and magnified each tiny defect, whereas the seller by as natural a process played up every virtue to the limit. But any man who inspected the goods was a potential buyer of the same, and Wiley had shown more than a passing interest in the fate of the unlucky Paymaster. And Wiley was a mining engineer.

They met in the glassed-in office of Blount in the ornate Bank of Vegas and for a half an hour or more Wiley sat tipped back in his chair while Blount talked of everything in general. It was a way he had, never to approach anything directly; but Wiley favored more direct methods.

"I understood," he remarked, bringing his chair down with a bang, "that you wanted to see me on business?"

"Yes, yes, Wiley," soothed Blount, "now please don't rush off—I wanted to see you about the Paymaster."

"Well, shoot," returned Wiley, "but don't ask my advice, unless you're ready to pay for it."

He tipped back his chair and sat waiting patiently while Blount unraveled his thoughts.

He could think closer than most men, but not quicker, and the Paymaster was a tangled affair.

"I have been told," he began at last, "that you are still buying Paymaster stock. Or at least—well, a check of yours came through here endorsed by Death Valley Charley, and Virginia Huff. Oh, yes, yes; that's your business, of course; but here's the point I'm coming to; it won't do you any good to buy in that stock because I've got a majority of it right here in my vault. If you want to control the Paymaster, don't go to someone else—I'm the man you want to see."

He tapped himself on the breast and smiled impressively, and Wiley nodded his head.

"All right," he said imperturbably, "when I want the Paymaster Mine I'll know right where to go."

"Yes, you come to me," went on Blount after a minute, "and I'll do the best I can." He paused expectantly, but Wiley did not speak, so he went on blandly, as before. "The stock, of course, is nonassessable and the taxes are very small. I intend from now on to keep them paid up, so there will be no further tax sales. The stock of Mrs. Huff, which I now hold as collateral security, is practically mine already, as she has defaulted on her first month's interest and is preparing to leave the state. Of course, there is the stock which your father is holding—as I calculate, something over two hundred thousand shares—and what little remains outside; but if you are interested in the mine I am the man to talk to, so what would you like to propose?"

"Well," began Wiley, and then he stopped and seemed to be lost in thought. "I'll tell you," he said, "I *was* interested in the Paymaster—I believe there's something there; but I've got some other propositions that I can handle a little easier, so if you don't mind we'll wait a while."

"No, but Wiley," protested Blount as his man rose up to go, "now just sit down; I'm not quite through. Now I know just as well as you do that you take a great interest in that mine. Your troubles with Mrs. Huff and Stiff Neck George prove conclusively that such is the case; and I am convinced that, either from your father or some other source, you have valuable inside information. Now I must admit that I'm not a mining man and my management was not a success; but with your technical education and all the rest, I am convinced that the results would be different. No, there's no use denying it, because I know myself that you've been buying up Paymaster stock."

"Sure," agreed Wiley, "I bought four hundred dollars' worth. That would break the Bank of Vegas. But you've got lots of money—why don't you hire a competent mining man and go after that lost ore-body yourself?"

"I may do that," replied Blount easily, "but in the meantime why not make me a reasonable offer, or take the mine on shares?"

"If the Paymaster," observed Wiley, "was the only mine in the world, I'd make you a proposition in a minute. But a man in my position doesn't have to buy his mines, and I never work anything on shares."

"Well, now Wiley, I've got another proposition, which you may or may not approve; but there's no harm, I hope, if I mention it. You know there's been a difference between me and your father since—well, since the Paymaster shut down. I respect him very much and have nothing but the kindliest feelings towards him but he—well, you know how it is. But I have been informed, Wiley, that since Colonel Huff's death, your father has been bidding for his stock. In fact, I have seen a letter written to Mrs. Huff in which he offers her ten cents a share. Now, of course, if you want to gain control of the company, I'm willing to do what's right; and so, after thinking it over, I have come to the conclusion that I will accept that offer now."

"Umm," responded Wiley, squinting his eyes down shrewdly, "how much would that come to, in all?"

"Well, twenty-one thousand, eight hundred dollars, for what I received from Mrs. Huff; but of course—well, he'd have to buy a little more of me in order to get positive control."

"How much more?" asked Wiley, but Blount's crooked mouth pulled down in a crafty smile.

"We can discuss that later," he suggested mildly. "Do you think he will buy the stock?"

"Not if he takes my advice," answered Wiley coldly. "I can buy the whole block for eight hundred."

"How?"

"Why, by loaning Mrs. Huff the eight hundred dollars with which to take up her note."

"I doubt it," replied Blount, and his mild, deceiving eyes took on the faintest shadow of a threat. "Mrs. Huff has defaulted on her first month's interest and, according to the terms of her note, the collateral automatically passes to me."

"Well, keep it, then," burst out Wiley, "and I hope to God you get stuck for every cent. Your old mine isn't worth a dam'!"

"Why—Wiley!" gasped Blount, quite shaken for the moment by this disastrous piece of news, "what reason have you for thinking that?"

"Give me a hundred dollars as an advising expert and I'll tell you—and show you, too."

"No, I hardly think so," answered Blount at last. "And, Wiley, you don't think so, either."

"No?" challenged Wiley. "Well, you just watch my smoke and see whether I do or not."

He had closed the door before Blount dragged

him back like a haggling, relentless pawn-broker.

"Make me a proposition," he clamored desperately, "and if it's anywhere in reason I'll accept it."

"All right," answered Wiley, "but show me what you've got—I don't buy any cat in a bag."

"And will you make me an offer?" demanded Blount hopefully. "Will you take the whole thing off my hands?"

"I will if it's good—but you'll have to show me first that you've got a controlling share of the stock. And another thing, Mr. Blount, since our time is equally valuable, let's cut out this four-flushing stuff. If I'd wanted your mine so awfully bad I'd have held on to it when the title was mine; but I turned it back to you, just to let you look it over, and to keep the peace for once. But now, if you're satisfied, I might look it over; but it'll be under a bond and lease. The parties I represent are strictly business, and we make it a rule to tie everything up tight before we put out a cent. I'll want an option on every share you have, and I can't offer more than ten per cent royalty; but to compensate for that I'll agree to pay in full or vacate within six months from date."

"But how much?" demanded Blount, brushing aside all the details, "how much will you pay me a share?"

"I'll pay you," stated Wiley, "what I paid Death Valley Charley, and that's five cents a share."

"Five cents!" shrilled Blount, rising up in protest, yet jumping at the price like a trout, "five cents—why, that's practically nothing!"

"Just five cents more than nothing," observed Wiley judicially and waited for Blount to rave.

"But your father," suggested Blount with a knowing leer, "is in the market at ten."

"No, not in the market. He offered that to the Widow, but now the deal is off, because all of her stock has changed hands."

"Well, the stock is the same," suggested Blount insinuatingly. "Give me seven and a half and split the profits."

"Now don't be a crook," rapped out Wiley angrily. "Just because you would rob your own father doesn't by any means prove that I will."

"Well, you certainly implied," protested Blount with injured innocence, "that this stock was to be sold to your father. And if it is worth that to him, why is it worth less to you? You must be working together."

"No, we're not," declared Wiley. "I'm in on this alone, and have been, from the start. And just to set your mind at rest—he didn't make that offer because he wanted the stock, but to kind of help out the Widow."

"Ah," smiled Blount, and nodded his head wisely, but there was a playful light in his eyes.

"Yes—*ah!*" flashed back Wiley, "and if you

think you're so danged smart I'll let you keep your old mine a few months."

He started for the door again but Blount dragged him back and laid a metal box on the table.

"Well, let's get down to business," he said with quick decision, and spread a heap of papers before his eyes. "There are all my Paymaster shares, and if you'll take them off my hands you can have them for six cents, cash."

"I said five," returned Wiley, as he ran through the papers, "and an option to buy in six months. But this stock of the Widow's—I can't take that at any price—the Colonel isn't legally dead."

"What?" yelled Blount, and sat down in a chair while he stared at the inscrutable Wiley.

"His body was never found and, under the law, he can't be declared dead for seven years. Mrs. Huff had no right to sell his stock."

"Oh, but he's dead, Wiley," assured Blount. "Surely there's no doubt of that. They found his burro, and his letters and everything; and where he had run wild through the sand. If that storm hadn't come up they would certainly have found his body—the Indian trailers said so; so why stick on a technicality?"

"That's the law," said Wiley. "You know it yourself. But of course, if you want to vote this stock at a directors' meeting we can still do business on that lease."

"Oh, my Lord!" sighed Blount, and after a heavy silence he rose up and paced the floor. As for Wiley, he ran through the papers, making notes of dates and numbers, and then grimly began to fill out a legal blank.

"There's the option," he said, passing over a paper, "and I see now how you double-crossed my father. So you don't need to sign unless you want to."

"Why—er—what's that?" exclaimed Blount, coming out of his abstraction as Wiley slapped down the bundle of certificates.

"I see by these endorsements," replied Wiley, "that you sold out before the panic and bought in all this stock afterwards."

Blount started and a red line mounted up to his eyes as he hastily glanced over the option.

"Well, I'll sign it," he mumbled, and reached for the pen, but Wiley checked his hand.

"No, you ring for a notary," he said. "I want that signature acknowledged."

The notary came and ran perfunctorily through his formula, after which he left them alone.

"Now here's the bond and lease," went on Wiley curtly, "so bring on your Board of Directors and let's get this business over. By rights I ought to kill you."

There was a special meeting then of the Board of Directors of The Paymaster Mining and Milling Company, and when the bond and lease was properly drawn up, they signed it and had it witnessed. Then once more the tense silence came over the room and Wiley rose to go.

"Well," he said, "I've been waiting for ten years just to get these papers in my hands. And now, you danged crook, just to hit you where you live, I'm going to make a fortune."

"A fortune!" echoed Blount, and then he clasped his hands and sank down weakly in a chair. "I knew it!" he moaned, "I knew it all the time—you've been trying to get that mine for months. But what is it, Wiley? Have you located the lost vein? Oh, I knew it; all the time!"

"Yes, you did," jeered Wiley, "you didn't know anything, except how to grab hold of the stock. What good was it to you after you'd got the old mine—you didn't know what to do with it! All you knew was how to rob the widow and the orphan and deprive better men of their good name. You wait till I tell my Old Man about this—and how you were selling him out, all the time. If it wasn't for you he'd never been called Honest John by a bunch of these tin-horns and crooks. But I'll show you who's honest—I'm going to skin you alive for what you did to my father. You wait till I make my clean-up!"

"But what is it, Wiley?" cried Blount, despairingly. "Have you really discovered the lost vein?"

"No," grinned Wiley, "but I've consulted

an expert and he tells me the mine is worth millions!"

"What—millions?" burst out Blount, struggling up to his feet. "Now here, Wiley Holman; I want that option back! You secured it by fraud and misrepresentation and by concealment of the actual facts. I'll have the law on you—I'll break the contract—you came here with intent to defraud!"

"Don't you think it!" returned Wiley, thrusting out his lip. "You thought you were trimming me, like taking candy from a baby. Why didn't *you* get an expert? I offered to hire out to you, myself!"

"Oh—hell!" choked Blount. "Well, tell me the worst—where was it he told you to dig?"

"Why right down the shaft," answered Wiley blandly. "He's a new kind of mining expert and he locates the gold by electricity."

"By electricity!" exclaimed Blount, and as he perceived Wiley's smile he straightened up in a rage. "I don't believe a word of it. Who is this man, anyway? I never heard of such a thing before!"

"Oh, yes!" said Wiley, as he stepped out the door, "you know the professor well. They call him Death Valley Charley."

CHAPTER XIII
A SACK OF CATS

The weary work of packing had gone on endlessly in the bare rooms of the old Huff house and now Virginia, with two kittens in her arms and the mother cat following behind, was passing it all in review. A solid row of packing boxes, arrayed on the front gallery, awaited the motor-truck; and here and there in corners lay piles of discarded treasures that were destined to go to Charley for loot. He was hanging about, with his pistol well in front, on the watch for Stiff Neck George; but up to that moment the Widow had not said the word that would start the mad rush for plunder. Her trunks were all packed, the china nested in barrels and the bedding sewed up in burlap; but still from day to day she put off the evil moment, and Virginia did not try to hurry her. The house had been their home for ten years and more and, though Los Angeles would be fine with its palm trees and bungalows, it was a strange land, far away. And what would they do in that city of strange faces and hustling, eager real-estate agents? It was that which held the Widow back.

In the city there would be rent and water to pay for, and electric lights and wood; but in desolate

Keno rent and water and wood were free, and the electric light company had taken down its poles. If the town were not so dead—if they could only make a living,—the Widow started up for the thousandth time, for she heard a racing auto down the street. It was Wiley Holman, as sure as shooting, and—well, Wiley was not so bad. It was his money, really, that had enabled them to pack up, and would enable them to go, when they started; and the Widow knew, as well as she knew anything, that he had designs upon the mine. He was after the Paymaster, and if he ever got hold of it—well, Keno would come back to its own. She rushed to the door and looked out into the street; and when she met Virginia, running away from meeting Wiley, she caught her and whirled her about.

"Now you go back there," she hissed in her ear, "and I want you to be nice to him—he may have come back about the mine."

Virginia went out the door and, as Wiley Holman saw her standing there, he leapt out and came up the steps.

"Well, well," he said, "just in time to say good-by. And I wanted to see you, too." He smiled down at her boyishly and Virginia's eyes turned gentle as he took both her hands in his. "I've got some news to tell you," he burst out eagerly; "not news that will buy you anything but something to remember when you're gone."

He led her to a box and, taking one of the kittens, sat down with his back to the door. Then he rose up hastily at a sudden rustle from behind and glanced inquiringly at Virginia.

"It's just Mother," she said and at the mention of her name Mrs. Huff came boldly out.

"Why, good morning, Wiley," she said, smiling over-sweetly. "Seems to me you're awful early."

"Yes," answered Wiley, trying vainly to seem polite, "I just stopped off to say good-by!"

He offered her his hand, but the Widow ignored the hint and took the conversation to herself.

"Well, I'm real glad you came," she went on sociably, "because I wanted to see you on a matter of business. In fact, I've been kind of waiting, on the chance that you might come through. Oh, I know that I don't count, but you can see Virginia afterwards; and I wanted to consult you about my stock. Yes, I know," she hastened on, as his face turned grim, "I haven't treated you fairly at all. I should have taken your offer, when you said you'd give ten cents for every share of stock that I had. But I took them to that Blount and he gave me next to nothing, and now he's holding the stock. But what I wanted to ask was: Isn't there some way we can arrange it to get it back and sell it to your father?"

"No, I don't think so," answered Wiley, putting down the kitten, "and—well, I guess I'd better go."

He rose up reluctantly, but the Widow would not hear to it and Virginia beckoned him to stay.

"Well, now listen," persisted the Widow. "That stock certainly must be worth something."

"Not to you," returned Wiley. "I saw Blount only yesterday and he says it belongs to him."

"Well, it does not!" declared the Widow, but as no one contradicted her, she took a different tack. "Are you coming back?" she asked, smiling brightly. "Are you going to open up the mine?"

Wiley's face fell for a moment.

"What gave you that idea?" he inquired bluffly, but the Widow pointed a finger and laughed roguishly.

"I knew it," she cried. "I've known it for months—and I wish you the best of good luck."

"Oh, you do, eh?" grunted Wiley, and stood undecided as Mrs. Huff continued her assurances. He had come there to see Virginia, but business was business and the Widow seemed almost reasonable. "Huh, that's funny," he said at last. "I thought you had it in for me. What's the chance for getting a quit-claim?"

"A quit-claim!" echoed the Widow, suddenly pricking up her ears. "Why, what do you want that for, now?"

"Well, you're going away," explained Wiley quietly, "and it might come in handy, later, if I should want to take over the mine. Of course you've got no title—and no stock, for that matter—but I'll give you a hundred dollars, all the same."

"I'll take it!" snapped the Widow and Wiley broke out laughing as he reached for his fountain pen.

"Zingo!" he grinned and then he bit his lip, for the Widow was quick to take offence. "Of course," he went on, "this doesn't affect your stock if you should ever get it back from Blount. That is still your property, according to law, and this quit-claim just guarantees me free entry and possession. We'll get Virginia to witness the agreement."

"All right," bridled the Widow and watched him cynically as he wrote out the quit-claim and check. "Oh! Actually!" she mocked as he put the check in her hands. "I just wanted to see if you were bluffing."

"Well, you know now," he answered and sat in stony silence until she departed with a triumphant smirk. Then he glanced at Virginia and motioned towards the street, but she sighed and shook her head.

"No," she said, "I can't leave the house—Mother is likely to start any time, now."

"I suppose you'll be glad to go," he suggested at last as she sat down and gathered up the kittens. "The old town is sure awful dead."

"Yes—I guess so," she agreed half-heartedly. "You'd think so, but we don't seem to go."

"Is there anything I can do for you?" he inquired after a silence. "You know what I told you once, Virginia."

"Yes, I know," she answered bitterly, "but—Oh, I'm ashamed to let you help me, after the way I acted up about Charley."

"Well, forget it," he said at length. "I guess I get kind of ugly when anyone doubts my good faith. It's on account of my father, and calling him Honest John—but say, I forgot to tell the news!"

Virginia looked up inquiringly and he beckoned her into the corner where no one could overhear his words.

"Blount sent for me yesterday—trying to sell me the mine," he whispered in her ear, "and I made him show me his stock. And when I looked on the back of his promotion certificates—the ones he got for promoting the mine—I found by the endorsements that he'd sold every one of them before or during the panic. Do you see? They were street certificates, passing from hand to hand without going to the company for transfer, but every broker that handled them had written down his name as a memorandum of the date and sale. Don't you see what he did—he set your father against my father, and my father against yours, and all the time, like the crook he is, he was selling them both out for a profit. I could have killed him, the old dog, only I thought it would hurt him more to whipsaw him out of his mine; but listen now, Virginia, don't you think we can be friends—because my father never robbed anybody of a cent! He thought more of the Colonel than he did of me; and I've started out, even if it is a little late, to prove that he was on the square."

He stopped abruptly, for in his rush of words he had failed to note the anger in her eyes, until now she turned and faced him.

"Oho!" she said, "so that's your idea—you're going to whipsaw Blount out of his mine?"

"If I can!" hedged Wiley. "But for the Lord's sake, Virginia, don't tell what I said to your mother! It won't make any difference, because she's given me a quit-claim—but what's the use of having any trouble?"

"Yes, sure enough!" murmured Virginia, with cutting sarcasm. "She might even demand her rights!"

"Well, maybe you *like* to fight!" burst out Wiley angrily, "and if you do, all right—hop to it! But I'll tell you one thing; if you can't be reasonable, I can be just as bullheaded as anybody!"

"Yes, you can," she agreed and then she sighed wearily, and waved it all away with one hand. "Well, all right," she said, "I'm so sick and tired of it that I certainly don't want any more. And since I've taken your money, as you know very well, I'm going to go away and give you peace."

Her eyes blinked fast, to hold back the tears, and once more the son of Honest John weakened.

"No, I don't want you to go away," he answered gently, "but—isn't there something I can do before you go? I have to fight my way, you know that yourself, Virginia; but don't let that keep us from being friends. I'm a mining engineer, and I can't tell you all my plans, because that sure would put me out of business; but why can't you trust me, and then I'll trust you and—what is it you've got on your mind?"

He reached for her hand but she drew it away and sat quiet, looking up the street.

"You wouldn't understand," she said with a sigh. "You're always thinking about money and mines. But a woman is different—I suppose you'll laugh at me, but I'm worried about my cats."

"About your cats!" he echoed, and she smiled up at him wistfully and then looked down at the kittens in her lap.

"Yes," she said, "you know they were left to me when the people moved out of town, and now I've got eight of them and I just know that old Charley—"

"He'll starve 'em to death," broke in Wiley, instantly. "I know the old tarrier well. You give 'em to me, Virginia, and I swear I'll take care of 'em just the same as I would of—you."

"Oh," smiled Virginia, and then she gave

him her hand and the old hatred died out in her eyes. "That's good of you, Wiley, and I certainly appreciate it; because no one would trust them with Charley. I'm going to take the two kittens, but you can have the rest of them and—you can write to me about them, sometimes."

"Every week," answered Wiley. "I'll take 'em back to the ranch and the girls will look after them when I'm gone. We'll have to put them in sacks, but that will be better—"

"Yes, that's better than starving," assented Virginia absently, and Wiley rose suddenly to go. There was something indefinable that stood between them, and no effort of his could break it down. He shook hands perfunctorily and started down the gallery and then abruptly he turned and swung back.

"Here," he said, throwing her stock down before her, "I told you to hold onto that, once."

CHAPTER XIV

THE EXPLOSION

There are moments when his great secret rises to every man's lips and flutters to wing away; but a thought, a glance, a word said or unsaid, turns it back and he holds it more closely. Wiley Holman had a secret which might have changed Virginia's life and filled every day with joy and hope, but he shut down his lips and held it back and spoke kind words instead. There was a look in her eyes, a brooding glow of resentment when he spoke of his father and hers; and, while he spoke from the heart, she drooped her dark lashes and was silent beyond her wont. He gave her much but she gave him little—and the reason she was sorry to leave Keno was the parting with six suffering cats.

There were girls that he knew who would have gone the limit and said something about missing Wiley Holman. So he gave her back her stock and put the cats in sacks and burnt up the road to the ranch. The next day the news came that he had bonded the Paymaster, but Wiley was far away. He caught the Limited and went speeding east, and then he came back, headed west; and finally he left Vegas followed by four lumbering auto trucks loaded down with freight and men. The time had come when he must put his fortunes to the test and Keno awaited him, anxiously.

A cold, dusty wind raved down through the pass, driving even old Charley to shelter; but as the procession moved in across the desert the city of lost hopes came to life. Old grudges were forgotten, the dead past was thrust aside, and they lined up to bid him welcome—Death Valley Charley and Heine, Mrs. Huff and Virginia, and the last of ten thousand brave men. For nine years they had lived on, firm in their faith in the mighty Paymaster; and now again, for the hundredth time, the old hope rose up in their breasts. The town was theirs, they had seen it grow from nothing to a city of brick and stone, and they loved its ruins still. All it needed was some industry to put blood into its veins and it would thrill with energy and life. Even the Widow forgot her envy and her anger at his deception and greeted Wiley Holman with a smile.

"Well—hello!" he hailed when he saw her in the crowd. "I thought you were going away."

"Not much!" she returned. "Bring your men in to dinner. I'm having my dishes unpacked!"

"Umm—good!" responded Wiley and, shrugging his shoulders, he led the way on to the mine. There were other faces that he would as soon have seen as the Widow's fighting mien, and he had brought his own cook along; but Mrs. Huff was a lady and as such it was her privilege to claim her woman's place in the kitchen. The town was part hers and the restaurant was her livelihood; and then, of course, there was Virginia. Having bidden her good-by, and taken care of her cats, he had reconciled himself to her loss, but not even the smile in her welcoming dark eyes could make him quite forget the Widow. She was an uncertain quantity, like a stick of frozen dynamite that will explode if it is thawed too soon; and there was a bombshell to come which gave more than even promise of producing spontaneous combustion. So Wiley sighed as he fired his cook, and told his men that they would board with the Widow.

The first dinner was not so much, consisting largely of ham and eggs with the chickens out on a strike; but there was plenty of canned stuff and the Widow promised wonders when she got all her boxes unpacked. Yet with all her work before her and the dishes unwashed, she followed the crowd to the mine. That was the day of days, from which Keno would date time if Wiley made his promise good; and every man in town, and woman and child, went over to watch them begin. Up the old, abandoned road the auto trucks crept and crawled, and the shed and the houses that had been prepared by Blount now gave shelter to his hated successor. Only one man was absent and he sat on the hill-top, looking down like a lonely coyote. It was Stiff Neck George, that specter at the feast, the harbinger of evil to come;

but as Wiley ordered the empty trucks to back up against the dump he glanced at the hill-top and smiled.

"We'll take back a load of tungsten," he announced to the drivers and the crowd of onlookers stared.

"Just load on that white stuff," he explained to the muckers and there was a general rush for the dump.

"What did you say that stuff was?" inquired Death Valley Charley, after a hasty look at his specimen; and Keno awaited the answer, breathless.

"Why, that's scheelite, Charley," replied Wiley confidentially, "and it runs about sixty per cent tungsten. It comes in pretty handy to harden those big guns that you hear shooting over in France."

"Oh, tungsten," muttered Charley, blinking wisely at the rock while everyone else grabbed a sample. "Er—what do you say they use it for?"

"Why, to harden high-speed steel for guns and turning-tools—haven't you read all about it in the papers?"

"How much did you say it was worth?" asked the Widow cautiously, and Wiley knew that the bombshell was ignited.

"Well, that's a question," he began, "that I can answer better when I get a report on this ore. It's all mixed up with quartz and ought to be milled, by rights, before I even ship it; but since the trucks are going back—well, if it turns out the way I calculate it might bring me forty dollars a unit."

"A unit!" repeated the Widow, her voice low and measured. "Well, I'd just like to know how much a unit is?"

"A hundredth of the standard of measure—in this case a ton of ore. That would come to twenty pounds."

"Twenty pounds! What, of this stuff? And worth forty dollars! Well, somebody must be crazy!"

"Yes, they're crazy for it," answered Wiley, "but it's just a temporary rage, brought on by the European war. The market is likely to break any time."

"Why—tungsten!" murmured the Widow. "Who ever heard of such a thing? And it's been lying here idle all the time."

"How much would that be a ton?" piped up someone in the crowd, and Mrs. Huff put her head to one side.

"Let's see," she said, "forty dollars a unit—that's one hundredth of a ton. Oh, pshaw, it can't be that. Let's see, twenty pounds at forty dollars—that's two dollars a pound; and two thousand pounds, that's—oh, I don't believe it! I never even heard of tungsten!"

"No, it's a new metal," replied Wiley ever so softly, "or rather, it's an acid. The technical magazines are full of articles that tell you all about it. It's found in wolframite, and hubnerite and so on; but this is calcium tungstate, where it is found in connection with lime. The others are combined variously with iron or manganese—"

"Yes, manganese," broke in Charley importantly. "I know that well—and wolfite and all the rest. It certainly is wonderful how they build them big cannons that will shoot for twenty-two miles. But it's tungsden that does it, tungsden in connection with electricity and the invisible rays of radium."

"Oh, shut up!" burst out the Widow, thrusting him rudely aside and seizing a fresh handful of the rock. "I just can't hardly believe it." She gazed at the glossy fragments and then at the muckers, industriously loading the trucks; and then she cocked her head on one side.

"Let's see—two times twenty—that's forty dollars a ton. No—four hundred! Why, no—*four thousand!*" She stopped short and made a hurried re-calculation, while a murmur ran through the crowd, and then Death Valley Charley gave a whoop.

"*Four thousand!*" he shouted. "I told ye! I knowed it! I claimed she was rich, all the time!"

"You did not!" snapped the Widow, putting her hand under his jaw and forcibly stifling his whoops. "You poor, crazy fool, you knew nothing of the kind—you sold out for five thousand dollars!" She pushed him away with a swift, disdainful shove that sent him reeling through the crowd and then she whirled on Wiley. "And I suppose," she accused, "that you knew all the time that this dump here was nothing but tungsten?"

"Well, I had a good idea," he admitted deprecatingly, "although it's yet to be tested out. This is just a sample shipment—"

"Yes, a sample shipment; and at two dollars a pound how much will it bring you in? Why, nothing, hardly; a mere bagatelle for a gentleman and a scholar like you; but what about me and poor Virginia, slaving around to cook your meals? What do we get for all our pains? Oh, I could kill you, you scoundrel! You knew it all the time, and yet you let me sell those shares!"

She choked and Wiley shifted uneasily on the ore-pile, for of course he had done just that. To be sure he had urged her to sell them to his father for the sum of ten cents a share; but the mention of that fact, in her heated condition, would probably gain him nothing with the Widow. She was gasping for breath and, if nothing intervened, he was in for the scolding of his life. But it was all in the day's work and he glanced about for Virginia, to seek comfort from her smiling eyes. She would understand now why he had given her back her stock, and advised her from the start not to sell; but—he looked again, for her dark orbs were blazing and her lips were moving as with threats.

"You knew it all the time!" screamed the Widow in a frenzy, but Wiley barely heard her. He heard her words, for they assaulted his ears in a series of screeching crescendos, but it was the unspoken message from the lips of Virginia that cut him to the quick. He had expected nothing else from the abusive Widow; but certainly, after all the kindnesses he had done her, he was entitled to something better from Virginia. Not only had he warned her to hold on to her stock, at a time when one word might ruin him; but he had bought it from Charley and then given it back, to show how he valued her friendship. And yet now, while the others were shouting with joy or rushing to stake out more claims, she stood by the Widow and with cruel, voiceless words added her burden to this paean of hate. And she looked just like her mother!

"You shut up, you old cat!" he burst out fiercely, as the Widow rushed in to assault him. "Shut your mouth and get off my ground!" He drew back his palm to launch a swift blow and then his hand fell slack. "Well, holler then," he said, "what do I give a dam' whether you like the deal or not? You'd be yammering, just the same. But it's lucky for you you're a woman."

CHAPTER XV
THE GOD OF TEN PER CENT

It was the nature of the Widow to resort to violence in every crisis of her life and at each fresh memory of the effrontery of Wiley Holman she searched the empyrean for words. From the very start he had come to Keno with the intention of stealing her mine. First it was his father, who pitied her so much he was willing to buy her shares; then it was the tax sale, and he had sneaked in at night and tried to jump the Paymaster; then he had deceived her and stood in with Blount to make her sell all her stock for a song; and then, oh hateful thought, he had actually sold out to Blount for a hundred dollars, cash; only to put Blount in the hole and buy the mine back again for the price of the ore on the dump!

The Widow poured forth her charges without pausing for breath or noticing that her audience had fled, and as Wiley went on about his business she raised her voice to a scream. The rest of the Kenoites, and some of the workmen, were out staking the nearby hills; but whenever she stopped she thought of some fresh duplicity which made reason totter on its throne. He had refused half the mine from Blount as a gift and then turned around and bought it all. He had refused to buy her shares, time and again, when he knew they were worth a million; and then, to cap the climax, he had let her sell to Blount and bought them for nothing from him. And even Death Valley Charley—poor, crazy, brain-sick Charley—he had robbed him of all ten of his claims!

It was a damning arraignment, and Wiley's men listened grimly, but he only twisted his lip and nodded his head ironically. With one eye on his accuser, who was becoming hysterical, he hustled the ore into the empty trucks and started them off down the road; and then, as Virginia led her mother away, he re-engaged his cook. They had supper that night in the old, abandoned cookhouse; and, so wonderfully do great minds work, that a complete bill of grub was discovered among the freight. Not only flour and beans and canned goods and potatoes, but baking powder and matches and salt; and the cook observed privately that you'd think Mr. Holman had intended to make camp all the time. It is thus that foresight leaps ahead into the future and robs life of half its ills; and the Widow Huff, still unpacking plates and saucers, was untroubled by clamorous guests. She had had her say and, as far as Wiley was concerned, there were no more favors to be expected.

Yet the Widow was wise in the ways of mining camps and she prepared to feed a horde—and the next day they came, by automobile and motor-truck, until every table was filled. The rush was on, for four-thousand-dollar ore will bring men from the ends of the world. Before the sun had set in the red glow of a sandstorm the desert was staked for miles. From the chimneys of old houses, long abandoned to the rats, rose the smokes of many fires and the rush and whine of passing automobiles told of races to distant grounds. All the old mines in the district, and of neighboring districts where the precious "heavy spar" occurred, were re-located—or jumped, as the case might be—and held to await future developments. The first thing was to stake. They could prospect the ground later. Tungsten now was king. Men who had never heard the name, or pronounced it haltingly, now spoke learnedly of tungsten tests; and he was a poor prospector indeed who lacked his bottle of hydrochloric acid and his test-tubes and strip of shiny tin. They swarmed about the base of the old Paymaster dump like bees around a broken pot of honey and when, pounded up and boiled in the hydrochloric acid, the solution bit the tin and turned bright blue, there was many a hearty curse at the fickle hand of fortune which had led Wiley Holman to that treasure.

It had lain there for years, trampled down

beneath their feet. Now this kid, this miningschool prospector, had come back and grabbed it all. Not only the Paymaster with its tons of mined ore, but the ten claims to the north, all showing good scheelite, which Death Valley Charley had located—he had held them down as well. Two hundred dollars down and a carefully worded option had tied them up for five thousand dollars, and there were tungsten-mad men in that crowd of boomers who would have given fifty thousand apiece. They came up to the mine where Wiley was working and waved their money in his face, and then went off grumbling as he refused all offers and went busily about his work. So they came, and went, until at last the great wave brought Samuel J. Blount himself.

He came up the trail smiling, for there was nothing to be gained by making belated complaints; but when he saw the pile of precious white rock the smile died away in spite of him. It was the boast of Blount that, buying or selling, he always held out his ten per cent; but that pile of ore had cost him dear and he had sold it out for next to nothing. And it was his other boast that he could read men's hearts when they came to buy or sell, but here was a young man who had seen him coming twice and gained the advantage both times. So the smile grew longer in spite of his best efforts and when at last he found Wiley

Holman in the office of the company it was perilously near a sulk.

"Well, good morning, Wiley," he began with unction, and then he looked grievously about. The expensive gas engine which he had bought and installed was already unwatering the mine; spare timbers were going down, the new blacksmith-shop was running and Wiley was sitting at his desk. Everything was there, just the way he had left it, except that it belonged to Wiley. Blount heaved a heavy sigh and then set his features resolutely, for the battle was not over yet. To be sure the mine was bonded for a measly fifty thousand dollars, and his stock was tied up under an option; but many things can happen in six months' time and Wiley was only a boy. Granted that he was a miner and understood ore, there is such a thing as an "Act of God." Cables break without reason, mines cave and timbers fall; and certainly if there is a God of Ten Per Cent his just wrath would be visited upon Wiley. Blount knew that great god and worshipped him continually and he felt certain that something would happen, for when boys out of college take money away from bank presidents it comes dangerously close to sacrilege.

"Well, well," murmured Blount, "quite a change, quite a change. Are you sure that stuff is tungsten, Wiley?"

"Yes," responded Wiley, affecting a becoming

modesty to cover up his youthful smirk. "Would you like to see it tested?"

"Very much," answered Blount, and followed after him to the assay office, which Wiley had hurriedly fitted up. Wiley took a piece of scheelite and pounded it in a mortar until it was fine as flour, then dropped it into a test-tube and boiled it over a flame in a solution of hydrochloric and nitric acids.

"Now," he said, when the tungstic acid had been dissolved, and he had dropped a small bar of tin into the solution. It turned a dark blue and Blount sighed again, for he had looked up the test in advance. "If it turns blue," a prospector had told him, "like the color of me overalls, then, sure as hell, it's tungsten."

"Well, well," commented Blount, gazing mildly about, for great men do not stop to repine, "and what do you use these big scales for?"

"That's for the quantitative test," explained Wiley importantly. "By weighing the sample first and extracting the tungsten we get the percentage, when it's been filtered and dried and weighed again, of the tungstic acid in the ore. But it's quite an elaborate process."

"Yes, yes," assented Blount, still managing to smile pleasantly. "Rather out of my line, I guess. What per cent do your samples average?"

"Oh, between sixty and seventy when I pick my specimens. I'm rigging up a jigger to separate the ore until I can get capital to start up the mill. It ought to be milled, by rights, and only the concentrates shipped; but while I'm getting started—"

"Oh, draw on me—any time," broke in Blount, smiling radiantly. "I'd be only too glad to accommodate you. That's my business, you know; loaning out money on good security, and you're good up to fifty thousand dollars."

"Do you mean it?" demanded Wiley after a startled silence, and Blount slapped him heartily on the back.

"Just try me," he said. "I've been looking up the market and tungsten is simply booming. It's quoted at forty-five for sixty per cent concentrates, and you must have tons and tons on the dump."

"Yes, lots of it," admitted Wiley, "and say, now that you mention it, I believe I'll take you up. I need a little money to install some machinery and get the old mill to running. How about ten thousand dollars?"

"Why—all right," assented Blount, after a moment's thought. "Of course you'll give some security?"

"Oh, sure," agreed Wiley. "My option on the mine—I suppose that's what you're after?"

Blount blinked for a moment, for such plain speaking was surprising from one as shrewd as Wiley, but he summoned up his smile and nodded. "Why—why, yes, that's all right. Say one per cent a month—payable monthly—those are our ordinary short-time terms."

"Suits me," said Wiley. "But no cut-throat clauses—none of this Widow Huff line of stuff. If I forget to pay my interest that doesn't make the principal due and the security forfeit and so on, world without end."

"Oh, no; no, certainly," cried Blount with alacrity. "We'll make it a flat loan, if you like, and endeavor to treat you right. Of course you'll start a checking account and—"

"No," said Wiley, "if I borrow the money I'll take it out of your bank and put it in another, right away. I never let friendship interfere with business or warp my business judgment."

"Yes, but Wiley," protested Blount, "what difference does it make? Isn't my bank perfectly safe and sound?"

"Undoubtedly," returned Wiley, "but—do you happen to remember a little check for four hundred dollars? It was made out by me in favor of Death Valley Charley and they cashed it through your bank—Virginia Huff, you know—in payment for Paymaster stock. Well, if you're going to keep track of my business like that—"

"Oh, no, no," exclaimed Blount, suddenly remembering the means by which he had detected Wiley's purchase of Virginia's stock, "you misunderstand me, entirely. If you want to wait a few days for the money you are welcome to put it anywhere."

"Well, hold on," began Wiley. "Now maybe I'd better go to the other bank—"

"Oh, no, no, no," protested Blount, "I wouldn't hear of it. I'll write you the check, this minute. On your personal note—that's good enough for me. You can put up the collateral later."

"Well, let's think this over," objected Wiley cannily. "I don't like to put up that option for security. That bond and lease is worth half a million dollars and—"

"Just give me your note," broke in Blount hurriedly, "and hurry up—here comes Mrs. Huff."

"All right," cried Wiley, and scribbled out the note while Blount was writing the check.

CHAPTER XVI
A SHOW-DOWN WITH THE WIDOW

If the benevolent Samuel Blount could have seen Wiley Holman's monthly statement from that mysterious "other bank" he would have crushed him with one blow of his ready, financial club and gone off with both bond-and-lease and option. But the pure, serene fire in those first water diamonds which graced the ring on Wiley's hand—that dazzled Samuel J. Blount as it had dazzled the Widow and many a store-keeper in Vegas. For it is hardly to be expected that a man with such a ring will have a bank account limited to three figures, any more than it is expected that a man with so little capital will be sitting in a game with millionaires. But Wiley was sitting in, holding his cards well against his chest, and already he had won ten thousand dollars. Which is one of the reasons why all mining promoters wear diamonds—and poker faces as well.

Yet Blount was playing a game which had once won him a million dollars from just such plungers as Wiley, and if he also smiled as he tucked away the note it was not without excuse. There had been a time when this boy's father had sat in the game with Blount and now he was engaged in raising cattle on a ranch far back in the hills. And Colonel Huff, that prince of royal plungers, had surrendered at last to the bank. It was twelve per cent, compounded monthly, with demand, protest and notice waived, which had brought about this miracle of wealth; and since it is well known that history repeats itself, Mr. Blount could see Wiley's finish. The thing to do first was to regain his confidence and get him into his power and then, at the first sign of financial embarrassment, to call his notes and freeze him out. Such were the intentions of the benevolent Mr. Blount—if the Widow Huff did not kill him.

She came toiling up the trail, followed by Virginia and Death Valley Charley and a crowd of curious citizens; and as they awaited the shock, Blount shuddered and smiled nervously, for he knew that she would demand back her stock. Wiley shuddered too, but instead of smiling he clenched his jaws like a vise; and as the Widow entered he signaled a waiting guard, who followed in close behind her. She halted before his desk, one hand on her hip the other on the butt of a six-shooter, and glanced insolently from one to the other.

"Aha!" she exclaimed, "so you're talking it over,—how to take advantage of a poor widow! But I want to tell you now, and I don't care who knows it, I've been imposed upon long enough. Here you sit in your office, both of you worth up into the millions, and discuss the division of your spoils; while the daughter and the widow of the man that found this mine are slaving away in a restaurant."

"Yes, I'm sorry, Mrs. Huff," interposed Blount, smiling gently. "We were just discussing your case. But it often happens that the best of us err in judgment, and in this case I've been caught worse than you were. Yes, I must admit that when I first heard about this tungsten and realized that I had sold out for nothing, I was moved for the moment to resent it; but under the circumstances—"

"Aw, what are you talking about?" demanded the Widow scornfully. "Don't you think I can see through your game? You pretend to be enemies until you get hold of my stock and then you come out into the open. I always knew you were partners, but now I can prove it; because here you are, thick as thieves."

"Yes, we're friendly," admitted Blount with a painful smile at Wiley, "but Wiley owns the mine. That is, he owns a bond and lease on the property, with the option of buying for fifty thousand dollars. And then besides that, I regret to say, he has an option on all my stock."

"Oh! Yes!" scoffed the Widow. "You've been cleaned by this whipper-snapper that's just a few months out of college! He's taken away your mine and your stock and everything—but of course you don't mind a little thing like that. But what I want to know, and I came here to find out, is which of you has got my stock—because I'll tell you right now—" she whipped out her pistol and brandished it in the air—"I'll tell you right now I intend to get it back or kill the one or both of you!"

Blount's lips framed a lie, and then he glanced at Wiley, who was standing with his hand by his gun.

"Well, now, Mrs. Huff," he began at a venture, "I—perhaps this can all be arranged."

"No! I want that stock!" cried the Widow in hot anger, "and I'm going to get it, too!"

"Why—why yes," stammered Blount, "but you see it was this way—I had no idea of the value of the stock. And so when Wiley came to see me I gave him an option on it for—well, I believe it was five cents a share."

"Ah!" triumphed the Widow, whirling to train her gun on Wiley, "so now I've got you, Mr. Man! You've been four-flushing long enough but I've got you dead to rights, and I want—that—Paymaster—stock!"

She threw down on him awkwardly, but as the pistol was not cocked, Wiley only curled his lip and smiled indulgently, with a restraining glance at his guard.

"Yes, Mrs. Huff," he agreed quite calmly, "I don't doubt you want it back. You want lots of things that you'll never get from me by coming around with these gun-plays. So put up that gun before you pull it off and I'll tell you about your husband's stock."

"My *husband's* stock!" cried the Widow in surprise, letting the six-shooter wobble down to her side. "Well I'd just like to tell you that that stock is *mine,* and furthermore—"

"Oh, yes! Sure! Sure!" shrugged Wiley scornfully. "Of course you know it all! But that stock wasn't yours, and you couldn't transfer it, and so I didn't take any option on it. It's in the bank yet; and if you want to get it, why, here's the man to talk to."

He jerked his thumb towards the cringing Blount, and exchanged scornful glances with Virginia. She was standing behind her mother and her glance seemed to say that he was passing the buck again; but his feeling for Virginia had suffered a great change and he replied to her head-toss with a sneer.

"Now—now Wiley!" protested Blount, rising weakly to his feet and regarding his pseudo-partner reproachfully, "you know very well—"

"Gimme that stock!" snapped the Widow, suddenly cocking the heavy pistol and throwing down savagely on Wiley; and then things began to happen. The watchful guard, who had been standing at her side, reached over and struck up the gun and as it went off with a bang, shooting a hole in the ceiling, he seized it and wrenched it away.

"You're under arrest, Madam," he said with some asperity, and flashed his officer's star.

"Well, who are you, sir?" demanded the Widow, vainly attempting to thrust him aside.

"I'm a deputy sheriff, ma'am," replied the officer respectfully, "and I'd advise you not to resist. It'll be assault with intent to kill."

"Why—I wouldn't kill anybody!" exclaimed the Widow breathlessly. "I was—I didn't intend to do anything."

"Will you swear out a warrant?" inquired the deputy and Wiley nodded his head.

"You bet I will," he said, "this is getting monotonous. She took a shot at me, once before."

"Oh, Wiley!" wailed the Widow suddenly weakening in the pinch. "You know I never meant it!"

"Well, maybe not," replied Wiley evenly, "but you hit me in the leg."

"But *he* pulled off my gun!" charged the Widow angrily, "I never went to do it!"

"Well, come on;" said the deputy, "you can explain to the judge." And he took her by the arm. She went out, sobbing violently, and in the succeeding silence Wiley found himself confronted by Virginia. He had seen her before when the wild light of battle shot forth from her angry eyes but now there was a glow of soft, feminine reproach and the faintest suggestion of appeal.

"Oh, Wiley Holman!" she cried, "I'll never forgive you! What do you mean by treating Mother like this?"

"I mean," replied Wiley, "that I've taken about enough, and now we'll leave it to the law. If your mother is right the judge will let her go, but I guess it's come to a show-down."

"What? Are you going to let them put my mother in jail?" she asked with tremulous awe, and then she burst into tears. "You ought to be ashamed!" she broke out impetuously. "I wish my father was here!"

"Yes, so do I," answered Wiley gravely. "I'd be dealing with a gentleman, then. But if your mother thinks, just because she is a woman, she can run amuck with a gun, then she gives up all right to be treated like a lady and she has to take what's coming to her."

"But Wiley!" she appealed, "just let her off this time and she'll never do it again. She's overwrought and nervous and—"

"Nope," said Wiley, "it's gone past me now—she'll have to answer before the judge. But if you think you can restrain her I'll be willing to let it go and have her bound over to keep the peace."

"Oh, that'll be fine! If she just promises not to bother you and—"

"And puts up a five-thousand-dollar bond,"

added Wiley. "And the next time she makes a gun-play or comes around and threatens me the five thousand dollars is gone."

"Oho!" she accused, "so that's your scheme! You've been framing this up, all the time!"

"Sure," nodded Wiley, with his old cynical smile, "I just love to be shot at. I got her to come over on purpose."

"Well, I'll bet you did!" cried Virginia excitedly. "Didn't you have that officer right there? You've just framed this up to rob us. And how are we going to give a five-thousand-dollar bond when you know we haven't a cent? Oh, I—I hate you, Wiley Holman; and if you put my mother in jail I'll—I'll come back and kill you, myself!"

She stamped her foot angrily, but a light leapt into Wiley's eyes such as had flamed there when he had faced Stiff Neck George.

"Very well," he said, "if you people think you can rough-house me I'll show you I can rough it, myself. I've tried to be friendly and to give you the best of it; but now it's all off, for good. I hate to fight a woman, but—"

"You do not!" she challenged. "You're a coward, that's what you are! And you can take your old stock back!"

She drew a package from her bosom and slammed it spitefully on the table and rushed out after her mother. Wiley picked up the envelope and regarded it absently, his lip curling to a twisted smile. It was the package of stock which he had bought from Death Valley Charley and returned, as a gift, to Virginia.

CHAPTER XVII
PEACE—AND THE PRICE

In the justice court at Vegas the Widow Huff met her match in the person of the magistrate, who warned her peremptorily that if she interrupted again he would commit her for contempt of court. Then the bailiff smote his desk a resounding blow and there was silence in the presence of the law. It was a new thing to her, this power called the law and that accuser of all offenders, The People; and before she had finished she learned the great truth that no one is above the law. It governs us all and, but for the mercy of the courts, would land most of our hot-heads in jail. But though it was proved beyond the peradventure of a doubt that the Widow had attempted violence it was tacitly understood that, being a woman, there would be no actual commitment.

Wiley Holman came forward and informed the court that the defendant had threatened his life and upon two occasions and had made assaults upon his person with the avowed intention of killing him. Upon being questioned by the judge he admitted recognizing a shotgun, and three buckshot which had been extracted from his leg; but in a voluntary statement he expressed the opinion that the defendant was hardly responsible. At the same time, he stated, since his place of business was not far from the defendant's home, he would respectfully request that she be placed in custody and bound over to keep the peace. The testimony of the officer and of other witnesses left no doubt as to the existence of a threat and after the Widow had made a chastened speech she was placed in the custody of the sheriff.

To this humiliation was added the greater pang of depositing all her jewels with her bondsmen and when it was over and she was back in her home the Widow's proud spirit was broken. She retired to the kitchen and the balm of a great peace was laid upon tumultuous Keno. For years the bold ego of Colonel Huff's wife had dominated the very life of the camp, but the son of Honest John had at last found a way of putting her anger in leash. Rage as she might in the privacy of her kitchen, or pour out her woes to the neighbors, when Wiley Holman came by she turned away her face and allowed him to pass in silence. And Wiley himself never gave her a glance, nor Virginia when he met her in the street; for the memory of their insults was still hot in his brain, and all he asked for was peace.

He was safe, at last, safe to remodel the mill and bring up the ore from the mine; but as his work grew and prospered the anger died in his breast and his heart turned back to Virginia. She was quiet now, with averted eyes and the sad, brooding face of a nun; and she worked early and late in the crowded dining-room, serving meals to the hard-rock miners. He had closed down his cookhouse to give them some patronage, when the first mad rush of prospectors was past; but though they fed his men and took the money that he had paid them, they owned no obligation to him.

In the Paymaster the pumps were working steadily now, clearing the water from the submerged passages, and as the first checks came back in payment for his tungsten he ordered more timbers and men. There was plenty of ore on the dump for the moment but, while he separated it from the waste and shipped it to town, he caught up the falling ground in the drifts and prepared to stope out the scheelite. In the old, dismantled mill he had a crew working over-time, installing a rock-crusher and a concentrating plant; and every truck that brought out timbers and supplies took back its tons of ore. The price of tungsten leapt from forty dollars a unit to sixty and sixty-five, and rival buyers clamored for his ore; the mills treated it for almost nothing in order to get control of it and his credit was all at the bank—but when he passed Virginia she turned her face away and his heart turned heavy as lead.

It was the price of success, and Wiley recognized it, but he rebelled against his fate. What fault was it of his that her father and his father had fallen out over the mine? He had shown by the stock that the treachery had been Blount's and neither of them was to blame. What fault was it of his that she had a shrewish mother who was bent upon ruining her life? Had he not endured abuse and suffered grievous wounds before he had asserted his rights? And with Virginia herself, when had there ever been a time when he had forgotten his lover's part—except on that last day, when he had turned like a trodden worm and protested his right to live? And yet she blamed him for all her misfortunes and for every day that she slaved; and even took the stock which he had returned as a peace-offering and hurled it in his face!

Wiley's lips set grimly as he gazed at the certificates for which men had striven and died. There were some from her father, transferred on her birthdays when the stock was around thirty and forty; and others from old prospectors like Henry Masters, who had left it to Virginia when they died. She had sent it to him by Charley, out of shame for her harsh words, and he had bought it for four hundred dollars, half the money that he had in the world. Those had been happy days, in spite of the anxiety, for he had made the sacrifice for her; and to prove his devotion—and make a peace-offering against the explosion that was bound to come—he had given the stock back to Virginia. That was when he was a prospector, doing business on a shoe-string, a racing car and a diamond ring; but now when he had made his *coup* and could write his check for thousands she threw the stock back in his face.

The stock had a value now for, under the terms of the bond and lease, one-tenth of the net mill returns were automatically withheld and turned in to the company as royalty; and if for any reason he failed to meet the payment when the fifty-thousand-dollar option expired, then this stock and all Paymaster stock would take a sudden jump to five or ten dollars a share. And the stock was hers—she had received it from her father when he was the mining king of the West, and from old man Masters when he was dying in the cabin where she had helped to care for him for months—yet she would not accept it as a gift. Wiley pondered a long time and then, as Christmas drew near, he sent for Death Valley Charley.

"Charley," he began, when he came up that night, "did I understand you to say one time that you were acting as a kind of guardian to Virginia? Well, now here's a bunch of stock that you sold to me once when you were slightly off your cabeza. There's over twelve thousand shares and all you asked was four hundred dollars, when you knew they were worth eight hundred at least."

"Yes, that's so," admitted Charley, blinking and rubbing his chin, "but you know them women, Wiley. They're crazy, that's all, and the Colonel he told me special not to let them lose their mine."

"Well, never mind the mine," said Wiley wincing. "I'm talking about this stock. Don't you think it's your duty, by George, as guardian, to turn around and buy it back? You've got five thousand dollars coming to you on those claims of yours and I'll tell you what I'll do. I'm short, right now on account of buying machinery, and so I can't pay you much cash; but if you'll take this stock back in part payment of your claims I'll give you four hundred more."

"Well, all right," agreed Charley after gazing at him thoughtfully, "but you ought to give back that mine. The Colonel, he told me—"

"What do you mean, give it back?" demanded Wiley, irritably. "It isn't my property yet. I've got to pay for it first and get it away from old Blount before I can give it to anybody. That's fifty thousand dollars that I've got to make clear between now and the twentieth of May; but believe me, Charley, if I once get it paid for I'm going to do something noble."

"That's good," assented Charley, "but you've got to pay me, right off—there's something going to happen!" His sun-dazed eyes opened up wide with excitement and he listened long and earnestly at the door before he tiptoed back to Wiley's desk. "I can hear 'em," he said. "They're going to blow up the mine and shake the mountains down. They're boring through the ground, but I can hear them working—it's like worms eating their way through wood."

"Is that so?" queried Wiley. "Well, maybe we can stop 'em. I'll look after it, right away. But now about this stock—"

"It's the Germans!" burst out Charley. "They've got boring machines that eat through mountains like wood. And then, *bumm,* it's them mines, and the dynamite bombs—"

"Yes, it's awful," agreed Wiley, "but here's your money, Charley; so maybe you'd better go. And you keep this stock now, until it comes Christmas; and then, Christmas Eve, you slip into the house and put it in Virginia's stocking."

"Oh—yes," agreed Charley, still listening to the Germans and then he became lost in deep thought. "The Colonel will kill me," he said at last. "It's Christmas, and I ain't brought his whiskey."

"Why, what's the matter?" joshed Wiley. "Why didn't you deliver it? Did you get caught in a sandstorm, or what?"

"Yes, a sandstorm," answered Charley, solemnly. "It came down the valley like a wall. And my burros got away; but the Colonel, he found me—I was digging a hole in the sand."

"Say, where are these Ube-Hebes?" broke in Wiley impulsively. "I'd like to go over there sometime."

"They're across Death Valley," answered Charley smiling craftily, "—on the west side, in the Funeral Range. The Coffin mine is there—I used to work in it—but they put me underground with a stiff for a pardner so I quit and come back to town."

"Yes, I heard about that; but you forgot something, Charley—how about that graveyard shift? But I'll tell you what I'll do, if you'll take me to the Colonel I'll help Virginia get back her mine."

He plumped the statement at him, for Charley was an innocent who spoke out the truth when he was jumped, but for once he detected the ruse.

"The Colonel's dead," he answered sulkily and picked up his hat to go.

"I doubt it!" scoffed Wiley. "I met a man the other day who said he'd seen him—in the Ube-Hebes mountains."

"He did?" exclaimed Charley, and then he drew back and his eyes flashed with angry resentment. "You're a liar!" he burst out. "The Colonel is dead. He never said anything of the kind."

"Yes, he did," insisted Wiley, "and you know the man well. He's got a little dog like Heine."

"He's a liar!" cried Charley savagely, "and don't you go to talking or I'll make you wish you hadn't."

"No, I won't," assured Wiley, "but here's the proposition—the Colonel left a lot of stock. And Mrs. Huff, being crazy, gave it all to Blount on a loan of eight hundred dollars. But if the Colonel should come back that transfer would be illegal and he could fix it to get back the mine. So don't talk to me about giving Virginia her mine—you go out and bring in the Colonel."

"He's dead!" yelled Charley, scrabbling madly out the door. "You're a liar—I tell you he's dead!"

"Yes, he's dead," observed Wiley, "just the same as I am. I'll have to get old Charley drunk."

CHAPTER XVIII
ON CHRISTMAS DAY

Christmas came to Keno in a whirling snowstorm that shrouded Shadow Mountain in white and, as he stepped out in the morning and looked up at the peak, Wiley Holman felt a thrill of joy. The black shadow had bothered him, now that he had come to live under it; and a hundred times a day as it caught his eye he would glance up to find the dark cloud. But now it was gone and in place of the lava cap there was a mantle of gleaming snow. He looked down at the town and, on every graceless house, there had been bestowed a crown of white; all the tin cans were buried, the burned spots were covered over, and Keno was almost beautiful. A family of children were out in the street, trying to coast in their new Christmas wagons, and Wiley smiled to himself.

He had brought back those children; he had brought the town to life and tenanted its vacant houses; and now, best of all, he had brought the spirit of Christmas, for he had sent a peace-offering to Virginia. She had spurned it once in the heat of passion, and called him a coward and a crook; but that package of stock would recall to her mind a time when she had known him for a friend. It would bring up old memories of their boy-and-girl love, which she knew he had never forgotten, and if there was anything to forgive she would know that he remembered it when he sent this offering by Charley.

He was a crazy old rat, but he had his uses; and he had promised to give her the stock, without fail. It was to come, of course, from Charley himself, in atonement for selling it for nothing; but Virginia would know, even if she missed his flowered Christmas card, that the stock was a present from him. It had a value now far above the price he had paid for it when Charley had thrust it upon him and the dividend alone from the royalties on his lease would be twelve hundred dollars and more. And then her pro rata share, when he paid his fifty thousand dollars, would add another six hundred; and she knew that, for the asking, she could have half of what he had—or all, if she would take him, too.

Wiley looked down on the house that sheltered Virginia and smiled to think of her there. She was waiting on miners, but the time would come when someone would be waiting on her. In the back of his brain a bold plan had been forming to feed fat his grudge against Blount and restore the Huffs to their own—and it needed but a word from her to put the plan into action. He held from Blount two separate and distinct papers; one a bond and lease on the mine, the other an option on his personal stock. But to grant the bond and lease—with its option for fifty thousand—Blount had been compelled to vote the Widow's stock; and if that stock was not his and had been illegally voted, then of course the bond and lease would be void.

Yet even so he, Wiley Holman, had fully safeguarded his interests, for by his other option he could buy all Blount's stock for the sum of five cents a share. The four hundred thousand-odd shares would come to only twenty thousand dollars, as against fifty thousand on the bond and lease; and yet, by buying the stock at once, he could effectually debar Blount from any share in the accumulating profits. The small payments on past royalties and his five cents a share would be all that Blount would receive; and then he would be left, a spectacle for gods and men—a banker who had been beaten by a boy. It was the chicanery of Blount which had ruined his father and driven Colonel Huff to his death, and what could be better, as poetic justice, than to see him hoist on his own petard. And if the Colonel was not dead—as would appear from Charley's maunderings—if he could be discovered and brought back to town, then surely Virginia would forget the old feud and consent to be his wife. All this lay before him, a fairyland of imaginings, waiting only her magic touch to make it real; just a word, a smile, a promise of forgiveness—

and of loyalty and love—and he, Wiley Holman, would go whirling on the errand that would win him wealth and renown.

It would all be done for her, and yet he would not be the loser, for his own father held two hundred thousand shares of Paymaster; and he himself would save a fifty-thousand-dollar payment at an expense of a little over twenty. And if the Colonel could be found quickly—or his death disproved to make illegal the Widow's transfer of his stock—then the mine could be claimed at once and Blount deprived even of his royalties. Of course this could all be done without the help of Virginia or the co-operation of any of the Huffs for, although his father had refused from the first to have anything to do with the mine, Wiley knew that he could talk him over and persuade him to pool his stock. That would make six hundred thousand, a clean voting majority and a fortune in itself; but for the sake of Virginia, and to heal the ancient feud, it would be better to unite with the Huffs.

Wiley paced up and down in the crisp, dry snow and watched for Virginia to come, and as his mind leapt ahead he saw her enthroned in a mansion, with him as her faithful vassal—when he was not her lord and king. For the Huffs were proud, even now in their poverty, and Virginia was the proudest of them all; and in this, their first meeting, he must remember what she had suffered and that it is hard for the loser to yield. It should be his part to speak with humility and dwell but lightly on the past while he pictured a future, entirely free from menial service, in which she could live according to her station. All her years of poverty and disappointment and loneliness would be forgotten in this sudden rise to wealth; and to complete the picture, Blount, the cause of all her suffering, would grovel, very unbankerlike, at their feet.

Blount would grovel indeed when he felt the cold steel that would deprive him of all his stock, for he was still playing the game with his loans and extensions in the hope of winning back what he had lost. For money was his god, before whom there was no other, and he worshiped it day and night; and all his fair talk was no more than a pretense to lure Wiley into the net. Yet not for a minute would Wiley put up his option, or his bond and lease on the mine; and for all the money that Blount had loaned him he had given his mere note of hand. It was his promise to pay, unsecured by any collateral, and yet it was perfectly good. The money came and went—he could pay Blount at any time—but it was better to rehabilitate the mine.

Wiley had a race before him, a race for big stakes, and he kept his eyes on the goal. To earn fifty thousand dollars in six months' time, earn it clean above all expense, required foresight and careful management, and a big daily output, for every day must count. The ore on the dump was in the nature of a grub-stake, a bonus for undertaking the game; and when it was all shipped the profits would drop to nothing unless he could bring up more ore. So he took his first checks, and what he could borrow, and timbered and cleaned out the mine; and, to save shipping out more ore, he had ordered expensive machinery to put the old mill into shape. It was the part of good judgment to spend quickly at first and build up the efficiency of his plant; and then the last few months, when Blount would begin to gloat, make a run that would put him in the clear. Clear not only of the bond and lease, but on Blount's stock as well, for it would pay for itself with the first dividend; and, to save paying any more royalties, Wiley was curtailing his wasteful shipments while he prepared to concentrate the ore in his mill.

There were envious people in town who prophesied his failure and claimed that success had gone to his head, but he was confident he could show them that a man can take chances and yet play his cards to win. He had taken chances with Blount when he had accepted his money, for there were other banks that would lend on his mine; but in what more harmless way could he engage his attention and keep him from actual sabotage? It was that which he dreaded, the resort to open warfare, the fire and vandalism, and dynamite; and day and night he kept his eye on the works, and hired a night-watchman, to boot. But as long as Blount was convinced he could win back the mine peaceably he would not resort to violence and, though Stiff Neck George still hung about the camp, he kept scrupulously away from the Paymaster.

As Christmas day wore on and the sun came out gleaming, Wiley swung off down the trail and through the town. He was a big man now, the man who had saved Keno after ten years of stagnation and lingering death; and yet there were those who disliked him. They recited old stories of his shrewd dealings with Mrs. Huff, and with Virginia and Death Valley Charley; and if any were forgotten the Widow undoubtedly recalled them. She was a shrewish woman, full of gossip and backbiting, and she let no opportunity pass; so that even old Charley cherished a certain resentment, though he disguised it as solicitude for the Huffs. And so on Christmas day, as Wiley walked down the street, many greetings lacked a holiday heartiness.

The front room of the Huff house was full of children and, as Wiley walked back and forth, he caught a glimpse of Virginia; but she did not come out and, after lingering around for a while, he climbed up the trail to the mine. He had caught but a glimpse, but it was clean-cut as a cameo—a classic head, eagerly poised; dark hair, brushed smoothly back; and a smile, for some neighbor's child. That was Virginia, high-headed and patrician, but kind to lame dogs and lost cats. She had invited in the children but he, Wiley Holman, who had loved her since she was a child, had been permitted to pass unnoticed. He wandered about uneasily, then went back to his office and began to run over his accounts.

Over a hundred thousand dollars had passed through his hands in less than a calendar month and yet the long haul across the desert from Vegas had put him in the hole. Besides the initial cost of cables and timbers—and of a rock-breaker and the concentrating plant—there was a charge of approximately twenty dollars a ton for every pound of supplies he hauled out. And, because of the war, all supplies were high and the machinery houses were behind with their orders; yet so eager were the buyers to get hold of his tungsten that they almost took it out of the bins. He was storing up the ore, preparatory to milling it and shipping only the concentrates; but if they could have their way they would wrest it from his hands and rush it to the railroad post haste. One mysterious buyer had even offered him a contract at seventy dollars a unit—three dollars and a half a pound!

Wiley opened up his notebook and made a careful estimate of what the ore on the dump would bring and his eyes grew big as he figured. At seventy dollars a unit it would come to more than he owed; and pay for the mine, to boot. It was a stupendous sum to come so quickly, before the mine was hardly opened up; but when the mill was running and the mine was sending up ore—he smiled dizzily and shook his head. A profit like that, if it ever became known, would make his position dangerous. It was too much of a temptation for Blount and his jumpers, and black-leg lawyers with fake claims. They could get out injunctions and tie up the work until he lost the mine by default!

But would they dare do it? And how long would it take to raise fifty thousand dollars elsewhere? Wiley studied it all over in the silence of his office, for the mine was closed down for Christmas; and then once more he turned to his notebook and figured the ore underground. Then he figured the outside cost for installing his machinery, for freight and supplies and the payroll; and, adding twenty per cent for wear and tear and accidents, he figured the grand total for six months. That was astounding too but, when he put against it his ore and the price per ton, not even the chances that stood out against him could keep down that dizzy smile. He was made, he was rich, if he could just hold things level and do a day's work every day.

The sun set at last as he sat planning details

and, rising up stiffly, he pushed his papers aside and went out into the night. The snow had melted fast on the roofs and bare ridges and, as the last rays of sunset touched the peak with ruddy fingers, he noticed that the shadow had come back. The barren lava cap had thrown aside its Christmas mantle, melting the snow before it could pack; and now, grim and black, it stood out like a death-head above the white valley below. Lights flashed out from miners' windows, the scampering children ceased their clamor, and he wandered through the darkness alone.

There was something he had forgotten, something big and significant, but his tired brain refused to respond. It was part of the scheme to beat Blount out of his stock, and the royalty from the shipments of ore; and—yes, it had to do with Virginia. It was going to make her rich, and both of them happy; but he could not recall it, at the moment. He was worn out, weary with the seething thoughts which had rioted through his mind all day, and he turned back dumbly to his office. It was dark and cold and as he groped for his matchbox his hand encountered a strange package. And yet it was not so strange—he seemed to remember it, somehow. He struck a hasty match and looked. It was the package of stock that he had sent to Virginia, but—The match burnt his fingers and he dropped it with a curse. She had refused his offer of peace.

CHAPTER XIX
THE ENIGMA

The heights and depths of life are sounded by emotions—cold reason lags behind. As thought cannot compass, so words cannot describe the anguished spirit's flight; and whether it soars to ecstasy or sinks to despair it comes back wide-eyed and silent. So any action which has been prompted by passion cannot be explained by a calculating mind, and to seek a reason where none exists is to stray still farther from the truth. Virginia Huff was poor and waited on the table for what she could eat and get to wear; and when she returned stock which was worth twelve hundred dollars without even a note of thanks it was not for any reason of the mind. It was a reason of the feelings, the soul, the human ego, which drives our minds and bodies to their tasks; a reason that soared up like a flaming aurora and stabbed the darkened sky with hate and passion. It was nothing to reason about, and yet Wiley reasoned.

He put down the stocks and lit his lamp and examined the package carefully. Then he looked inside for some note of explanation and paused and swore to himself. No note was there, nor any sign that the stocks had ever passed through her hands. He rose up craftily and stepped out the door, passing silently from house to house, and then as he came back he threw his door open and examined the snow for tracks. If Death Valley Charley had failed of his mission, if he had neglected to place the shares in her stocking and then sneaked back to get rid of them—but Wiley put all thought of Charley aside for there in the snow was the print of a woman's shoe. Small and dainty it was and he knew in his heart that Virginia had been there and gone. She might have been watching him as he sat at his work, she might even be watching him now; but again something told him that, however she had come, she had gone away in a rage. The stab of the high heel, the heedless step into a mud-puddle, the swinging stride down the trail; all spoke of defiance, of a coming in the open and a return without fear of man or devil. She had come there to see him and finding him away, she had thrown down the papers and gone home. And that was the answer to his love.

Wiley sat down by the fire and tried to account for it. He imagined himself a woman, young and beautiful, but poor; working hard, as Virginia now worked, for her board and keep. Before her there was nothing—her father was dead or lost, her mother a hopeless scold, her fortune irretrievably gone—and yet she closed the only door out.

As an earnest of his love, without asking anything in return, he had restored to her a portion of her stock; and she had promptly flung it back. Had Charley made some break in his method of presentation? But no, she would not mind if he had; it was something deeper, behind. He battered his brain, recalling every little incident that might have turned her heart against him, and it all brought him back to the trial.

When he had had her mother arrested for coming into his office and demanding—what was it she had demanded? He remembered the six-shooter, and the deputy and Blount, and the Widow's rage and tears; and Virginia's return and all she had said to him—but what was it her mother had demanded? Her stock! All her stock! The stock she had refused to sell for ten cents a share and then had turned around and put up with Blount as security on a quick-action note. She had demanded it all back, without reason, without compensation, simply because she was a woman with a gun; and because he had invoked the law to protect him in his rights Virginia had sworn she would kill him. Wiley rose up swiftly and pulled the curtain across the window, and then he considered the matter again.

It was not like Virginia to resort to any violence—she had been humiliated too often by her mother's—but she must still think he had deprived her of her rights. By what process of reasoning could they fix the blame on him for this stock which had been purloined by Blount, was beyond his strictly masculine mind; but women sometimes think by jumps. They skip a few processes, like a mathematical prodigy, and then arrive at some mammoth result. But, even if they exaggerated their grievance—was there anything behind it, any peg on which to hang this senseless hate?

Well, of course he had deceived them about the mine. He had known it contained scheelite the moment he picked up that white rock that Virginia had placed in her collection, but naturally he had not announced it from the house-tops. With the Widow as a partner, or even as a stockholder, the best-natured man in the state of Nevada could not have worked the Paymaster at a profit. For that reason alone he had been fully justified in letting her freeze herself out; and if Virginia had taken his advice—but then, the poor girl had been distracted. She had been worn out and discouraged, hag-ridden by her mother and facing a trip to the city; and she had sold out for what she could get. She was a good girl, a brave girl, and a sweet and lovely one too; and it was foolish to blame her for anything. The thing to do, after all, was to find ways and means of bringing her back to her own. Just a word from Virginia and he could change her whole life, he could get back all her stock and her mother's as well and pour money into their laps—but first he must win her love. He must teach her to trust him, break down her suspicion and show her that he was her friend.

Wiley thought a long time and the next morning at dawn he was up in his car and away. Virginia was a child. She did not reason about this and that, but was swayed by the impulses of the moment. Her life was ruled, not by her head but by her heart; and he had forgotten until that moment the sacks full of cats that he had taken from her house to the ranch. They were all her pets, and he had taken them as a trust when she was about to start for Los Angeles; but the mine had made him forget. They were safe at the ranch, with his sisters to look after them; but how many times since their estrangement began must some question have risen to her lips as to how they were, or if he would bring them back, or whether any had died or been lost? Yet she had turned her head away and refused to speak to him, even to demand back the pets she loved.

The road was bad out across the desert, and on through Vegas to the ranch, but he came thundering back the next night. He had left the mine to run itself, for his thoughts were of Virginia, but as he slowed down at the sand-wash and listened for the pumps he noticed that the engine had stopped. Well, he had an engineer and that was his business—to keep the sump-hole pumped out; perhaps he had shut down for repairs. But the big thing, after all, was to restore Virginia her pets and win his way to a place in her heart. He drove boldly up the street and stopped before the house, but nobody came to the door. He waited a while, then leapt out uncertainly and released the mother of Virginia's pet kittens. She ran under the house and, as no one came out, Wiley let the rest of them go and turned disconsolately back towards the mine. If he had ever thought, when he had the Widow arrested, that Virginia was going to take it so hard—but then, of course, it had been absolutely necessary—and just wait till she found her kittens!

There was trouble in the engine-house. He knew that the minute he saw the dancing torches in the dark, and he went up the trail on the run; but when he saw the wreckage, and the gear-wheel dismounted, he burst into a wailing curse. The mine had been all right, pumps operating, hoist running, when he had left the day before; but the minute he turned his back—

"What's the matter?" he demanded and then, pushing the engineer aside, he flashed a torch on the wreck. Wedged in the gearing of the shattered gear-wheel was a pair of engineer's overalls. They had jammed tight in the teeth and the resistless driving of the engine had cracked the great gear-wheel like an eggshell. Held solid by its base in the bolted concrete there had not been a half-inch's play and, since something must give, and the opposing wheel had stood, the enormous casting had smashed. The engineer and his helpers were pottering about, trying guiltily to remove the cause of the accident, but one look was enough to tell Wiley Holman that his mine was closed down for a week. No welding could ever repair that broken gear-wheel—he would have to wire for another.

"Whose overalls are those?" he asked at last as the men sought to evade his eye and the engineer himself confessed ownership.

"They're an old pair of mine," he explained, "that got caught when I was wiping up the grease."

"What? Wiping up grease when the machinery was in motion? Why didn't you wait until it stopped?"

"Well—I didn't; that's all. There was a big puddle of grease gathering dirt underneath there—and I thought I'd wipe it up."

"I see," observed Wiley and his eyes narrowed down as he caught the aroma of whiskey. "Well, clear up this mess," he said at last and hurried to his office to telephone. A single line of wire stretched out across the plain, connecting Keno with Vegas and the world, and within half an hour he had dictated a rush order to be wired to his supply-house in Los Angeles. If money would buy it he would grab a new gear-wheel and have it shipped out by express; but if there was none in stock he would have to wait for it; and the machine-shops were months behind. Yet his whole mine was shut down on account of this accident and, if he only had the money, he could almost afford to buy a new engine and be done with it. He stopped and thought if there was one in the country that he could get hold of, second-hand, and then he thrust the matter aside. The problem of getting an engine on the ground was one that could be worked out later, but in the meanwhile the water was rising in the sump and the pumps would soon be submerged. There were two shifts of miners who would have to be discharged and—yes, the engine crew, too. It was against all the rules for an engineer to be wiping up his engine while it was running, and it was only by a miracle that the engineer himself had escaped unhurt from the smash?

But was it a miracle? A swift stab of suspicion made Wiley's heart stand still. Was this the first treacherous move in Blount's battle to win back the mine? Had Blount, or some agent, suggested to the engineer that an accident would be followed by a reward; and then had not the engineer, when no one was looking, fed his overalls into the gearings? He was a surly young brute and he met Wiley's eyes with a stare that bordered on defiance, yet there was nothing to be gained by accusing him. If Blount had bribed his men it was best to get rid of them without the faintest suggestion of suspicion; and then take on a new crew, shipped in from San Francisco or some equally distant place.

Wiley went underground with his men, opening up the air-cocks in the pumps, and bringing out the powder and steel; and then the next morning, just before the stage went out, he gave them all their time. They had a certain constraint, a sullen silence in his presence, that argued them against him at heart and, since the mine was closed down for some time to come, he made a clean sweep of them all. Yet it pained him somehow, being new at the game, to see all these miners against him and as they piled their rolls on the stage he lingered to see them off. He had paid them union wages and treated them right but now, with their time-checks in their pockets, they looked past him in stony silence. It puzzled him somehow, leaving him vaguely uneasy; but just as the stage pulled out he found the answer to his enigma. On the gallery of the Huff house as the automobile sped past there was a sudden flash of white and as Virginia appeared the young engineer rose up drunkenly and wafted her a kiss. After that the answer was plain.

CHAPTER XX

AN APPEAL TO CHARLEY

What is a kiss waved by a drunken hand, to a man whose love is like the hills? And yet that kiss, wafted so amorously to Virginia, stirred up a rage in Wiley Holman's heart. Was it not enough to wait on the table, without cultivating the acquaintance of her boarders? And this foolish affair, whatever it was, had cost him at least ten thousand dollars. It would come to that before he was through with it—in lost time and new machinery and unearned profits—and all because Virginia had smiled at this drunken engineer, who had promptly sent his overalls through the driving-gear. Yet that was the natural result of letting his men board in town where they could hear the Widow's ravings against him.

In the midst of his telephoning and giving directions to his mill-crew, who were still rushing their work on the mill, Wiley turned the matter over in his mind and it left him sick with doubts. He had counted upon the opposition of Blount, but Virginia's almost staggered him. It would make a difference, before his six months was up, if she set all his men against him, and yet he could not stop her. If he withdrew his men and boarded them himself that would only inflame the neighborhood the more, for it would deprive the Huffs of their livelihood; and if he let things go on it might result in more wrecks that would seriously interfere with his plans. No, the thing to do was to see Virginia at once and come to an understanding.

A telegram from his supply-house reported the engine an old type with all parts out of stock, and he worked for hours making tedious measurements before he ordered the new gear-wheel made. Then he sent an urgent wire to rush him the new engine that had been ordered to supply power to the mill, only to be told once more that it was held up by previous orders and could not be delivered for a month. A month! And with the water mounting up in his shaft like the interest on his notes. It was no time for half measures. He leapt into his racer and burned up the road to Vegas. Three days later he returned with an old gas engine that he had salvaged from an abandoned mine and by the end of the week, by working day and night, he had the pumps lifting water. And then again he remembered Virginia.

He had thought of her, of course, when he was speeding to and fro, but he was hardly in the mood for sentiment. There were more things to go wrong than he had thought humanly possible in the management of a mine, and between ordering his machinery and taking on new men he had had scant leisure for affairs of the heart. He was young and inexperienced and the dealers took advantage of it to foist off old stock and odd parts, and then his engineers became fractious and disgruntled because he expected quick results. It was all very different from what he had expected when he had taken over the Paymaster lease, and yet it had to be endured and muddled through somehow until the mine was safely his own. Then out would come the engines, and all second-hand machinery and makeshift parts, and with a superintendent who knew his job he would lean back in comfort and learn the mining business by proxy.

Wiley shaved that evening and went down through the town, but when he put his hand on the Widow's gate his resolution failed him. He had placed her under bonds to keep the peace, and she had lived up to the undertaking scrupulously, but within her own house she had certain rights and privileges which even he dared not invade. If he stepped in that doorway she would order him out; and unquestionably she would be within her rights, since every man's house is his castle. So, on the very threshold of Virginia's retreat, he drew back and went to see Death Valley Charley.

Death Valley was drunk, but his conscience was still active and he burst into a voluble explanation.

"No, I gave her that stock," he protested earnestly, "but she made me take it back.

"'It ain't mine,' she says, 'and I'll work my hands off before I'll take charity from anybody.'

"'No, you keep it,' I says, just exactly like you tole me, 'because I'm your guardian, and all; and Wiley he says that I'm a hell of a poor one, because I sold him that stock for nothing. No,' I says, just exactly like you tole me, 'I want you to keep this stock.'"

"Well?" inquired Wiley, as Charley paused to take a drink, "and what did Virginia say, then?"

"Oh, I couldn't repeat it," answered Death Valley virtuously. "She don't seem to like you now. She says you stole her mine."

"Huh!" grunted Wiley, and looked about the cabin which was littered with bottles and flasks. "Well, where've *you* been?" he went on at last, the better to change the subject, and Charley leered at him shrewdly.

"Over across Death Valley," he chanted drunkenly, "—on the east side, in the Funeral Range. But they put me to work on the graveyard shift so I quit and come back to town."

"Ye-es," jeered Wiley, "you've been on a big drunk. What are you doing with this demijohn of whiskey?"

"Why, I got it for the Colonel," replied Charley, laughing childishly, "and I started to take it over to him, but my burros got away at Daylight

Springs, so I made camp and drunk it all up."

"But it's full!" objected Wiley.

"Yes, I refilled it," answered Charley and helped himself to another nip. "Thas second time now I took that whiskey to the Colonel and both times I drunk it up. Thas bad—the Colonel will kill me."

"Yes, and do a danged good job," grumbled Wiley morosely. "You sure got me in Dutch with Virginia."

"She says you stole her mine," defended Charley stoutly. "And don't you say nothing against Virginia. She's noblest girl the sun ever shined. I'll *kill* any man that says different!"

"Oh yes, sure," agreed Wiley, "I'd do that myself. But Charley, I didn't steal her mine. I got it from Blount, and if she wants it back—say, Charley, you tell her I want to see her!"

He leaned over eagerly and laid his hand on Charley's shoulder, but Death Valley shook him off.

"No!" he declaimed. "The Huffs are poor but proud—they don't take charity from no one!"

"Aw, but, Charley," he argued, "this isn't charity. We'll get it away from Blount!"

"You're drunk!" declared Charley and turned sternly to the demijohn which was rapidly going down.

"Well, maybe I am," admitted Wiley craftily, "but that's all right, isn't it, between friends?"

190

"Sure thing—have another!" responded Charley cordially, and Wiley poured out a generous portion.

"Here's to you," he said, "Old Chuckawalla Charley—the man that put the Death in Death Valley. You're some desert rat, now ain't you, Charley? You helped pack the mud to build the butte and stoped out the guest chamber down in hell! Well, here's luck!" and he nodded his health.

"Yes, you bet I'm an old-timer," boasted Death Valley vaingloriously. "I was at Panamint and Ballarat, and all them camps. Me and old Shorty Harris—we used to lead every rush—we was first at Greenwater and Skidoo. But these damned lizzies can beat us to it now—the old burro-man is too slow."

"But crossing the sand, Charley, you've got us there; and climbing up these rocky washes. I've got a good machine—it'll take me most anywhere—but when it comes to crossing Death Valley, give me some burros and old Uncle Charley." He slapped him on the back and Uncle Charley smiled doubtfully and took another drink. "You bet," went on Wiley, with method in his madness. "I'd like nothing better, when I get a little time, than to have you take me out across Death Valley. What's it like, over there, Charley? Is it very far to water? But I'll bet you know every trail!"

"I know 'em all," announced Charley proudly, "but here's one that nobody knows. It's the trail to the Ube-Hebes. First you go from here to Daylight Springs, but they ain't no feed around there, so you go over the divide and down six miles and camp at Hole-in-the-Rock. And there they's good feed and plenty of good water and a tin house where the freighters used to camp; and then you fill your tanks and the next day you follow the wash till it takes you down to Stove-Pipe Wells. That water is bad but the burros will drink it if you bail the hole out first, and the next day you cross the sandhills and the Death Valley Sink and head for Cottonwood wash. Many is the man that has started for that gateway and died before he reached the water, but the Colonel—"

Charley stopped abruptly and looked around for Heine and then he poured out a drink.

"He's dead now," he concluded, but Wiley caught his eye and shook his head disapprovingly.

"Not between friends," he said. "Ain't we drunk here together? Well, tell me the truth now—where is he? And listen here, Charley; I'll tell you something first that will make it all right with the Colonel. All he has to do is to come back to Keno and I'll give him his share in the mine. Then we can throw in together, and, when we get through, old Blount will be left holding the sack. Do you get the idea? I'm trying to be friends, but you've got to take me over to the Colonel!"

"The Colonel is dead!" repeated Charley doggedly and then he cocked his head to one side. "Don't you hear 'em?" he asked, "it's them Germans or something—"

"Never mind!" said Wiley sharply. "I'm talking about the Colonel, and I'll tell you what I'll do. I can't give the mine to Virginia because she won't take it; but the Colonel is a gentleman. He's reasonable, Charley, and I'd get along with him fine; so come on, now—go over and tell him!"

He patted him on the back and a look of indecision crept into Charley's drink-dimmed eyes, but in the end he shook his head.

"Nope," he muttered, "the Colonel is dead!" And Wiley threw up his hands.

"Well, then here," he ran on, "you know me, Charley; and you know I'm not trying to steal that mine. Now here's what I want you to do. You tell Virginia I want to see her; and then some night you bring her over and—well, maybe that will do just as well."

"Will you give her back her mine?" inquired Charley pointedly, and Wiley rose up in a rage.

"Yes!" he yelled, "for cripes' sake, what's the matter with you? You talk like everybody was a crook. Didn't I give her back her stock? Well then, I'll give her back her mine! But she's got to accept it, hasn't she?"

"That was her I heard coming," answered Charley simply, but when Wiley looked out she was gone.

CHAPTER XXI

THE DRAGON'S TEETH

It is the curse of success that it raises up enemies as Jason's dragon teeth brought forth armed men. When he was skating around the country, examining mines and taking out options, Wiley could safely count every man his friend; but now that he had made his big *coup* on the Paymaster they were against him, from Virginia down. If he went to her politely with a thousand-dollar bill and asked her to take it as a gift she would refuse to so much as look at him. And yet, as a matter of fact, he was the same old laughing Wiley—only now he did not laugh. It was not right, but it could not be helped.

A long and weary month, full of vexatious delays and nerve-racking demands from his creditors, left its mark on Wiley's face; but in six weeks the mine and mill were running. Three shifts of men broke the ore at the face and sent it up the shaft to the grizzly and from there it was fed down through the enormous rock-crusher and then on through the ball-mills and rollers to the concentrating tables below. It was crushed and sorted and crushed again and ground fine in the revolving tubes, and then it was screened and washed and separated on vanners until nothing but the concentrates remained. The tail sluicings were sluiced off down the gulch, to add to the mighty dump that the Paymaster had left there in its prime. But even at its best, when it was working in gold ore that ran three or four thousand to the ton, even then the famous Paymaster had not turned out treasure like this.

The banks were full of gold—they were shipping it to America in lots of ten and twelve million at a time—but tungsten was rare, it was necessary, almost priceless, and the demand for it increased by leaps and bounds. How could ironmasters harden the tools that were to turn out the mighty cannon that this gold had been sent over to buy, unless they could get the tungsten? Molybdenum, vanadium, manganese, and all the substitutes were commandeered to take its place; but month by month the price of tungsten crept up until now all the West was tungsten-mad. It had gone up from forty dollars to sixty, and now seventy, for a twenty-pound unit of concentrates—running sixty per cent or better of tungstic acid—and as Wiley resumed his shipments he received a frantic offer of seventy-five dollars a unit. And then once more he smiled.

There had been a time when he had felt the cold hand of Blount closing down on his precious mine—and the other banks had refused to take over his notes. The property was not his, there was nothing tangible upon which to make a loan; and then, Blount had passed the word around. Wiley was indebted to him, and heavily indebted, and when he took the apple there would be no core for the rest. But now in a week the whole situation had changed and Wiley's smile brought forth answering smiles. The general store in Vegas extended his credit, even his supply-house had heard the good news; and Blount, who had grown arrogant, became suddenly friendly and fawning, trying vainly to cover up his hand. He was like a man who had clutched at a treasure and discovered himself a little too soon. The treasure was still Wiley's but—well, Blount was used to waiting, so he smiled and extended the notes.

At three dollars and more a pound it would not take many tons of tungsten to put Wiley safely out of the hole, but when he ran over his accounts he was startled by the bills that were piling up against him. A thousand dollars was nothing to these mining machinery houses and his payroll was over two hundred a day; and then there was powder and timber and steel, and gasoline and oil, *and* the freight across the desert. That went on everything, twenty dollars a ton whether they hauled both ways or one; and with so much at stake he had to treat everyone generously or run the chance of being tied up by a strike. Nor was there lacking the sinister evidence of some unfriendly if not hostile force, and as breakdowns recurred and unexpected accidents happened, Wiley came and went like a ghost. His gun was always on him and he watched each man warily, seeking out his enemies from his friends.

As for Virginia and her mother, he had long since given up hope of stopping their venomous tongues; and Death Valley Charley, finding the pressure too strong, had conveniently dropped out of sight. In all that town, which he had found dead and unpeopled and had changed in a few months to a live camp, there was not a single soul that he could truthfully say was honestly and unquestionably his friend. It was not that they were against him, for most of them realized that their own success was bound up with his; but they were not actively for him, they did not boost and help him, but joined in on the old anvil chorus. He had cheated the Widow, he had beaten Virginia out of her stock, he had taken advantage of Death Valley Charley! But, they added—and this was what galled him—what else could you expect from the son of Honest John?

Wiley gritted his teeth, but he did not speak his mind for the hour of vindication was at hand. When he had paid off his notes and his bills for supplies the first thing he would do, even before he took over the mine, would be to buy in Blount's Paymaster stock. And with that stock in his hands, with every tell-tale endorsement to prove the damning story of Blount's guilt, he would go to these old-timers and make them eat their words when they said his father was not honest. But as far as he was concerned, what difference did it make whether they considered him honest or not? Would they feel any more kindly towards his honest old father when he had proved that he had been faithful to the end? No, they thought they were virtuous and only denouncing injustice, but when that charge was taken out of their mouths they would clack on out of jealousy at his success. It was envy that really poisoned their minds and made them spit forth spleen, envy and chagrin at their own lack of foresight.

The Paymaster dump had lain right at their doorway where all of them could inspect its ore, but no one had noticed the heavy spar. They had called it white quartz and dismissed it from their minds, but he had come among them with different eyes. He had gone to a school of mines, where he had learned to identify minerals, and he had kept up with the mining magazines; and while these poisonous knockers had been lamenting the results of the war he had jumped in and turned it to his advantage. He had done something practical, to the improvement of industry, something that might change in a certain measure, the very destiny of the world; but the moment he succeeded they had accused him of robbing half-wits and of oppressing the widow and the orphan. Wiley shut down his jaws and smiled dourly.

There was small hope now of changing the widow and her "orphan" but if he could not convert them he could show them. As sure as he knew anything he was convinced that Colonel Huff had simply fled from his wife's nagging tongue and, when he got the time, Wiley intended to hire a pack-train and set out across Death Valley to find him. Virginia came and went, but always she avoided him scrupulously. Not once since she had returned from Vegas had she met his questioning eyes; and to all his advances she turned a deaf ear, if the statements of Charley could be trusted. The carefully thought-out scheme of getting back the Huff stock and then forming an alliance against Blount had died before it was born; or it remained at best in suspended animation, pending Death Valley Charley's return. He had gone off with his burros but the longer Wiley waited on him the more he saw that Charley was a broken reed. No, the trimming of Blount, if it was done at all, would have to be done by him—and all he needed was time.

Two months and a little more lay between him and the day of reckoning—the twentieth day of May. In that short time he must meet heavy obligations, pay off his notes, buy Blount's stock and purchase the mine; and if anything should happen—if the hoist should break down, the mill blow up, the market for tungsten fail—well, he could kiss the Paymaster good-by. The market and other influences were on the knees of the gods, but Wiley decided that there should be no more accidents. That was something preventable and no more love-sick engineers were going to use his gearings for a clothes mangle. He engaged two watchmen who were mechanics as well and then he kept watch over his watchmen. Neither by day nor by night did he go down the hill for more than a few minutes at a time and on dark, stormy nights he wandered about like a specter watching the shadows for Stiff Neck George. He was out there somewhere, Wiley knew it as instinctively as he knew that Virginia hated him, and yet he never appeared. He never made threats nor showed himself in the open but, somewhere, he was out there in the darkness; and sooner or later he would strike.

The days dragged on slowly, with cold, March winds and sandstorms boiling in over Shadow Mountain; and then driving rain followed by bright, sunny weather and struggling flowers in the swales. It was spring, in a way, but not the spring of yester-year, with its songs and laughter and high hopes. Wiley felt the old call to be up and away, but his racer remained in its shed. He paced about restlessly, waiting for something to happen, observing the slightest signs—and then he found her tracks in the dust. Virginia had come up the trail in the night and had gone down past the mill. He knew her tracks well and, among the broad brogans of the miners, they stood out like the footprints of a fairy. Wiley's heart leapt up in his breast—and then it stood still. Had she come as an enemy or a friend?

He followed her trail to where it had been trampled out by the watchman in making his regular rounds; and then, below the mill, he picked it up again as it went on down the path. Not once had she hesitated or turned from the beaten trail, but she had gone down after the graveyard shift. That went on at eleven and her tracks were superimposed on the hob-nailed boot-marks of the miners. When they had come off shift they had trampled them out again, except for a print here and there; and by the color of the dust Wiley shrewdly judged that she had visited him between twelve and one. Between the windblown footprints of the night-shift and the fresh red of the day shift as they had mounted the trail at seven, her high-arched steps had been made about midnight, for the dust had been whitened by the air. Wiley followed them silently, trampling them out as he went, and that night as the graveyard shift came on he slipped out and hid by the trail. What kind of a watchman was this, who let a woman come and go and never even saw her tracks in the dust? He could watch for Virginia; and meanwhile, incidentally, he could keep tab on this sleepy-headed guard.

The *chuh, chuh* of the engine echoed loud in the canyon as the hoist brought up the first cars, and then the rumble of the trams as they were pushed down the track and the clatter of the ore down the grizzly. A sharp *blap, blap,* from the compressor showed that the machine-men had set up their drills; and beneath all the rest there was the hushed rumble of the mill and the thunderous *rhump, rhump,* of the rock-breaker. It was a ponderous affair of the old jaw-type, surmounted by a fly-wheel of a full ton's weight that drove it rhythmically on; and as Wiley listened it made a music for his ears as sweet as any bass viol. In this mine of his there was an orchestration of busy sounds, from the clang of the bell to start or stop the engine, to this deep, rumbling undertone of the crusher; and every clang and crunch brought him that much nearer to the day when he would be free.

He took shelter within the black mouth of a short tunnel by the trail and looked out at his little world—the huge mill, dimly lighted, the gaunt gallows-frame against the sky, and the sleeping town below. He had made them his own and now he must fight for them; and watch over them, day and night. Above him the stars shone out clean and cold, a million of them in the dry, desert air; and in the east the half moon rose up slowly above Gold Hill, where the wealth of ages lay hid. It had given up its gold but his hand had struck the blow that would open up its treasure vaults of tungsten. All it needed now was watchfulness and patience. The moon rose up higher and he dozed within the shadow and then a sound brought him to with a start. It was the crunch of gravel on the trail before him and as he looked out he saw Virginia.

CHAPTER XXII
VIRGINIA EXPLAINS—NOTHING

She was covered by a cloak and there was a man's hat on her head, but Wiley knew her—it was Virginia Huff. The moon had mounted high and the chill of the morning was in the air, so he could hardly flatter himself that she had come to see him. Perhaps it was just to see the mine. But if, beneath that cloak, she carried some instrument of destruction—he stepped out and watched her covertly. She tiptoed up the trail, glancing nervously about her, starting back as a trammer dumped his ore; and then, very slowly, she crept past his house and disappeared in the direction of the mill. Instantly he whipped out of his tunnel and started after her, running swiftly up the trail; but as he neared the summit she came catapulting against him, running as swiftly the other way.

"Here! Stop!" he commanded as she leapt back with a stifled scream and then as she made a dash he plunged resolutely after her and caught her like a child.

"You let go of me!" she panted, but he flung one arm about her and held both her hands to her side.

"No," he said, and she struck out violently only to find herself clutched the tighter.

"Wiley Holman!" she exploded, "if you don't let me go! You'd better—I saw a man back there!"

"It's my watchman," answered Wiley. "I keep him to guard the mill. But what are you doing up here?"

"No! It wasn't! It was Stiff Neck George! And he had something heavy in his hand! You'd better go and watch him!"

She was struggling in his arms, her breath hot against his cheek, fear and rage in every word, but he crushed her roughly to his side.

"Never mind about George," he said. "What are *you* doing up here, now?"

"But he'll blow up your mine! I've heard him threaten to! I just came up to tell you!"

"Oh, that's different!" returned Wiley, relaxing his grip, "but never mind—my watchman will get him."

"No! The watchman is asleep—I didn't see him anywhere! Oh, Wiley; please run and stop him!"

"Nope," replied Wiley, "he can blow the whole mill up—I want to ask you a question."

He released her reluctantly, for the touch of her had thrilled him, and the sweetness of her breath on his cheek—but she darted down the trail like a rabbit.

"Here! Wait!" he ordered and outran her in ten

jumps, at which she stooped and snatched up a rock.

"Put that down!" he said, and as she swung back the rock, he braved it and caught her anyway. "Now," he went on, trembling from the smash of the blow, but holding her in a grip of steel, "we'll see what all this is about!"

"You will not!" she hissed back, "because I won't answer you a word! And I hope old George ruins your mill!"

"That's all right," he said, shaking his bloody head, "but, Judas, you did smash me with that stone! After that, I guess, I've got something coming to me!" And he reached down and kissed her lips.

"You—stop!" she panted. "Oh, I—I'll kill you for that!" But Wiley only laughed recklessly.

"All right!" he said, "what's the difference—I'd die happy! I almost wish you'd hit me again."

"Well, I will!" she threatened, but when he released her she drew back and hung her head. "That isn't fair," she said, "you know I can't protect myself, and—"

"Well, all right," he agreed, "we'll call it square then. But—I want to tell you something, Virginia."

"Are you going to stand here," she burst out sharply, "and let him blow up your mill?"

"Yes, I am," he answered. "I don't care what happens to me if you and I can be friends. I love you, Virginia, you know it as well as I do, and that's all I want in the world. Let's just be friends, the way we used to be when we were playing around town together. I've been trying to see you for months—it's seemed like forty years—and Virginia, you've got to listen to me!"

He paused and drew nearer, and she stood waiting passively, as if daring him to touch her again; but he stooped and peered into her face. The night was not dark and in the ghostly moonlight he could see the cold anger in her eyes.

"Yes, I know," he said, "you hate me like poison—but Virginia, this is going too far. It's all right to hate me, if that's the way you're built, but you ought to give me a chance. It looks very much as if you'd come up here to-night to do some damage to my mine; but I'll let that pass and say nothing about it if you'll only give me a chance. Let me tell you how I feel and then, some other time—"

"Well, go on," she said, "but if your old mine blows up—"

"I wish it would!" he burst out passionately. "If it would make any difference, I wish it was blown off the map. I can't bear to fight you, Virginia; it makes my life miserable, and I've tried to be friendly from the first. But is it right to blame a man for something he can't help and not even give him a chance to explain? If you think I've stolen your mine, why, go ahead and say so and let me give it back. I'll do it, so help me God, if you'll only say the word."

"What word?" she asked, and he threw out his hands in a helpless appeal to her pity.

"Any word," he said, "so long as it's friendly. But I just can't stand it to be without you!"

"Oh," she said, and looked back up the trail as if meditating another dash to escape.

"Well, what is it?" he asked at last. "Won't you even listen to me? I've got a plan to propose."

"Why, certainly," she responded, "go ahead and tell it. And then, when it's done, can I go?"

"Yes, you can go," he answered eagerly, "if you'll only just listen reasonably and think what this means to us both. We used to be friends, Virginia, and while I was working up this deal I did everything I could to help you. I didn't have much money then or I'd have done more for you, but you know my heart was right. I wasn't trying to take advantage of you. But the minute I got the mine it seems as if everybody turned against me—and you turned against me, too. That hurt me, Virginia, after what I'd tried to do for you, but I know you had your reasons. You blamed me for things that I never had done and—well, you wouldn't even speak to me. But that was all right—it was perfectly natural—and on Christmas I sent you back your stock. I only bought it from Charley to help you get to Los Angeles, and I considered that I was holding it in trust; so I sent it back by Charley, but I suppose he made some break, because I found it on my table that night. But you'll take it back now; won't you, Virginia?"

His voice broke like a boy's in the earnestness of his appeal and yet it was hopeless, too, for he saw that she stood unmoved. He waited for an answer, then as she shifted her feet impatiently he went on with dogged persistence. It was useless, he knew it; and yet, sometime in the future, she might recall what he had said and take advantage of it.

"Well, all right, then," he assented, "but the stock's yours if you want it. I'm holding it for you, in trust. But now here's what I wanted to tell you—I'd hoped we could do it together; but you ought to do it, anyway. You know that stock that your mother lost to Blount? Well, I know how you can get it back."

He paused for her to speak, to exclaim perhaps at his magnanimity in offering to help her against her will, but she shrouded herself pettishly in her cloak.

"Oh, you don't care, eh?" he asked with a bitter laugh. "Well, I wish to God, then, I didn't. But I do, Virginia! I can't stand it to see you slaving when there's anything in the world that I can do. Now here's the proposition: according to law your father isn't legally dead—he won't be for seven years—and so your mother, not being his heir yet, had no right to hypothecate that stock. It still belongs to your father's estate and all you have to do is to go to a lawyer and demand the property back. You're his daughter, you see, and a co-heir with your mother, and Blount will not dare to oppose it!"

"Yes, thanks," returned Virginia. "Is that all?"

"Why—no!" he said at last, clutching his hands at his side. "There's—I'll lend you the money, Virginia."

"No, thank you!" she answered, and started off down the trail, but he stepped in her way and stopped her. His mood had changed, for his voice was rough and threatening, but he struggled to keep it down.

"Is that all?" he demanded and without waiting for the answer he reached out and caught her by the arm. "Virginia," he said, "I've tried to be good to you, but maybe you don't appreciate it. And maybe I've made a mistake. There's something about you when I'm around that reminds me of a man with a grouch—only a man would speak out his mind. Now I've given you a chance to clean up twenty thousand dollars and I expect something more than: 'No, thanks!' "

"Well, what *do* you expect?" she asked, struggling feebly against his grasp.

"I expect," he answered, "that you'll state your

grievance and tell me why you won't have me?"

"And if I do, will you let me go?"

"When I get good and ready," he responded grimly. "I don't know whether I'm in love with you or not."

"Well, my grievance," she went on defiantly, "is that you went to work deliberately and robbed me and mother of our mine. And as for winning *me,* that's one thing you can't steal—and I'll kill you if you don't let go of that hand!"

"Yes," he said, "I've heard that before—it seems to run in the family. But don't you think for a minute that I'm afraid of getting killed—or that I'm trying to steal you, either. If you were an Indian squaw you might be worth stealing, because I could beat a little sense into your head; but the way things are now I'll just turn you loose—and kindly keep off my ground."

He flung back her hand and stepped out of the trail but Virginia did not pass. Her breast heaved tumultuously and she turned upon him as she sought for a fitting retort; but while they stood panting, each glowering at the other, there was a crash from inside the old mill. Its huge bulk was lit up by a flash of light which went out in Stygian darkness and as they listened, aghast, the ground trembled beneath them and a tearing roar filled the air. It began at the stone-breaker and went down through the mill, like the progress of a devastating host, and as Wiley sprang forward, there was a terrifying smash which seemed to shake the mill to its base. Then all was silent and as he looked around he saw Virginia dancing off down the trail.

CHAPTER XXIII
ON DEMAND

If there was anything left of his mill but the frame, Wiley's ears had played him false; and yet he stood and looked after Virginia. This grinding crash, this pandemonium of destruction which had left him sick with fear, had put joy into her dancing feet. Yes, she had danced—like a child that hears good news or runs to meet its father—and he had thought her worthy of his love! He had battered his brain for weeks to devise some plan whereby he could make his peace; he had taken her blows like a dog; and she had answered with this. Whether it was Stiff Neck George or some other man, she had known both his presence and his purpose; and now she rejoiced in the catastrophe. A hundred dollars would buy him a squaw more worthy of confidence and love.

There was darkness in the mill, but when they brought the flares, Wiley saw that the ruin was complete. From the rock-breaker to the concentrators there was nothing but splintered wood, twisted iron and upturned tanks; and the demon of destruction which had raged down through its length was nothing but the fly-wheel of the rock-crusher. What power had uprooted it he was at a loss to conjecture but, a full ton in weight, it had jumped from its frame and plowed its way down through the mill. The ore-bins were intact, for the fly-wheel had overleapt them, but tables and tanks and concentrating jigs were utterly smashed and ruined. Even the wall of the mill had given way before it and the cold light of dawn crept in through a jagged aperture that marked its resistless course. The fly-wheel was gone and the damage was done; but there was still, of course, the post mortem. What had caused that massive shafting, with its ponderous speeding wheels, to leap from its bearings and go crashing down the descent, laying everything before it in ruins? Wiley summoned his engineer and, in the shattered jaws of the rock-breaker, they found the innocent-looking instrument of destruction. It was not a stick of dynamite, but a heavy steel sledge-hammer that had been cast into the jaws of the crusher. They had closed down upon it, the hammer had resisted, and then all the momentum of that whirling double fly-wheel had been brought to bear against it. Yet the hammer could not be crushed and, as the wheel had applied its weight, the resistance to its force had caused it to leap from its bearings and go hurtling down the incline.

It was a very complete job, even better than dynamiting, and yet Wiley did not blame it on Stiff Neck George. Some miner, some millman, who had seen it done before, had repeated the performance for his benefit. Or was it, perhaps, for Virginia's? He remembered the engineer who had fed his greasy overalls into the gearings of the hoist. He had boarded with Virginia and had waved her a parting kiss—but this time it would be some trammer. Wiley gave them all their time on general principles, but he did not go down to witness the farewell. Whether the trammer kissed her good-by or simply kissed her hand was immaterial to him now—and, in case it might have been a millman or some miner underground, he laid off the whole night shift. The night-watchman went too, and the stage the following evening brought out a cook to start up the boarding-house.

Wiley did not guess it—he knew it—Virginia Huff was the witch who had mixed the hell-broth that had raised up all this treachery against him. She had poisoned his men's minds and incited them to vandalism, but it would not happen again. He had been a fool to endure it so long; but she could starve now, for all that he cared. If she thought she could twist him like a ring around her finger while she egged on these men to wreck his mill, she had one more guess coming and then she would be right, for he had come to his senses at last. This was not the Virginia that he had known and loved—the Virginia he had played with in his youth—but a warped and embittered Virginia, a waspish, heartless vixen who had never been anything but cold. She had worked him deliberately, resorting to woman's wiles to gain what was not her due, and now when his mill was smashed into kindling wood, she danced and laughed for joy.

What kind of a mind could a woman have, to do such a senseless thing and then laugh at the man who had helped her? She was kind to her cats, the neighbors all liked her, to everyone else she seemed human; but when it came to him she was a devil of hate, a fiend of ruthless cunning. She would tell him to his face—at three in the morning, when he had caught her running away from the mill—that she hoped his old mill would be ruined. And now, when the trammer or some other softhead had sent one of his sledges through the crusher, she was laughing up her sleeve. But there was a hereafter coming for Virginia and her mother and they would get no more favors from him. If they crept to his feet and said they were starving he would tell them to get out and hustle. Meanwhile they had sent him broke.

There would be no more ore concentrated in the Paymaster mill during the life of his bond and lease; and unless he could raise some money, and raise it quick, he was due to lose his mine. Whether he had abetted it or not, Blount would not fail to take advantage of this last, staggering blow to his fortunes; and there were notes and paper due which would easily serve as a pretext for a writ of attachment on his mine. Bad news travels fast, but Wiley set out to beat it by snatching at his one remaining chance. His mill was ruined, his output was stopped, but he still had the ore underground—and the buyers were crazy to get it. He sent out identical messages to ten big consumers and then sat down to await the results. They came with a rush, ten scrambling frantic bids for his total output for one year—and one of them was for eighty-four dollars! It was from the biggest buyer of them all, a man who was reputed to be the representative of a foreign government, a man who had paid cash on the nail. Wiley pondered a while, looked up his obligations to Blount, and accepted immediately by wire. But there was one proviso—he demanded an advance payment, which the buyer promptly wired to his bank. Then Wiley twisted up his lip and waited.

Blount appeared the next day, dropping in casually as was his wont; but there was a cold, killing look in his eye and he had a deputy sheriff as a witness. They looked through the mill and Blount asked several leading questions before he ventured to come to the point, but at last he cleared his throat and spoke up.

"Well, Wiley," he said, drawing some papers from his pocket, "I'm sorry, but I'll have to call your notes. If it were my money it would be different; but I'm a banker, you understand, and your paper is long overdue. I've extended it before because I admired your courage and thought you might possibly pull through, but this accident to your mill has impaired the property and I can't let it run any longer."

"Oh, that's all right," said Wiley, "but you don't need to apologize, because there won't be any attachments and judgments. Just tell me how much it comes to and I'll write you out a check." He took the notes from Blount's palsied hand and spread them on the desk before him, but as he was jotting down the totals Blount grabbed them wildly away.

"Not much!" he exclaimed, "I don't surrender those notes until the money is put in my hands! Your check isn't worth a pen stroke!"

"Well, I don't know," returned Wiley. "There may be two opinions about that. I had a hunch, Mr. Blount, that you might spring something like this and so I made arrangements to accommodate you."

"But you're strapped! You owe everybody!" cried Blount in a passion. "I don't believe you've got a cent!"

"Just a minute," said Wiley, and took down his telephone. "Hello," he called, "get me the First National Bank." He waited then, twiddling his pencil placidly, while Blount's great neck swelled out with venom. "I figure," went on Wiley, as he waited for the connection, "that I owe you twenty-two thousand dollars, with interest amounting to two-eighty-three, sixty-one. Here's your check, all filled out, and when I get the bank you can ask the cashier if it's good."

"But, Wiley—," began Blount.

"Hello! Hello! Is this the First National? This is Holman, out at the Paymaster. Mr. Blount is here and, as I'm closing my account with him—"

"No! No!" cried Blount in a panic, but Wiley went on with his talk.

"Yes," he said, "the check is for twenty-two thousand, two eighty-three, sixty-one. Will you please set that amount aside to meet the payment on this check? All right, Mr. Blount, here's the bank."

He held out the instrument and Blount seized it roughly, for he had heard of fake telephone messages before, but when he listened he recognized the voice.

"Oh, Agnew?" he hailed, smiling genially at the 'phone. "Well, sorry to have troubled you, I'm sure. Oh, yes, yes; I know Wiley is all right; he's good with us for twenty thousand more. No, never mind the certification; we may let the matter drop. Yes, thank you very much—good-by!"

He hung up the receiver and turned to Wiley; but the cold, killing look was gone.

"Wiley," he chuckled, slapping him heartily

on the back, "you certainly have put one over. It isn't every day that I find a man waiting with the check all made out to a cent; and somehow—well, I hate to take the money."

"Yes, I know how you suffer," replied Wiley, grimly, "but let's get the agony over." He held out the check and Blount accepted it reluctantly, passing over the notes with a sigh.

But for the trifling detail that "demand" had not been waived Blount could have gone into court without even asking for his money and secured an attachment against the property. But Wiley's firm insistence that all cut-throat clauses should be omitted had compelled Blount to demand payment on the notes; and then, by some process which still remained a mystery, he had raised the full amount to meet the payment. And so once more, after going to all the trouble of bringing a deputy sheriff along, Blount found himself balked and his dreams of judgment and lien permanently banished to the limbo of lost hopes.

Wiley's over-prompt payment had confused Blount for the moment and thrown him into a panic. He had counted confidently upon crushing him at a blow and cutting short his inimical activities, but now of a sudden he found himself threatened with the loss of all his interests. If Wiley had made profits beyond his calculations—but no, he could not, for under the terms of their bond and lease one-tenth of the net profit on all his shipments was sent direct to Blount. And if what Wiley had received was only ten times the Company's royalty, he was still in debt to someone. Blount had followed him closely and he knew that his expenses had absorbed all his profits, up to date. But perhaps—and Blount paused—perhaps the other bank, or some outside parties, were backing him in his enterprise. He would have to look that matter up—first. But if not—if he was still running his mine as he had from the first, on his nerve and his diamond ring—then there were ways and means which should be speedily invoked to prevent him from meeting his payments.

Scarcely a month remained before the bond and lease lapsed—and Wiley's option on Blount's personal stock—but any day he might raise the money and, by taking over Blount's stock, place him out of the running for good. These tungsten buyers who were so avid for its product might purchase an interest in the mine; they might advance the fifty thousand and take it over under the bond and lease, and bring all his plans to naught. As Blount paced about the office he suddenly saw himself defrauded of that which he had worked for for years. He saw his stock bought up first, to deprive him of the royalties, and then the mine snatched from his hands; and all he would have left would be the forfeited Huff stock and the small payment it would earn from the sale.

Something would have to be done, and done every minute, to prevent him from carrying out his purpose.

Blount paused in his nervous pacing and held out a flabby hand to Wiley, who was writing away at his desk.

"Well, Wiley," he said, "I guess I must be going. But any time you need money—" He stopped and smiled amiably, in the soft, easy way he had when he wished to appear harmless as a dove, and Wiley glanced up briefly from his work.

"Yes, thank you, Mr. Blount," he said. But he did not take his hand.

CHAPTER XXIV

DOUBLE TROUBLE

The next two weeks of Wiley Holman's life were packed so full of trouble that there were those who almost pitied him, though the word had been passed around to lay off. It was Samuel J. Blount who was making the trouble, and who notified the rest to keep out, and so great was his influence in all the desert country that no one dared to interfere. What he did was all legal and according to business ethics, but it gloved the iron hand. Blount was reaching for the mine and he intended to get it, if he had to crush his man. The attachments and suits were but the shadow boxing of the bout; the rough stuff was held in reserve. And somehow Wiley sensed this, for he sat tight at the mine and hired a lawyer to meet the suits. His job was mining ore and he shoveled it out by the ton.

The distressing accidents had suddenly ceased since he began to board his own men at the mine and, while his lawyer stalled and haggled to fight off an injunction, he rushed his ore to the railroad. It was too precious to ship loose, for at eighty-four dollars a unit it was worth over four dollars a pound; he sent it out sacked, with an armed guard on each truck to see that it was delivered and receipted for. As the checks came back he paid off all his debts, thus depriving Blount of his favorite club; and then, while Blount was casting about for new weapons, he began to lay aside his profits.

They rolled up monstrously, for each five-ton truck load added several thousand dollars to his bank account, but the time was getting short. Less than three weeks remained before the bond and lease expired, and still Wiley was playing to win. He crammed his mine with men, snatching the ore from the stopes as the bonanza leasers had done at Tonopah, and doubling the miner's pay with bonuses. Every truck driver received his bonus, and night and day the great motors went thundering across the desert. The ore came up from below and was dumped on a jig, where it was sorted and hastily sacked; and after that there was nothing to do but sent it under guard to the railroad. There was no milling, no smelting, no tedious process of reduction; but the raw picked ore was rushed to the East and the checks came promptly back.

Blount was fully informed now of the terms of his contract and of the source of his sudden wealth, but there was no way of reaching the buyer. A great war was on, every minute was precious—and every ounce of the tungsten was needed. The munitions makers could not pause for a single day in their mad rush to fill their contracts. The only ray of hope that Blount could see was that the price had broken to sixty dollars a unit. Wiley's contract called for eighty-four, throughout the full year—but suppose he should lose his mine. And suppose Blount should win it. He could offer better terms, provided always that the buyer would accommodate him now. Suppose, for instance, that the fat daily checks should cease coming during the life of the lease. That could easily be explained—it might be an error in bookkeeping—but it would make quite a difference to Wiley. And in return for some such favor Blount could afford to sell the tungsten for, say, fifty-five dollars a unit.

Blount was a careful man. He did not trust his message to the wires, nor did he put it on paper to convict him; he simply disappeared—but when he came back Wiley's lawyer was waiting with a check. It was for twenty thousand dollars, and in return for this payment the lawyer demanded all of Blount's stock. Four hundred thousand shares, worth five dollars apiece if the bond and lease should lapse, and called for under the option at five cents! In those few short days, while Blount had been speeding East, Wiley had piled up this profit and more—and now he was demanding his stock!

"No!" said Blount, "that option is invalid because it was obtained by deception and fraud, and therefore I refuse to recognize it."

"Very well," replied the lawyer, who made his living out of controversies, and, summoning witnesses to his offer, he placed the money in the hands of the court and plunged into furious litigation. It was furious, in a way, and yet not so furious as the next day and the next passed by; for the lawyer was a business man and dependent upon the good will of Blount. It was a civil suit and, since Wiley could not appear to state his case in Court, it was postponed by mutual consent.

It had come over Wiley that, as long as he stood guard, no accident would happen at the mine; but he was equally convinced that, the moment he left it, the unexpected would happen. So, since Blount had elected to fight his suit, he let the fate of his option wait while he piled up money for his *coup*. As an individual, Blount might resist the sale of his stock; but as President of the Company he and his Board of Directors had given Wiley a valid bond and lease and, acting under its terms, Wiley still had an opportunity to gain a clear title to the mine. What happened to the stock could be thrashed out later, but with the Paymaster in his possession he could laugh his enemies to scorn—and he did not intend to be jumped! For who could tell, among these men who swarmed about him, which ones might be hired emissaries of Blount; and, once he was out of sight, they might seize the mine and hold it against all comers.

It was a thing which had been done before, and was likely to be done again; and as the days slipped by, bringing him closer to the end, he looked about for some agent. Had he a man that he could trust to hold the mine, while he went into town to gain title to it? He looked them all over but, knowing Blount as he did, and the weakness of human nature, he hesitated and decided against it. No, it was better by far that *he* should hold the mine—for possession, in mining, is everything—and send someone to pay over the money. That would be perfectly legal, and anyone could do it, but here again he hesitated. The zeal of his lawyer was failing of late—could he trust him to make the payment, in a town that was owned by Blount? Would he offer it legally and demand a legal surrender, and come out and put the deed in his hand? He might, but Wiley doubted it.

There was something going on regarding the payments for his shipments which he was unable to straighten out over the 'phone, and his lawyer was neglecting even that. And yet, if those checks were held up much longer it might seriously interfere with his payment. He had wired repeatedly, but either the messages were not delivered or his buyer was trying to welch on his contract. What he wanted was an agent, to go directly to the buyer and get the matter adjusted. Wiley thought the matter over, then he 'phoned his lawyer to forget it and wrote direct to an express company, enclosing his bills of lading and authorizing them to collect the account. When it came to collecting bills you could trust the express company—and you could trust Uncle Sam with your mail—but as to the people in Vegas, and especially the telephone girl, he had his well-established doubts. His telegraphic messages went out over the 'phone and were not a matter of record and if she happened to be eating a box of Blount's candy she might forget to relay them. It was borne in upon him, in fact, more strongly every day, that there are very few people you can trust. With a suitcase, yes—but with a mine worth millions? That calls for something more than common honesty.

The fight for the Paymaster, and Wiley's race against time, was now on every tongue, and as the value of the property went up there was a sudden flurry in the stock. Men who had hoarded it secretly for eight and ten years, men who had moved to the ends of the world, all heard of the fabulous wealth of the new Paymaster and wrote in to offer their stock. Not to offer it, exactly, but to place it on record; and others began as quietly to buy. It was known that the royalties had piled up an accruing dividend of at least twenty cents a share; and with the sale of it imminent—and a greater rise coming in case there was no sale— there would be a further increase in value. It was good, in fact, for thirty cents cash, with a gambling chance up to five dollars; and the wise ones began to buy. Men he had not seen for years dropped in on Wiley to ask his advice about their stock; and one evening in his office, he looked up from his work to see the familiar face of Death Valley Charley.

"Hello there, Charley," he said, still working. "Awful busy. What is it you want?"

"Virginia wants her stock," answered Charley simply and blinked as he stood waiting the answer. There was a war on now between the Huffs and Holmans into which Wiley's father had been drawn; and since Honest John had repudiated his son's acts and disclaimed all interest in his deal, Charley knew that Wiley was bitter. He had cut off the Widow from her one source of revenue but, when she had accused him of doing it for his father, Wiley had forgotten the last of his chivalry. Not only did he board all his men himself but he promised to fire any man he had who was seen taking a meal at the Widow's. It was war to the knife, and Charley knew it, but he blinked his eyes and stood firm.

"What stock?" demanded Wiley, and then he closed his lips and his eyes turned fighting gray. "You tell her," he said, "if she wants her stock, to come and get it herself."

"But she sent me to get it!" objected Charley obstinately.

"Yes, and I send you back," answered Wiley. "I gave her that stock twice, and I made it what it is, and if she wants it she can come and ask for it."

"And will you give it to her?" asked Charley, but Wiley only grunted and went ahead with his writing.

It was apparent to him what was in the wind. The Widow had written to demand of his father some return for the damage to her business; and Honest John had replied, and sent Wiley a copy, that he was in no wise responsible for his acts. This letter to Wiley had been followed by another in which his father had rebuked him for persecuting Mrs. Huff, and Wiley had replied with five pages, closely written, reciting his side of the case. At this John Holman had declared himself neutral and, beyond repeating his offer to buy the Widow's stock, had disclaimed all interest in her affairs. But now, with her stock still in Blount's hands and this last source of revenue closed to her, the Widow was left no alternative but to appeal indirectly to Wiley. What other way then was open, if she was ever to win back her stock, but to get back Virginia's shares and sell them to raise the eight hundred dollars? Wiley grumbled to himself as Death Valley Charley turned away and went on writing his letter.

It had been a surprise, after his break with Virginia, to discover that it left him almost glad. It had removed a burden that had weighed him down for months, and it left him free to act. He could protect his property now as it should be protected, without thought of her or anybody; and he could board his own men and keep the gospel of hate from being constantly dinned into their ears. They were honest, simple miners, easily swayed by a woman's distress, but equally susceptible to the lure of gold; and now with a bonus after the minimum of work they were tearing out the ore like Titans. They were loyal and satisfied, greeting his coming with a friendly smile; but if Virginia got hold of them, or her venomous mother, where then would be his discipline?

He was deep in his work when a shadow fell upon his desk and he looked up to see—Virginia.

CHAPTER XXV

VIRGINIA REPENTS

"I came for my stock," said Virginia coolly as she met his questioning eye and Wiley turned and rummaged in a drawer. The stock was hers and since she came and asked for it—he laid it on the desk and went ahead with his work. Virginia took the envelope and examined it carefully, but she did not go away. She glanced at him curiously, writing away so grimly, and there was a scar across his head. Could it be—yes, there her rock had struck him. The mark was still fresh, but he had given her the stock; and now he was privileged to hate her. That wound on his head would soon be overgrown and covered, but she had left a deeper scar on his heart. She had hurt his man's pride; and now he had hurt hers, and humbled her to ask for her stock. He looked up suddenly, feeling her eyes upon him, and Virginia drew back and blushed.

"Oh—thank you," she stammered and turned to go, and yet she lingered to see what he would say.

"You're welcome," he answered evenly, and took a fresh sheet of paper, but she refused to notice the hint. A sense of pique, of wonder at his politeness and half-resentment at his obliviousness of her presence, drew her back and she leaned against his desk.

"What are you writing?" she asked as he glanced at her inquiringly. "Is it a letter to that squaw?"

A sudden twitch of passion passed over his face at this reference to a dark page in their past and he drew the written sheet away.

"No," he said, "I happened to remember a white girl—"

"What?" burst out Virginia before she could check herself and he curled his lip up scornfully.

"Yes," he nodded, "and she seems to think I'm all right."

"Oh," she said and turned away her head with a painful twisted smile. Somehow she had always thought—and yet he must have met other girls—he was meeting them all the time! She tried to summon her anger, to carry her past this fresh stab, but the tears rose to her eyes instead.

"I—we'll be going away soon," she went on hurriedly. "That is, if he gives us back our stock. Do you think he'll do it, Wiley? You know—the plan you spoke of. We're going to sell this stock to a broker and then pay Mr. Blount back."

"I don't know," mumbled Wiley, and humped up over his letter, but it did not produce the effect he had hoped for.

"Well—I'm sorry I hurt you," she broke out

impulsively, rebuked by the long gash in his hair, "but you shouldn't have tried to stop me! I wasn't doing you any harm—I just came up there that night to see what was going on. And I did see Stiff Neck George, you can smile all you want to, and he had something heavy in his hand."

She ran on with her explanation, only to trail off inconclusively as she saw his face growing grim. He did not believe her, he did not even listen; he just sat there patiently and waited.

"Are you waiting for me to go?" she asked, smiling wanly, but even then he did not respond. There had been a time, not many weeks ago, when he would have risen up and offered her a chair; but he had got past that now and seemed really and sincerely to prefer his own company to hers. "I thought you might help us," she went on almost tearfully, "to get back our stock from Blount. It was nice of you to tell me, after the way I acted; but—oh, I don't know what it was that came over me! And I never even thanked you for telling me!"

A cynical smile came into Wiley's eyes as he sat back and put down his pen, but even after that she hurried on. "Yes, I know you don't like me—you think I tried to wreck your mine and turned all your men against you—but I do thank you, all the same. You—you used to care, Wiley; but anyhow, I thank you and—I guess I'll be going now."

She started for the door but he did not try to stop her. He even picked up his pen, and she turned back with fire in her eyes.

"Well, you might say something," she said defiantly, "or don't you care what happens to me?"

"No; I don't, Virginia," he answered quietly, "so just let it go at that. We can't get along, so what's the use of trying? You go your way and let me go mine."

"Oh, I know!" she sighed, "you think I'm ungrateful—and you think I just came for my stock. But I didn't, altogether; I wanted to say I'm sorry and—oh, Wiley, *do* you think he's alive?"

"Who?" he asked; but he knew already—she was thinking about the Colonel.

"Why, Father," she ran on. "I heard you that time when you got old Charley drunk. Do you think he's really alive? Because if he is!" She raised her eyes ecstatically and suddenly she was smiling into his. "Because if he is," she said, "and I can find him again—oh, Wiley; won't you help me find him?"

"I'll think about it," responded Wiley, but his eyes were smiling back and the anger had died in his heart. After all, she was human; she could smile through her tears and reach out and touch his rough hand, and he could not bring himself to hate her. "After I pay for the mine," he suggested gently. "But now you'd better go."

"Oh, no," she protested, "please tell me about it. Is he hiding in the Ube-Hebes? Oh, you don't know how glad I was when I heard you talking with Charley—I never did think he was dead. He sent me word once, not to worry about him, but—the Indians said he had died. That is—well, they said if it hadn't been for that sandstorm they would surely have found the body. And he'd thrown away his canteen, so he couldn't have had any water; and there wasn't any more for miles. He was lost, you know, and out of his head; and heading right out through the sandhills. Oh, it's awful to talk about it, but of course we don't know for certain; and it might have been somebody else. Don't you think it was some other man?"

"I don't know," answered Wiley, and sat staring straight ahead as she ran on with her arguments and entreaties. After all, what did he have to base his belief upon, except the babblings of brain-cracked Charley? They had found the Colonel's riding-burro, and his saddle-bags and papers, besides his rifle and canteen; and the Shoshone trailers had followed the tracks of a man until they were lost in the drifting sandhills. And yet Charley's remarks, and his repeated attempts to get across the valley with some whiskey; there was something there, certainly, upon which to build hope—and Virginia was very insistent.

"Yes, I think it was another man," he said at length. "Either that or your father escaped. He might have lost one canteen and still have had another, or he might have found his way to some water-hole. But from the way Charley talks, and tries to cover up his breaks, I feel sure that your father is alive."

"Oh, goodie!" she cried and before he could stop her she had stooped over and kissed his bruised head. "Now you know I'm sorry," she burst out impulsively, "and will you go out and look for him at once?"

"Pretty soon," said Wiley, putting her gently away. "After I make my payment on the mine. They'd be sure to jump me, now."

"Oh, but why not now?" she pleaded. "They wouldn't jump your mine."

"Yes, they would," he replied. "They'd jump me in a minute! I don't dare to go off the grounds."

"But what's the mine," she demanded insistently, "compared to finding Father?"

"Well, not very much," he conceded frankly, "but this is the way I'm fixed. I've got the whole world against me, including you and your mother, and I've got to play out my hand. There's nobody I can trust—even my father has turned against me—and I've got to fight this out myself."

"What? Just for the money? Do you think more of that than you do of finding my father?"

"No, I don't," he said, "but I can't go now, and so there's no use talking."

"No," she answered, drawing resentfully away from him, "there's no use talking to *you!* He might be dying, or out of food, but you don't think of anything but that money!"

"Well, maybe so," he retorted tartly, "but if you'd just left me alone, instead of siccing all your dogs on me, I'd've been over there looking for him, long ago. Of course I'm wrong—that's understood from the start; but—"

"What dogs did I set on you?" she demanded, flaring up, and he fixed her with sullen eyes.

"Never mind," he said. "You know what you've done as well or better than I do. All I've got to say is that my conscience is clear and we'd better quit talking while we're friends."

"Yes—friends!" she repeated, and then she stopped and at last she heaved a sigh. "Well, I don't care," she defended. "You drove me to it. A woman must protect herself, somehow."

"Well, you can do it," he said, feeling tenderly of his head, and Virginia flew into a rage.

"I told you I was *sorry!*" she cried, stamping her foot. "Isn't that enough? I'm sorry, I said!"

"Yes, and I'm sorry," he answered, but his eyes were level and his jaw jutted out like a crag.

"Sorry for what?" she demanded, and he sprang his trap.

"Sorry I can't go out and hunt for your father."

"Oh," she said, and drooped her head.

"If we could pay for what we've done by just being sorry," he went on with a ghost of a smile, "we wouldn't be where we are. But you know we can't, Virginia. I'm sorry for some things myself, and I expect to pay for them, but I can't stop to do it now."

"But will you go for him—sometime?" she asked, smiling wistfully. "Then—oh, Wiley; why can't we be friends?" She held out her hands and he rose up and took them, but with a startled look in his eyes. "You know that I'm sorry," she said, "and I'm willing to pay, too; if there's anything that I can do. Can't I help you, Wiley? Isn't there something I can do to help you pay for your mine? And I'll never oppose you again—if you'll only go and find my father!"

She raised his hands and put them against her cheek and the quick tears sprang to his eyes.

"I'll do it," he promised, "just the minute I can go. And—I'll try to be good to you, Virginia. Won't you give me a kiss, just to show it's all right? I'm sorry I treated you so rough. But it'll be all right now and we'll try to be friends again—I wasn't writing to any other girl."

"Oh, weren't you?" she smiled. "Well, I'll kiss you, then—just once. But somehow, I'm afraid it won't last."

CHAPTER XXVI
THE CALL

The long quarrel was over, they had made up—and kissed—and yet to Wiley it all seemed unreal. That is, all but the kiss. It was that, perhaps, which made the rest seem unreal, for it had changed the color of his life. Before, he had thought in terms of hard fact, but the kiss put a rainbow in the sky. It roused a great hope, a joy, an ecstasy, a sense of well-wishing for mankind; and yet it was only he who had changed. The world was the same; Samuel Blount was the same; and the miners, and Stiff Neck George. They were all there together in a rough-and-tumble fight to see who would get the Paymaster Mine and, even with the madness of her kiss in his soul, he pressed on towards the one, fixed goal.

He had set out to win the Paymaster and win it he would if he had to shoot his way to victory. For Stiff Neck George, like a watchful coyote, had taken up his post on the hill; and from that sign alone Wiley knew that Blount had changed his tactics and appealed to the court of last resort. His attachments had failed, his injunction suit had failed, and his cheap attempt to cut off Wiley's checks. The money had come, promptly forwarded by the Express Company with a note of apology from the buyer, and it lay now in Wiley's office safe. All that was left to do was to send it to Blount and get back the deed to the property. Three days remained before the bond and lease expired, but that was not a day too much. The question was—who to send? Wiley thought the matter over, glanced at George up on the hill, and sent a note down to Virginia.

She came up the trail smiling, for her proud reserve had vanished, and she even allowed him a kiss; but when he asked her to take the money to Blount she drew back and shook her head.

"I'm afraid," she said, "—I'm afraid something might happen. Can't you send it by somebody else?"

"No, that's just the point," he answered gravely. "Something is likely to happen if I do. My lawyer has turned crooked, and the bank won't touch it; so there's nobody to send but you. You can hide the money till you get there, so that no one will rob you on the way; and if anybody asks you, you can tell them about that stock deal and that you're going down to hold up Blount."

"Why don't you go?" she objected and he pointed out the doorway at Stiff Neck George on the hill.

"There he sits," he said, "like a red-necked old buzzard, just waiting for a chance to jump my mine. He may do it, anyhow—I wouldn't put it past him—but if he comes he'd better come a-shooting. You see, here's the point: the man that holds this mine can turn out ten thousand dollars a day, and that amount of money would hire enough lawyers to fight the outsiders to a standstill. If I get jumped I'm licked, because I haven't got any more money; and I'm going to stay right here and fight 'em. But you take this money—there's fifty-two thousand dollars—and go down and make that payment. If you can't find Blount, then hunt up the clerk of the Superior Court and deposit the fifty thousand with him. Just bring me his receipt, with a memorandum of the payment, and he'll notify Blount himself."

"I don't like to," she shuddered. "I'm afraid they won't take it, and then you'll—"

"They've got to take it!" he broke in eagerly. "Just get the stage driver to go along as witness, and I'll give you a full power of attorney. And then listen, Virginia; you take the rest of this money and buy back your father's stock."

"Oh, can I?" she cried and, reaching out for the money, she held it with tremulous hands. There were fifty thousand-dollar bills, golden yellow on the back and a rich, glossy black on the front; and others of smaller denominations, making fifty-two thousand in all. It was a fortune in itself, but in what it was to buy it was well worth over a million.

"Aren't you afraid to trust me?" she asked at

last, and when he smiled she hid it away. "All right," she said, "and as soon as I've paid it I'll call you up on the 'phone."

She went out the next morning on the early stage and Wiley watched it rush across the plain. It was green as a lawn, that dry, treeless desert with its millions of evenly spaced creosote bushes; but as the sun rose higher it turned blood-red like an omen of evil to come. Many times before, in the glow of evening, he had seen the green change to red; but now it was ominous, with Stiff Neck George on the hill-top and Shadow Mountain frowning down behind. He paced about uneasily as the day wore on and at night he listened for the 'phone. She was to call him up, as soon as she had paid over the money; but it did not ring that night.

The morning of the last day dawned fair and pleasant, with the fresh smell of dew in the air, and he awoke with a sense that all was well. Virginia was in Vegas and, when Blount came to his office, she would make the payment in his stead. There was no chance to fail, once she had found her man; and if Blount refused to accept it, which he could hardly do, she could simply leave the money with the court. There were no papers to confuse her, no forms to go through; Blount had made a legal contract to sell the property and she had a full power of attorney. All it called for was loyalty and faithfulness to her trust, and

Wiley knew Virginia too well to think she would fail him now. She was proud and hot-headed, and she had fought him in the past; but, once she had given her word, she would keep her promise or die.

As the sun rose higher he imagined her at the bank with the sheaf of bills hidden in her bosom, and Blount's surprise and palavering when he found he was caught and that his deep-laid plans had failed. He had schemed to catch Wiley between the horns of a dilemma, and either jump his mine when he went in to make the payment or force him to lose it by default. But, almost by a miracle, Virginia had appeared at the very moment when he was seeking a messenger; and by an even greater miracle, they had composed all their difficulties just in time for him to send her to town. It was like an act of Providence, an answer to prayer, if people any longer prayed; and, more, even, than the money and the joy of success, was the consciousness of Virginia's love. She had seemed so hostile, so distant and unattainable; but the moment that he forgot her and abandoned all hope she fluttered to his hand like a dove.

The noon hour came and went and as Wiley watched the 'phone it seemed to him strangely silent. To be sure, few people called him, but— he snatched the receiver from the hook. He had guessed it—the 'phone was dead! He rattled the hook and listened impatiently, then he shouted and listened again, and black fancies rose up in his brain. What was the meaning of this? Had they cut the wire on him? And why? It really made no difference! Virginia was there; he had heard it from the stage-driver who had driven her in the day before—and yet, there must be a reason. Perhaps it was an accident, for the line was old and neglected, but why should it happen now? He hung up the receiver and reviewed it all calmly. There were a hundred things which might happen to the line, for it passed through rough country near Vegas; but the weather was fair and there was no wind blowing to topple over the poles. No one used the line but him—it had been connected up by Blount when he had first taken over the mine—and yet the wire had been cut. But by whom? As he sat there pondering he raised his eyes to the hill-top, and Stiff Neck George was gone!

"The dastard!" cursed Wiley, leaping furiously to his feet and reaching for his rifle, but though he scanned the line through his high-power field-glasses there was not a man in sight. Wiley ran down to the shed and got out his racer that had lain there idle for months, but as his motor began to thunder, a head popped up and he saw Stiff Neck George on the ridge. He too had a rifle and, as he saw Wiley watching him, he dropped back and hid from sight.

"Oho!" said Wiley, and, leaving his machine, he strode angrily back to the mine. So that was their game, to get him to leave and then slip in and jump his mine. Perhaps it was all arranged with the men he had working for him and George would not even have a fight. Neither his foremen nor the guards were men he would care to trust in a matter involving millions—and yet something was wrong in Vegas. There was treachery somewhere or they would not cut the line to keep him from getting the news. He lingered irresolutely, his hands itching for the steering wheel, his eyes searching for Stiff Neck George.

There was a feud between them—he had braved George's killing gun and rushed in and kicked him down the dump. Would George, then, withhold his hand? But, down in Vegas, Blount was framing up some game to deprive him of title to his mine. Wiley weighed them in the balance, the two forces against him, and decided to stay with the mine. As long as he held it there were lawyers a-plenty to prove that his title was good, but if Stiff Neck George jumped it he would have to kill him to get back possession of the property. Or rather, he would have to fight him, for George was a gunman with notches on the butt of his six-shooter. No, he would have to get killed, or give up the Paymaster, whether Blount was right or wrong.

He set his teeth and settled down to endure it—

but he knew that Virginia would not fail him. He had given her the money, she knew what to do, and as sure as she hoped to save her father, he knew that she would do it. His part was to hold down the mine. The men came and went, the engine puffed and panted, and the long, dragging hours went by. As the darkness came on Wiley stalked in the shadows, looking out into the night for Stiff Neck George; but nothing stirred, the work went on as usual, and at midnight he gave up the search. His option had expired and either the mine was his or the title had reverted to the Company. There was nothing to watch for and so he slept, but at dawn his telephone jangled.

Wiley rose up breathlessly and took down the receiver but no one answered his call. The 'phone was dead and yet it had rung—or was it only a dream? He hung up in disgust and went back to bed but something drew him back to the 'phone. He held down the hook and, with the receiver to his ear, let the lever rise slowly up. There was talking going on and men laughing in hoarse voices and the tramp of feet to and fro, but no one responded to his shouts. He hung up once more and then suddenly it came over him, a foreboding of impending disaster. Something was wrong, something big that must be stopped at once; and a voice called insistently for action. He leapt into his clothes and started for the door—then turned back and strapped on his pistol. As the sun rose up he was a speck in the desert, rushing on through a blood-red sea.

CHAPTER XXVII
THE THUNDER CLAP

The broad streets of Vegas were swarming with traffic as Wiley glided swiftly into town and he noticed that people looked at him curiously. Perhaps it was all imagination but it seemed to him they eyed him coldly. Yet what they thought or felt was nothing to him then—his business was with Samuel J. Blount. The mine was unprotected—he had not even told his foreman that he was leaving, or where he was going—and there was no time for anything but business. If there was any trouble for him, Samuel J. Blount was at the bottom of it, and he drove straight up to the bank. It was a huge, granite structure with massive onyx pillars and smiling young clerks at the grilles; but he hurried past them all and turned down a hall to a room that was marked: President—Private. This was no time for dallying or sending in cards—he opened the door and stepped in.

Samuel Blount was sitting at the head of a table with other men grouped about him, but as Wiley Holman entered they were silent. He glanced at Blount and then again at the men—they were the directors of the Paymaster Mining and Milling Company!

"Good morning, Mr. Holman," spoke up Blount with asperity. "Please wait for me out in the hall."

"Since when?" retorted Wiley and then, leaping to the point, "what about that deed to the Paymaster?"

"Why—you must be misinformed," replied Blount slowly, at the same time pressing a button, "this is a meeting of the Board of Directors."

"So I see," returned Wiley, "but I sent the money by Virginia to take up the option on the mine. Did you receive it or did you not?"

A broad-shouldered man, very narrow between the eyes, came in and stood close to Wiley, and Blount smiled and cleared his throat.

"No," he said, "we did not receive it?"

"Oh, you didn't, eh?" said Wiley, glancing up at the janitor. "Perhaps you will tell me if it was offered to you?"

"No, it was not offered to us," replied Blount, smiling blandly, "although Miss Huff did make a deposit."

"Of fifty thousand dollars?"

"No, it was more than that—fifty-two, I believe. It was deposited to your account."

"Oh," observed Wiley, and looked them over again as the directors turned around to scowl. "Well, perhaps I can see Miss Huff?"

"She is not here at present," replied Blount with finality, "and so I must ask you to withdraw."

"Just a moment," said Wiley, as the janitor

moved expectantly. "I came here on a matter of business with you and this Board of Directors and, since the matter is urgent, I must request an immediate hearing. You don't need to be alarmed—all I want is my answer and then I'll leave you alone. In the first place, Mr. Blount, will you please tell me the circumstances under which this deposit was made? I gave Miss Huff instructions to offer the money to you in payment for the Paymaster Mine."

"Oh! Instructions, eh?" piped Blount with a satirical smile, and the Board stirred and nodded significantly. "Well, since you've just come in and are evidently unaware of the wide interest that has been taken in this case, I'll tell you a few things, Mr. Holman. The people of this town do not approve of the manner in which you have treated Mrs. Huff; and as for your 'instructions' to Virginia, let me tell you right now that we have saved her from becoming your victim."

"My victim!" repeated Wiley, moving swiftly towards him, but the janitor caught him by the arm.

"Yes, your victim," answered Blount with a venomous sneer, "or, at least, your intended victim. The people of Vegas had nothing to say when you deprived Virginia and her mother of their livelihood—it was your privilege as lessee of the mine to board your own men if you chose—but when you had the effrontery to send Virginia to this Board with 'instructions' to jeopardize her own interests, we felt called on to interfere."

"Why, you're crazy!" burst out Wiley. "What interests did she jeopardize by making that payment for me? As a matter of fact it was just the contrary—I gave her the money to get back the stock that you had practically stolen from her mother!"

"Now! Now!" spoke up Blount, "we won't have any personalities, or I'll ask Mr. Jepson to remove you. You must know if you know anything that Virginia herself had over twelve thousand shares of stock; while her mother left with me, as collateral on a note, more than two hundred thousand shares more. Yet you asked this innocent girl, who trusted you so fully, to wipe out her whole inheritance at one blow. You asked her to come here and make a payment that would beat her out of half a million dollars—*for fifty thousand dollars!*"

He paused and the men about the table murmured threateningly among themselves.

"And now!" went on Blount with heavy irony, "you come here and ask for your deed!"

"Yes, you bet I do!" snapped back Wiley, "and I'm going to get it, too. If Virginia came here and offered you that money, that's enough, in the eyes of the law. It was a legal payment under a legal contract, entered into by this Board of Directors;

and I call you gentlemen to witness that she came here and offered the money."

"She came to *me!*" corrected Blount, "and in no wise as the President of this Board!"

"Well, you're the man that I told her to go to—and if she offered you the money, that's enough!"

"Oh, it's enough, is it? Well, it may be enough for you, but it is not enough for the citizens of this town. We have organized a committee, of which Mr. Jepson is a member, to escort you out of Vegas; and I would say further that your bond and lease has lapsed and the Company will take over the mine."

"We'll discuss that later," returned Wiley grimly, "but I'll tell you right now that there aren't men enough in Vegas to run me out of town—not if you call in the whole town and the Janitors' Union—so don't try to start anything rough. I'm a law-abiding citizen, and I know my rights, and I'm going to see this through." He put his back to the wall and the burly Jepson took the hint to move further away. "Now," said Wiley, "if we understand each other let's get right down to brass tacks. It's all very well to organize Vigilance Committees for the protection of trusting young ladies, but you know and I know that this is a matter of business, involving the title to a mine. And I'd like to say further that, when a Board of Directors talks a messenger out of her purpose and persuades her to disregard her instructions—"

"Instructions!" bellowed Blount.

"Yes—instructions!" repeated Wiley, "—instructions as my agent. I sent Miss Huff down here to make this payment and I gave her instructions regarding it."

"Do you realize," blustered Blount, "that if she had followed those instructions she would have defrauded her own mother out of millions; that she would have ruined her own life and conferred her father's fortune upon the very man who was deceiving her?"

"No, I do not," replied Wiley, "but even if I did, that has nothing to do with the case. As to my relations with Miss Huff, I am fully satisfied that she has nothing of which to complain; and since it was you, and the rest of the gang, who stood to lose by the deal, your indignation seems rather far-fetched. If you were sorry for Miss Huff and wished to help her you have abundant private means for doing so; but when you dissuade her from her purpose in order to save your own skin you go up against the law. I'm going to take this to court and when the evidence is heard I'm going to prove you a bunch of crooks. I don't believe for a minute that Virginia turned against me. I know that she offered you the money."

"Oh, you know, do you?" sneered Blount as his

Directors rallied about him. "Well, how are you going to prove it?"

"By her own word!" said Wiley. "I know her too well. You just talked her out of it, afterward."

"So you think," taunted Blount, "that she offered the money in payment, and demanded the delivery of the deed? And will you stand or fall on her testimony?"

"Absolutely!" smiled Wiley, "and if she tells me she didn't do it I'll never take the matter into court."

"Very well," replied Blount and turned towards the door, but the Directors rushed in and caught him. They thrust their heads together in a whispered, angry conference, now differing among themselves and now flying back to catch Blount, but in the end he shook them all off. "No, gentlemen," he said, "I have absolute confidence in the justice of my case. If you stand to lose a little I stand to lose a great deal—and I know she never asked for that deed!"

"Well, bring her in, then," they conceded reluctantly, and turned venomous eyes upon Wiley. They knew him, and they feared him, and especially with this girl; for he was smiling and waiting confidently. But Blount was their czar, with his great block of stock pitted against their tiny holdings, and they sat down to await the issue.

She came at last, ushered in through the back

door by Blount, who smiled benevolently; and her eyes leapt on the instant to meet Wiley's.

"Here is Miss Huff," announced Blount deliberately and the light died in Wiley's shining eyes. He had waited for her confidently, but that one defiant flash told him that Virginia had turned against him. She had thrown in her lot with Blount, and against her lover, and by her word he must stand or fall. She had been his agent, but if she had not carried out her trust—

"Any questions you would like to ask," went on Blount with ponderous calm, "I am sure Virginia will answer."

He turned reassuringly and she nodded her head nervously, then stepped out and stood facing Wiley.

"It is a question," began Wiley, speaking like one in a dream, "of the way you paid Mr. Blount that money. When you took it to him first, before they had talked to you, did you tell him it was my payment on the option?"

Virginia glanced at Blount, then she took a deep breath and drew herself up very straight.

"No," she said, "I spoke to him first about buying back father's stock."

"But after that," he said, "didn't you hand him over the money and say it was sent by me?"

"No, I didn't," she answered. "After the way you had treated me I didn't think it was right."

"Not right!" he repeated with a slow, dazed

smile. "Why—why wasn't it right, Virginia?"

"Because," she went on, "you were trying to deceive me and beat me and mother out of our rights. You knew all the time that father's stock was still ours—and that Mr. Blount never even claimed it!"

"Never claimed it!" cried Wiley, suddenly roused to resentment. "Well, Virginia, he most certainly did! He offered to sell it to me for five cents a share when I took out that option on the Paymaster!"

"Now, now, Wiley!" began Blount, but Virginia cut him short with a scornful wave of the hand.

"Never mind," she said. "I'll attend to this myself. I just want to tell him what I think!"

"What you *think!*" raved Wiley, suddenly coming up fighting. "You've been fooled by a bunch of crooks. Never mind what you think—did you give him the money and tell him it came from me?"

"I did not!" answered Virginia, her eyes flashing with hot anger, "and while I may not be able to think, I certainly wasn't fooled by *you*. No, I took your money and put it in the bank, and I let your option expire!"

"My—God!" moaned Wiley, and groped for the door, but in the hall he stopped and turned back. There was some mistake—she had not understood. He slipped back and looked in once more. She was shaking hands with Blount—and smiling.

CHAPTER XXVIII
THE WAY OUT

When a woman treads the ways of deceit she smiles—like Mona Lisa. But was the great Leonardo deceived by the smile of his wife when she posed for him so sweetly? No, he read her thoughts—how she was thinking of another—and his master hand wove them in. There she smiles to-day, smooth and pretty and cryptic; but Leonardo, the man, worked with heavy heart as he laid bare the tragedy of his love. The message was for her, if she cared to read it, or for him, that rival for her love; or, if their hearts were pure and free from guilt, then there was no message at all. She was just a pretty woman, soft and gentle and smiling—as Virginia Huff had smiled.

She had not smiled often, Wiley Holman remembered it now, as he went flying across the desert, and always there was something behind; but when she had looked up at Blount and taken his fat hand, then he had read her heart at a glance. If he had taken his punishment and not turned back he would have been spared this great ache in his breast; but no, he was not satisfied, he could not believe it, and so he had received a worse wound. She had been playing with him all the time and, when the supreme moment arrived, she had landed him like a trout; and then, when she had left him belly-up from his disaster, she had turned to Blount and smiled. There was no restraint now; she smiled to the teeth; and Blount and the Directors smiled.

Wiley cursed to himself as he bored into the wind and burned up the road to Keno. The mine was nothing; he could find him another one, but Virginia had played him false. He did not mind losing her—he could find a better woman—but how could he save his lost pride? He had played his hand to win and, when it came to the showdown, she had slipped in the joker and cleaned him. The Widow would laugh when she heard the news, but she would not laugh at him. The road lay before him and his gas tanks were full. He would gather up his belongings and drift. He stepped on the throttle and went roaring through the town, but at the bottom of the hill he stopped. The mine was shut down, not a soul was in sight, and yet he had left but a few hours before.

He toiled wearily up the trail, where he had caught Virginia running and held her fighting in his arms, and the world turned black at the thought. What madness had this been that had kept him from suspecting her when she had opposed his every move from the start. Had she not wrecked his engine and ruined his mill? Then why had he trusted her with his money? And that last innocent visit, when she had asked for her stock, and thanked him so demurely at the end! She would not be dismissed, all his rough words were wasted, until in the end she had leaned over and kissed him. A Judas-kiss? Yes, if ever there was one; or the kiss of Judith of Bethulia. But Judith had sold her kisses to save her people—Virginia had sold hers for gold.

Yes, she had sold him out for money; after rebuking him from the beginning she had stabbed him to the heart for a price. It was always he, Wiley, who thought of nothing but money; who was the liar, the miser, the thief. Everything that he did, no matter how unselfish, was imputed to his love of money; and yet it had remained for Virginia, the censorious and virtuous, to violate her trust for gain. It was not for revenge that she had withheld the payment and snatched a million dollars from his hand; she had told him herself that it was because Blount had returned their stock and she would not throw it away. How quick Blount had been to see that way out and to bribe her by returning the stock—how damnably quick to read her envious heart and know that she would fall for the offer. Well, now let them keep it and smile their smug smiles and laugh at Honest Wiley; for if there ever was a curse on stolen money then Virginia's would buy her no happiness.

He raised his bloodshot eyes to look for the last time at the Paymaster, which he had fought for and lost. What had they done to save it, to bring it to what it was, to merit it for their own? For years it had lain idle, and when he had opened it up they had fought him at every step. They had shot him down with buckshot, and beaten him down with rocks and threatened his life with Stiff Neck George. His eyes cleared suddenly and he looked about the dump—he had forgotten his feud with George. Yet if his men were gone, who then had driven them out but that crooked-necked, fighting fool? And if George had driven them out, then where was he now with his ancient, filed-down six-shooter? Wiley drew his gun forward and walked softly towards the house, but as he passed a metal ore-car a pistol was thrust into his face. He started back, and there was George.

"Put 'em up!" he snarled, rising swiftly from behind the car, and the hot fury left Wiley's brain. His anger turned cold and he looked down the barrel at the grinning, spiteful eyes behind.

"You go to hell!" he growled, and George jabbed the gun into his stomach.

"Put 'em up!" he ordered, but some devil of resistance seized Wiley as his hands went up. It was close, too close, and George had the drop on him, but one hand struck out and the other clutched the gun while he twisted his lithe body aside. At the roar of the shot he went for his own gun, leaping back and stooping low. Another bullet clipped his shirt and then his own gun spat back, shooting blindly through the smoke. He emptied it, dodging swiftly and crouching close to the ground, and then he sprang behind the car. There was a silence, but as he listened he heard a gurgling noise, like the water flowing out of a canteen, and a sudden, sodden thump. He looked out, and George was down. His blood was gushing fast but the narrow, snaky eyes sought him out before they were filmed by death. It was over, like a rush of wind.

Wiley flicked out his cylinder and filled it with fresh cartridges, then looked around for the rest. He was calm now, and calculating and infinitely brave; but no one stepped forth to face his gun. A boy, down in town, started running towards the mine, only to turn back at some imperative command. The whole valley was lifeless, yet the people were there, and soon they would venture forth. And then they would come up, and look at the body, and ask him to give up his gun; and if he did they would take him to Vegas and shut him up in jail, where the populace could come and stare at him. Blount and Jepson would come, and the Board of Directors; and, in order to put him away, they would tell how he had threatened George. They would make it appear that he had come to jump the mine, and that George was defending the property; and then, with the jury nicely packed, they would send him to the penitentiary, where he wouldn't interfere with their plans.

In a moment of clairvoyance he saw Virginia before him, looking in through the prison bars and smiling, and suddenly he put up his gun. She had started this job and made him a murderer but he would rob her of that last chance to smile. There was a road that he knew that had been traveled before by men who were hard-pressed and desperate. It turned west across the desert and mounted by Daylight Springs to dip down the long slope to the Sink; and across the Valley of Death, if he could once pass over it, there was no one he need fear to meet. No one, that is, except stray men like himself, who had fled from the officers of the law. Great mountain ranges, so they said, stretched unpeopled and silent, beneath the glare of the desert sun; and though Death might linger near it was under the blue sky and away from the cold malice of men.

From his safe in the office Wiley took out a roll of bills, all that was left of his vanished wealth; and he took down his rifle and belt; and then, walking softly past the body of Stiff Neck George, he cranked up his machine and started off. Every doorway in town was crowded with heads, craning out to see him pass, and as he turned down the main street he saw Death Valley

Charley rushing out with a flask in his hand.

"We seen ye!" he grinned as Wiley slowed down, and dropped the flask of whiskey on the seat.

"You killed him fair!" he shouted after him, but Wiley had opened up the throttle and the answer to his praise was a roar.

The sun was at high noon when Wiley topped the divide and glided down the canyon towards Death Valley. He could sense it in the distance by the veil of gray haze that hung like a pall across his way. Beyond it were high mountains, a solid wall of blue that seemed to rise from the depths and float, detached, against the sky; and up the winding wash which led slowly down and down, there came pulsing waves of heat. The canyon opened out into a broad, rocky sand-flat, shut in on both sides by knife-edged ridges dotted evenly with brittle white bushes; and each jagged rock and out-thrust point was burned black by the suns of centuries.

He passed an ancient tractor, abandoned by the wayside, and a deserted, double-roofed house; and then, just below it where a ravine came down, he saw a sign-board, pointing. Up the gulch was another sign, still pointing on and up, and stamped through the metal of the disk was the single word: Water. It was Hole-in-the-Rock Springs that old Charley had spoken about and, somewhere up the canyon, there was a hole in the limestone cap, and beneath it a tank of sweet water. On many a scorching day some prospector, half dead from thirst, had toiled up that well-worn trail; but now the way was empty, the freighter's house given over to rats, and the road led on and on.

A jagged, saw-tooth range rose up to block his way and the sand-flat narrowed down to a deep wash; and, then, still thundering on, he struggled out through its throat and the Valley seemed to rise up and smite him. He stopped his throbbing motor and sat appalled at its immensity. Funereal mountains, black and banded and water-channeled, rose up in solid walls on both sides and, down through the middle as far as the eye could see, there stretched a white ribbon, set in green. It swung back and forth across a wide, level expanse, narrow and gleaming with water at the north and blending in the south with gray sands. The writhing white band was Death Valley Sink, where the waters from countless desert ranges drained down and were sucked up by the sun. Far from the north it came, when the season was right and the cloudbursts swept the Grape-Vines and the White mountains; the Panamints to the west gave down water from winter snows that gathered on Telescope Peak; and every ravine of the somber Funeral Range was gutted by the rush of forgotten waters.

The Valley was dry, bone-dry and desiccated,

and yet every hill, every gulch and wash and canyon, showed the action of torrential waters. The chocolate-brown flanks of the towering mountain walls were creased, and ripped out and worn; and from the mouth of every canyon a great spit of sand and boulders had been spewed out and washed down towards the Sink. On the surface of this wash, rising up through thousands of feet, the tips of buried mountains peeped out like tiny hill-tops, yet black, and sharp and grim. The great ranges themselves, sweeping up from the profundity till they seemed to cut off the world, looked like molded cakes of chocolate which had been rained on and half melted down. They were washed-down, melted, stripped of earth and vegetation; and down from their flanks in a steep, even slope, lay the debris and scourings of centuries.

The westering sun caught the glint of water in the poisonous, salt-marshes of the Sink; but, far to the south, the great ultimate Sink of Sinks was a-gleam with borax and salt. It was there where the white band widened out to a lake-bed, that men came in winter to do their assessment work and scrape up the cotton-ball borax. But if any were there now they would know him for a fugitive and he took the road to the west. It ran over boulders, ground smooth by rolling floods and burned deep brown by the sun, and as he twisted and turned, throwing his weight against the wheels, Wiley felt the growing heat. His shirt clung to his back, the sweat ran down his face and into his stinging eyes and as he stopped for a drink he noticed that the water no longer quenched his thirst. It was warm and flat and after each fresh drink the perspiration burst from every pore, as if his very skin cried out for moisture. Yet his canteen was getting light and, until he could find water, he put it resolutely away.

The road swung down at last into a broad, flat dry-wash, where the gravel lay packed hard as iron, and as his racer took hold and began to leap and frolic, he tore down the valley like the wind. The sun was sinking low and the unknown lay before him, a land he had never seen; yet before the night came on he must map out his course and stake his life on the venture. Other automobiles might follow and snatch him back if he delayed but an hour in his flight; but, once across Death Valley and lost in those far mountains, he would leave the law behind. The men he met would be fugitives like himself, or prospectors, or wandering Shoshones; and, live or die, he would be away from it all—where he would never see Virginia again.

The deep wash pinched in, as the other had done, before it gave out into the plain; and, then, as he whirled around a point, he glided out into the open. The foothills lay behind him and, straight athwart his way, stretched a sea of motionless sand-waves. As far north as he could see, the ocean of sand tossed and tumbled, the crests of its rollers crowned with brush and grotesque driftwood, the gnarled trunks and roots of mesquite trees. To the east and west the high mountains still rose up, black and barren, shutting in the sea of sand; but across the valley a pass led smoothly up to a gap through the wall of the Panamints. It was Emigrant Wash, up which the hardy Mormons had toiled in their western pilgrimage, leaving at Lost Wagons and Salt Creek the bones of whole caravans as a tribute to the power of the desert.

A smooth, steep slope led swiftly down to the edge of the Valley of Death and as Wiley looked across he saw as in a vision a massive gateway of stone. It was flung boldly out from the base of a blue mountain, enclosing a dark valley behind; and from between its lofty walls a white river of sand spread out like a flower down the slope. It was the gateway to the Ube-Hebes, just as Charley had described it, and it was only a few miles away. It lay just across the sand-flat, where the great, even waves seemed marching in a phalanx towards the south; and then up a little slope, all painted blue and purple, to the mysterious valley beyond. The sun, swinging low, touched the summits of distant sand-hills with a gleam of golden light and all the dark shadows moved toward him. A breath of air fanned his cheek, and as he drank deep from his canteen he nodded to the Gateway and smiled.

CHAPTER XXIX

ACROSS DEATH VALLEY

The way to the Ube-Hebes lay across a low flat, glistening white with crystals of alkali; and as his car trundled on Wiley came to a strip of sand, piled up in the lee of a prostrate salt bush. Other bushes appeared, and more sand about them, and then a broad, smooth wave. It mounted up from the north, gently scalloped by the wind, and on the south side it broke off like a wall. He drove along below it, glancing up as it grew higher, until at last it cut off his view. All the north was gone, and the Gateway to his hiding-place; but the south and west were there. To the south lay mud flats, powdery dry but packed hard; and the west was a wilderness of sand.

A giant mesquite tree, piled high with clinging drifts, rose up before the crest of his wave, and as he plowed in between them the edge of the crest poured down in a whispering cascade. Then more trees loomed up, and hundreds of white bushes each mounted on its pedestal of sand; and at the base of each salt-bush there were kangaroo-rat holes and the tracery of their tails in the dust. Men called it Death Valley, but for such as these it was a place of fullness and joy. They had capered about, striking the ground with their tails at the end of each playful jump, and the dry, brittle salt-bushes had been feast enough to them, who never knew the taste of grass or water.

The sand-wave rose higher, leaving a damp hollow behind it where ice-plants grew green and rank; and as he crept along the thunder of his exhaust started tons of sliding silt. His wheels raced and burrowed as he struck a soft spot, and then abruptly they sank. He dug them out carefully and backed away, but a mound of drifted sand barred his way. Twist and turn as he would he could not get around it and at last he climbed to its summit. The sun was setting in purple and fire behind the black shoulder of the Panamints and like a path of gold it marked out the way, the only way to cross the Valley. At the south was the Sink with its treacherous bog-holes and further north the sandhills were limitless—the only way, where the wagon-wheels had crossed, was buried deep in the sand. Three great mountains of sand, like huge breakers of the sea, had swept in and covered the wheel-tracks; and far to the west in the path of the sun their summits loomed two hundred feet high.

He went back to his car and drove it desperately at the slope, only to bury the rear wheels to the axles; and as he dug them out the sand from the wave crest began to whisper and slip and slide. He cleared a great space and started his motor, but at the first shuddering tug the sand began to tremble and in a rush the wave was upon him. It buried him deep and as he leapt from his machine little rills of singing sand flowed around it. So far it had carried him, this high-powered, steel-springed racer; but now he must leave it for the sand to cover over and cross the great Valley alone. On many a rocky slope and sliding sandhill it had clutched and plunged and fought its way, but now it was smothered in the treacherous, silt-fine sand and he must leave it, like a partner, to die. Yet if die it must, then in its desert burial the last trace of Wiley Holman would be lost. The first wind that blew would wipe out his foot-prints and the racer would sink beneath the waves. Wiley took his canteen, and Charley's bottle of whiskey, his rifle and a small sack of food and dared the great silence alone.

While his motor had done the work he had not minded the heat and the pressure of blood in his head, but as he toiled up the sandy slope, sinking deeper at each stride, he felt the breath of the sand. All day it had lain there drinking in the sun's rays and now in the evening, when the upper air was cool, it radiated a sweltering heat. Wiley mounted to the summit of wave after wave, fighting his way towards the Gateway to the north; and then, beaten at last and choking with the exertion, he turned and followed a crest. The sand piled up before him in a vortex of sharp-edged ridges, reaching their apex in a huge pyramid to the west, and as he toiled on past its flank he felt a gusty rush of air, sucking down through Emigrant Wash. It was the wind, after all, that was king of Death Valley; for whichever way it blew it swept the sand before it, raising up pyramids and tearing them down. Along the crest of the high wave a feather-edge of sand leapt out like a plume into space and as he stopped to watch it Wiley could see that the mountain was moving by so much across the plain.

A luminous half-moon floated high in the heavens and the sky was studded thick with pin-point stars. In that myriad of little stars, filling in between the big ones, the milky way was lost and reduced to obscurity—the whole sky was a milky way. Wiley sank down in the sand and gazed up sombrely as he wetted his parching lips from his canteen, and the evening star gleamed like a torch, looking down on the world he had fled. Across the Funeral Range, not a day's journey to the east, that same star lighted Virginia on her way while he, a fugitive, was flung like an atom into the depths of this sea of sand. It was deeper than the sea, scooped out far below the level of the cool breakers that broke along the shore; deep and dead, except for the wind that moved the drifting sand across the plains. And even as he lay there, looking up at the stars and wondering at the riddle of the universe, the busy wind was bringing grains of sand and burying him, each minute by so much.

He rose up in a panic and hurried along the slope, where the sand of the wave was packed hardest, and he did not pause till he had passed the last drift and set his foot on the hard, gravelly slope. The wind was cooler now, for the night was well along and the bare ground had radiated its heat; but it was dry, powder dry, and every pore of his skin seemed to gasp and cry out for water. There was water, even yet, in the bottom of his canteen; but he dared not drink it till the Gateway was in sight, and the sand-wash that led to the valley beyond.

An hour passed by as he toiled up the slope, now breaking into a run from impatience, now settling down doggedly to walk; and at last, clear and distinct, he saw the Gateway in the moonlight, and stopped to take his drink. It was cool now, the water, and infinitely sweet; yet he knew that the moment he drained the last drop he would feel the clutch of fear. It is an unreasoning thing, that fear of the desert which comes when the last drop is gone; and yet it is real and known to every wanderer, and guarded against by the bravest. He screwed the cap on his canteen and hurried up the slope, which grew steeper and rockier with each mile, but the phantom gateway seemed to lead on before him and recede into the black abyss of night. It was there, right before him, but instead of getting nearer, the Gateway loomed higher and higher; and daylight was near before he passed through its portals and entered the dark valley beyond.

A gaunt row of cottonwoods rose up suddenly before him, their leaves whispering and clacking in the wind, and at this brave promise all fear for water left him and he drained his canteen to the bottom. Then he strode on up the canyon, that was deep and dark as a pocket, following the trail that should lead him to the spring; but as one mile and two dragged along with no water, he stopped and hid his rifle among the rocks. A little later he hid his belt with its heavy row of cartridges, and the sack of dry, useless food. What he needed was water and when he had drunk his fill he could come back and collect all his possessions. Two miles, five miles, he toiled up the creek bed with the cottonwoods rustling overhead; but though their roots were in the water, the sand was still dry and his tongue was swelling with thirst.

He stumbled against a stone and fell weakly to the ground, only to leap to his feet again, frightened. Already it was coming, the stupifying lassitude, the reckless indifference to his fate, and yet he was hardly tired. The Valley had not been hot, any more than usual, and he had walked twice as far before; but now, with water just around the corner, he was lying down in the sand. He was sleepy, that was it, but he must get to water first or his pores would close up and he would die. He stripped off his pistol and threw it in the sand, and his hat, and the bottle of fiery whiskey; and then, head down, he plunged blindly forward, rushing on up the trail to find water.

The sun rose higher and poured down into the narrow valley with its fringe of deceptive green; but though the trees became bigger and bushier in their tops the water did not come to the surface. It was underneath the sand, flowing along the bed-rock, and all that was needed was a solid reef of country-rock to bring it up to the surface. It would flow over the dyke in a beautiful waterfall, leaping and gurgling and going to waste; and after he had drunk he would lie down and wallow and give his whole body a drink. He would soak there for hours, sucking it up with his parched lips that were cracked now and bleeding from the drought; and then—he woke up suddenly, to find himself digging in the sand. He was going mad then, so soon after he was lost, and with water just up the stream. The creek was dry, where he had found himself digging, but up above it would be full of water. He hurried on again and, around the next turn, sure enough, he found a basin of water.

It was hollowed from the rock, a round pool, undimpled, and upon its surface a pair of wasps floated about with airy grace. Their legs were outstretched and on the bottom of the hole he could see the round shadows of their tracks. It was a new kind of water, with a skin that would bend down and hold up the body of a wasp, and yet it seemed to be wet. He thrust in a finger and the wasps flew away—and then he dropped down and drank deep. When he woke from his madness the pool was half empty and the water was running down his face. He was wet all over and his lips were bleeding afresh, as if his very blood had been dry; but his body was weak and sick, and as he rose to his feet he tottered and fell down in the sand. When he roused up again the pool was filled with water and the wasps were back, floating on its surface.

When he looked around he was in a little cove, shut in by towering walls; and, close against the cliff where the rock had been hollowed out, he saw an abandoned camp. There were ashes between the stones, and tin cans set on boxes, and a walled-in storage place behind, and as he looked again he saw a man's tracks, leading down a narrow path to the water. They turned off up the creek—high-heeled boots soled with rawhide and bound about with thongs—and Wiley rushed recklessly at the camp. When he had eaten last he could hardly remember, (it was a day or two back at the best), and as he peered into cans and found them empty he gave vent to a savage curse. He was weak, he was starving, and he had thrown away his food—and this man had hidden what he had. He kicked over the boxes and plunged into the store-room, throwing beans and flour sacks right and left, and then in the corner behind a huge pile of pinon nuts he found a single can of tomatoes.

Whoever had treasured it had kept it too long, for Wiley's knife was already out and as he cut out the top he tipped it slowly up and drained it to the bottom.

"Hey, there!" hailed a voice and Wiley started and laid down the can. Was it possible the officers had followed him? "Throw up your hands!" yelled the voice in a fury. "Throw 'em up, or I'll kill you, you scoundrel!"

Wiley held up his hands, but he raised them reluctantly and the fighting look crept back into his eyes.

"Well!" he challenged, "they're up—what about it?"

A tall man with a pistol stepped out from behind a tree and advanced with his gun raised and cocked. His hair was hermit-long, his white beard trembled, and his voice cracked and shrilled with helpless rage.

"What about it!" he repeated. "Well, by Jupiter, if you sass me, I'll shoot you for a camp-robbing hound!"

"Well, go ahead then," burst out Wiley defiantly, "if that's the way you feel—all I took was one can of tomatoes!"

"Yes! One can! Wasn't that all I had? And you robbed me before, you rascal!"

"I did not!" retorted Wiley, and as the old man looked him over he hesitated and lowered his gun.

"Say, who are you, anyway?" he asked at last and glanced swiftly at Wiley's tracks in the sand. "Well—that's all right," he ran on hastily, "I see you aren't the man. There was a renegade came through here on the twentieth of last July and stole everything I had. I trailed him, dad-burn him, clear to the edge of Death Valley—he was riding my favorite burro—and if it hadn't been for a sandstorm that came up and stopped me, I'd have bored him through and through. He stole my rifle and even my letters, and valuable papers besides; but he went to his reward, or I miss my guess, so we'll leave him to the mercy of hell. As for my tomatoes, you're welcome, my friend; it's long since I've had a guest."

He held out his hand and advanced, smiling kindly, but Wiley stepped back—it was Colonel Huff.

CHAPTER XXX

AN EVENING WITH SOCRATES

How the Colonel had come to be reported dead it was easy enough now to surmise. Some desperate fugitive, or rambling hobo miner seeking a cross-cut to the Borax Mines below, had raided his camp in his absence; and, riding off on his burro, had met his death in a sandstorm. His were the tracks that the Indians had followed and somewhere in Death Valley he lay beneath the sand-dunes in place of a better man. But the Colonel—did he know that his family had mourned him as dead, and bandied his stock back and forth? Did he know that the Paymaster had been bonded and opened up, and lost again to Blount? And what would be his answer if he knew the man before him was the son of Honest John Holman? Wiley closed down his lips, then he took the outstretched hand and looked the Colonel straight in the eye.

"I'm sorry, sir," he said, "that I can't give you my name or tell you where I'm from; but I've got a bottle of whiskey that will more than make up for the loss of that can of tomatoes!"

"Whiskey!" shrilled the Colonel and then he smiled benignly and laid a fatherly hand upon his shoulder. "Never mind, my young friend, what you have done or not done; because I'm sure it was nothing dishonorable—and now if you will produce your bottle we'll drink to our better acquaintance."

"I threw it away," answered Wiley apologetically, "but it can't be very far down the trail. I was short of water and lost, you might say, and—well, I guess I was a little wild."

"And well you might be," replied the Colonel heartily, "if you crossed Death Valley afoot; and worn out and hungry, to boot. I'll just take the liberty of going after that bottle myself, before some skulking Shoo-shonnie gets hold of it."

"Do so," smiled Wiley, "and when you've had your drink, perhaps you'll bring in my rifle and the rest."

"Whatever you've dropped," returned the Colonel cordially, "if it's only a cartridge from your belt! And while I am gone, just make yourself at home. You seem to be in need of rest."

"Yes, I am," agreed Wiley, and before the Colonel was out of sight he was fast asleep on his bed.

It was dark when he awoke and the light of a fire played and flickered on the walls of his cave. The wind brought to his nostrils the odor of cooking beans and as he rose and looked out he saw the Colonel pacing up and down by the fire. His hat was off, his fine head thrown back and he was humming to himself and smiling.

"Come out, sir; come out!" he cried upon the moment. "I trust you have enjoyed your day's rest. And now give me your hand, sir; I regret beyond words my boorish conduct of this morning."

He shook hands effusively, still continuing his apologies for having taken Wiley for less than a gentleman; and while they ate together it became apparent to Wiley that the Colonel had had his drink. If there was anything left of the pint bottle of whiskey no mention was made of the fact; but even at that the liquor was well spent, for it had gained him a friend for life.

"Young man," observed the Colonel, after looking at him closely, "I am a fugitive in a way, myself, but I cannot believe, from the look on your face, that your are anything else than honest. I shall respect your silence, as you respect mine, for your past is nothing to me; but if at any time I can assist you, just mention the fact and the deed is as good as done. I am a man of my word and, since true friends are rare, I beg of you not to forget me."

"I'll remember that," said Wiley, and went on with his eating as the Colonel paced up and down. He was a noble-looking man of the Southern type, tall and slender, with flashing blue eyes; and the look that he gave him reminded Wiley of Virginia, only infinitely more kind and friendly. He had been, in his day, a prince of entertainers, of the rich and poor alike; and the kick of the whiskey had roused up those genial qualities which had made him the first citizen of Keno. He laughed and told stories and cracked merry jests, yet never for a moment did he forget his incognito nor attempt to violate Wiley's. They were gentlemen there together in the heart of the desert, and as such each was safe from intrusion. The rifle and cartridge belt, Wiley's pistol and the sack of food, were fetched and placed in his hands; and then at the end the Colonel produced the flask of whiskey which had been slightly diluted with water.

"Now," he said, "we will drink a toast, my farfaring-knight of the desert. Shall it be that first toast: 'The Ladies—God bless them!' or—"

"No!" answered Wiley, and the Colonel silently laughed.

"Well said, my young friend," he replied, nodding wisely. "Even at your age you have learned something of life. No, let it be the toast that Socrates drank, and that rare company who sat at the Banquet. To Love! they drank; but not to love of woman. To love of mankind—of Man! To Friendship! In short, here's to you, my friend, and may you never regret this night!"

They drank it in silence, and as Wiley sat thinking, the Colonel became reminiscent.

"Ah, there was a company," he said, smiling

mellowly, "such as the world will never see again. Agatho and Socrates, Aristophanes and Alcibiades, the picked men of ancient Athens; lying comfortably on their couches with the food before them and inviting their souls with wine. They began in the evening and in the morning it was Socrates who had them all under the table. And yet, of all men, he was the most abstemious—he could drink or let it alone. Alcibiades, the drunkard, gave witness that night to the courage and hardihood of Socrates—how he had carried him and his armor from the battlefield of Potidaea, and outfaced the enemy at Delium; how he marched barefoot through the ice while the others, well shod, froze; and endured famine without complaining; yet again, in the feasts at the military table, he was the only person that appeared to enjoy them. There was a man, my friend, such as the world has never seen, the greatest philosopher of all time; but do you know what philosophy he taught?"

"No, I don't," admitted Wiley, and the Colonel sighed as he poured out a small libation.

"And yet," he said, "you are a man of parts, with an education, very likely, of the best. But our schools and Universities now teach a man everything except the meaning and purpose of life. When I was in school we read our Plato and Xenophon as you now read your German and French; but what we learned, above the language itself, was the thought of that ancient time. You learn to earn money and to fight your way through life, but Socrates taught that friendship is above everything and that Truth is the Ultimate Good. But, ah well; I weary you, for each age lives unto itself, and who cares for the thoughts of an old man?"

"No! Go on!" protested Wiley, but the Colonel sighed wearily and shook his head gloomily in thought.

"I had a friend once," he said at last, "who had the same rugged honesty of Socrates. He was a man of few words but I truly believe that he never told a lie. And yet," went on the Colonel with a rueful smile, "they tell me that my friend recanted and deceived me at the last!"

"*Who* told you?" put in Wiley, suddenly rousing from his silence and the Colonel glanced at him sharply.

"Ah, yes; well said, my friend! *Who* told me? Why, all of them—except my friend himself. I could not go to him with so much as a suggestion that he had betrayed the friendship of a lifetime; and he, no doubt, felt equally reluctant to explain what had never been charged. Yet I dared not approach him, for it was better to endure doubt than to suffer the certainty of his guilt. And so we drifted apart, and he moved away; and I have never seen my good friend since."

Wiley sat in stunned silence, but his heart leapt

up at this word of vindication for Honest John. To be sure his father had refused him help, and rebuked him for heckling the Widow, but loyalty ran strong in the Holman blood and he looked up at the Colonel and smiled.

"Next time you go inside," he said at last, "take a chance and ask your friend."

"I'll do that," agreed the Colonel, "but it won't be for some time because—well, I'm hiding out."

"Here, too," returned Wiley, "and I'm *never* going back. But say, listen; I'll tell *you* one now. You trusted your friend, and the bunch told you that he'd betrayed you; I trusted my girl, and she told me to my face that she'd sold me out for fifty thousand dollars. Fifty thousand, at the most; and I lost about a million and killed a man over it, to boot. You take a chance with your friends, but when you trust a woman—you don't take any chance at all."

"Ah, in self-defense?" inquired the Colonel politely. "I thought I noticed a hole in your shirt. Yes, pretty close work—between your arm and your ribs. I've had a few close calls, myself."

"Yes, but what do you think," demanded Wiley impatiently, "of a girl that will throw you down like that? I gave her the stock and to make it worth the money she turned around and ditched me. And then she looked me in the face and laughed!"

"If you had studied," observed the Colonel,

"the Republic of Plato you would have been saved your initial mistake; for it was an axiom among the Greeks that in all things women are inferior, and never to be trusted in large affairs. The great Plato pointed out, and it has never been controverted, that women are given to concealment and spite; and that in times of danger they are timid and cowardly, and should therefore have no voice in council. In fact, in the ideal State which he conceived, they were to be herded by themselves in a community dwelling and held in common by the state. There were to be no wives and no husbands, with their quarrels and petty bickerings, but the women were to be parceled out by certain controllers of marriage and required to breed men for the state. That is going rather far, and I hardly subscribe to it, but I think they should be kept in their place."

"Well, they are cowardly, all right," agreed Wiley bitterly, "but that's better than when they fight. Because then, if you oppose them, everybody turns against you; and if you don't, they've got you whipped!"

"Put it there!" exclaimed the Colonel, striking hands with him dramatically. "I swear, we shall get along famously. There is nothing I admire more than a gentle, modest woman, an ornament to her husband and her home; but when she puts on the trousers and presumes to question and dictate, what is there left for a gentleman to do?

He cannot strike her, for she is his wife and he has sworn to cherish and protect her; and yet, by the gods, she can make his life more miserable than a dozen quarrelsome men. What is there to do but what I have done—to close up my affairs and depart? If there is such a thing as love, long absence may renew it, and the sorrow may chasten her heart; but I agree with Solomon that it is better to dwell in a corner of the house-top than with a scolding woman in a wide house."

"You bet," nodded Wiley. "Gimme the desert solitude, every time. Is there any more whiskey in that bottle?"

"And yet—" mused the Colonel, "—well, here's to our mothers! And may we ever be dutiful sons! After all, my friend, no man can escape his duty; and if duty should call us to endure a certain martyrdom we have the example of Socrates to sustain us. If report is true he had a scolding wife—the name of Xanthippe has become a proverb—and yet what more noble than Socrates' rebuke to his son when he behaved undutifully towards his mother? Where else in all literature will you find a more exalted statement of the duty we all owe our parents than in Socrates' dialogue with Lamprocles, his son, as recorded in the Memorabilia of Xenophon? And if, living with Xanthippe and listening to her railings, he could yet attain to such heights of philosophy is it not possible that men like you and me might come, through his philosophy, to endure it? It is that which I am pondering while I am alone here in the desert; but my spirit is weak and that accursed camp robber made off with my volume of Plato."

"Well, personally," stated Wiley, his mind on the Widow, "I think I agree more with Plato. Let 'em keep in their place and not crush into business with their talk and their double-barreled shotguns."

"I beg your pardon, sir," said the Colonel, drawing himself up gravely, "but did you happen to come through Keno?"

"Never mind;" grumbled Wiley, "you might be the Sheriff. Tell me more about this married man, Socrates."

CHAPTER XXXI
THE BROKEN TRUST

To seek always for Truth and Justice and the common good of mankind has seldom had its earthly reward but, twenty-three hundred and fifteen years after he drank the cup of hemlock, the soul of Socrates received its oration. Not that the Colonel was hipped upon the subject of the ancients, for he talked mining and showed some copper claims as well; but a similar tragedy in his own domestic life had evoked a profound admiration for Socrates. And if Wiley understood what lay behind his words he gave no hint to the Colonel. Always, morning, noon and night, he listened respectfully, his lips curling briefly at some thought; and at the end of a week the Colonel was as devoted to him as he had been formerly to his father.

Yet when, as sometimes happened, the Colonel tried to draw him out, he shook his head stubbornly and was dumb. The problem that he had could not be solved by talk; it called for years to recover and forget; and if the Colonel once knew that his own daughter was involved he might rise up and demand a retraction. In his first rush of bitterness Wiley had stated without reservation that Virginia had sold him out for money, and the pride of the Huffs would scarcely allow this to pass unnoticed—and yet he would not retract it if he died for it. He knew from her own lips that Virginia had betrayed him, and it could never be explained away.

If she argued that she was misled by Blount and his associates, he had warned her before she left; and if she had thought that he was doing her an injustice, that was not the way to correct it. She had accepted a trust and she had broken that trust to gain a personal profit—and that was the unpardonable sin. He could have excused her if she had weakened or made some mistake, but she had betrayed him deliberately and willfully; and as he sat off by himself, mulling it over in his mind, his eyes became stern and hard. For the killing of Stiff Neck George he had no regrets, and the treachery of Blount did not surprise him; but he had given this woman his heart to keep and she had sold him for fifty thousand dollars. All the rest became as nothing but this wound refused to heal, for he had lost his faith in womankind. Had he loved her less, or trusted her less, it would not have rankled so deep; but she had been his one woman, whose goings and comings he watched for, and all the time she was playing him false.

He sat silent one morning in the cool shade of a wild grapevine, jerking the meat of a mountain sheep that he had killed; and as he worked mechanically, shredding the flesh into long strips, he watched the lower trail. Ten days had gone by since he had fled across the Valley, but the danger of pursuit had not passed and, as he saw a great owl that was nesting down below rise up blindly and flop away he paused and reached for his gun.

"Never mind," said the Colonel who had noticed the movement. "I expect an old Indian in with grub. But step into the cave and if it's who you think it is you can count on me till the hair slips."

Wiley stepped in quietly, strapping on his belt and pistol, and then the Colonel burst into a roar.

"It's Charley," he cried, leaping nimbly to his feet and putting up his gun. "Come on, boy—here's where we get that drink!"

Wiley looked out doubtfully as Heine rushed up and sniffed at the pans of meat, and then he ducked back and hid. Around the shoulder of the cliff came Death Valley Charley; but behind him, on a burro, was Virginia. He looked out again as the Colonel swore an oath and then she leapt off and ran towards them.

"Oh—*Father!*" she cried and hung about his neck while the astonished Colonel kissed her doubtfully.

"Well, well!" he protested as she fell to weeping, "what's the cause of all this distress? Is your mother not well, or—"

"We—we thought you were *dead!*" she burst out indignantly, "and Charley there knew—all the time!"

She let go of her father and turned upon Death Valley Charley, who was solicitously attending to Heine, and the Colonel spoke up peremptorily.

"Here, Charley!" he commanded, "let that gluttonous cur wait. What's this I hear from Virginia? Didn't you tell her I was perfectly well?"

"Why—why yes, sir; I did, sir," replied Charley, apologetically, "but—she only thought I was crazy. I told her, all the time—"

"Oh, Charley!" reproached Virginia, "didn't you know better than that? You only said it when you had those spells. Why didn't you tell me when you were feeling all right—and you denied it, I know, repeatedly!"

"The Colonel would kill me," mumbled Charley sullenly. "He told me not to tell. But I brought you the whiskey, sir; a whole big—"

"Never mind the whiskey," said the Colonel sharply. "Now, let's get to the bottom of this matter. Why should you think I was dead when I had merely absented myself—"

"But the body!" clamored Virginia. "We got word you were lost when your burro came in at the Borax works. And when we hired trackers, the Indians said you were lost—and your body was out in the sandhills!"

"It was that cursed camp-robber!" declared the

Colonel with conviction. "Well, I'm glad he's gone to his reward. It was only some rascal that came through here and stole my riding burro—did they care for old Jack at the Works? Well, I shall thank them for it kindly; and anything I can do—but what's the matter, Virginia?"

She had drawn away from him and was gazing about anxiously and Charley had slunk guiltily away.

"Why—where's Wiley?" she cried, clutching her father by the arm. "Oh, isn't he here, after all?"

"Wiley?" repeated the Colonel. "Why, who are you talking about? I never even heard of such a man."

"Oh, he's dead then; he's lost!" she sobbed, sinking down on the ground in despair. "Oh, I knew it, all the time! But that old Charley—"

She cast a hateful glance at him and the Colonel beckoned sternly.

"What now?" he demanded as Charley sidled near. "Who is this Mr. Wiley?"

"Why—er—Wiley; Wiley Holman, you know. I followed his tracks to the Gateway. Ain't he around here somewhere? I found this bottle——"
He held up the flask that he had given to Wiley, and the Colonel started back with a cry.

"What, a tall young fellow with leather puttees?"

"Oh, yes, yes!" answered Virginia, suddenly

springing to her feet again. "We followed him—isn't he here?"

The Colonel turned slowly and glanced at the cave, where Wiley was still hiding close, and then he cleared his throat.

"Well, kindly explain first why you should be following this gentleman, and—"

"Oh, he's here, then!" sighed Virginia and fell into her father's arms, at which Charley scuttled rapidly away.

"Mr. Holman," spoke up the Colonel, as Wiley did not stir, "may I ask you to come out here and explain?"

There was a rustle inside the cave and at last Wiley came out, stuffing a strip of dried meat into his hip pocket.

"I'll come out, yes," he said, "but, as I'm about to go, I'll leave it to your daughter to explain."

He picked up his canteen and started down to the water-hole, but the Colonel called him sternly back.

"My friend," he said, "it is the custom among gentlemen to answer a courteous question. I must ask you then what there is between you and my daughter, and why she should follow you across Death Valley?"

"There is nothing between us," answered Wiley categorically, "and I don't know why she followed me—that is, if she really did."

"Well, I did!" sobbed Virginia, burying her face

on her father's breast, "but I wish I hadn't now!"

"Huh!" grunted Wiley and stumped off down the trail where he filled his canteen at the pool. He was mad, mad all over, and yet he experienced a strange thrill at the thought of Virginia following him. He had left her smiling and shaking hands with Blount, but a curse had been on the money, and her conscience had forced her to follow him. It had been easy, for her, with a burro to ride on and Death Valley Charley to guide her; but with him it had been different. He had fled from arrest and it was only by accident that he had won to the water-hole in time. But yet, she had followed him; and now she would apologize and explain, as she had explained it all once before. Well, since she had come—and since the Colonel was watching him—he shouldered his canteen and came back.

"My daughter tells me," began the Colonel formally, "that you are the son of my old friend, John Holman; and I trust that you will take my hand."

He held out his hand and Wiley blinked as he returned the warm clasp of his friend. Ten days of companionship in the midst of that solitude had knitted their souls together and he loved the old Colonel like a father.

"That's all right," he muttered. "And—say, hunt up the Old Man! Because he thinks the world of you, still."

"I will do so," replied the Colonel, "but will you do me a favor? By gad, sir; I can't let you go. No, you must stay with me, Wiley, if that is your name; I want to talk with you later, about your father. But now, as a favor, since Virginia has come so far, I will ask you to sit down and listen to her. And—er—Wiley; just a moment!" He beckoned him to one side and spoke low in his ear. "About that woman who betrayed your trust—perhaps I'd better not mention her to Virginia?"

Wiley's eyes grew big and then they narrowed. The Colonel thought there was another woman. How could he, proud soul, even think for a moment that Virginia herself had betrayed him? No, to his high mind it was inconceivable that a daughter of his should violate a trust; and there was Virginia, watching them.

"Very well," replied Wiley, and smiled to himself as he laid down his gun and canteen. He led the way up the creek to where a gnarled old cottonwood cast its shadow against the cliff and smoothed out a seat against the bank. "Now sit down," he said, "and let's have this over with before the Colonel gets wise. He's a fine old gentleman and if his daughter took after him I wouldn't be dodging the sheriff."

"Well, I came to tell you," began Virginia bravely, "that I'm sorry for what I've done. And to show you that I mean it I gave Blount back his stock."

Wiley gazed at her grimly for a moment and then he curled up his lip. "Why not come through," he asked at last, "and acknowledge that he held it out on you?"

Virginia started and then she smiled wanly.

"No," she said, "it wasn't quite that. And yet—well, he didn't really give it to me."

"I knew it!" exploded Wiley, "the doggoned piker! But of course you made a clean-up on your other stock?"

"No, I didn't! I gave that away, too! But Wiley, why won't you listen to me? I didn't intend to do it, but he explained it all so nicely—"

"Didn't I tell you he would?" he raged.

"Yes, but listen; you don't understand. When I went to him first I asked for Father's stock and—he must have known what was coming. I guess he saw the bills. Anyway, he told me then that he had always loved my father, and that he wanted to protect us from you; and so, he said, he was just holding my father's stock to keep you from getting it away from us. And then he called in some friends of his; and oh, they all became so indignant that I thought I couldn't be wrong! Why, they showed me that you would make millions by the deal, and all at our expense; and then—I don't know, something came over me. We'd been poor so long, and it would make you so rich; and, like a fool, I went and did it."

"Well, that's all right," said Wiley. "I forgive

you, and all that; but don't let your father know. He's got old-fashioned ideas about keeping a trust and—say, do you know what he thinks? I happened to mention, the first night I got in, that a woman had thrown me down; and he just now took me aside and told me not to worry because he'd never mention the lady to you. He thinks it was somebody else."

"Oh," breathed Virginia, and then she sat silent while he kicked a hole in the dirt and waited. He was willing to concede anything, agree to anything, look pleasant at anything, until the ordeal was over; and then he intended to depart. Where he would go was a detail to be considered later when he felt the need of something to occupy his mind; right now he was only thinking that she looked very pale—and there was a tired, hunted look in her eyes. She had nerves, of course, the same as he had, and the trip across Death Valley had been hard on her; but if she suffered now, he had suffered also, and he failed to be as sorry as he should.

"You'll be all right now," he said at last, when it seemed she would never speak up, "and I'm glad you found your father. He'll go back with you now and take a fall out of Blount and—well, you won't feel so poor, any more."

"Yes, I will," returned Virginia, suddenly rousing up and looking at him with haggard eyes. "I'll always feel poor, because if I gave you back all

I had it wouldn't be a tenth of what you lost."

"Oh, that's all right," grumbled Wiley. "I don't care about the money. Are they hunting me for murder, or what?"

"Oh, no; not for anything!" she answered eagerly. "You'll come back, won't you, Wiley? Mother was watching you through her glasses, and she says George fired first. They aren't trying to arrest you; all they want you to do is to give up and stand a brief trial. And I'll help you, Wiley; oh, I've just got to do something or I'll be miserable all my life!"

"You're tired now," said Wiley. "It'll look different, pretty soon; and—well, I don't think I'll go in, right now."

"But where will you go?" she entreated piteously. "Oh, Wiley, can't you see I'm sorry? Why can't you forgive me and let me try to make amends, instead of making both our lives so miserable?"

"I don't know," answered Wiley. "It's just the way I feel. I've got nothing *against* you; I just want to get away and forget a few things that you've done."

"And then?" she asked, and he smiled enigmatically.

"Well, maybe you'll forget me, too."

"But Father!" she objected as he rose up suddenly and started off down the creek. "He thinks we're lovers, you know." Wiley stopped and the cold anger in his eyes gave way to a look of doubt. "Why not pretend we are?" she suggested wistfully. "Not really, but just before him. I told him we'd quarreled—and he knows I followed after you. Just to-day, Wiley; and then you can go. But if my father should think—"

"Well, all right," he broke in, and as they stepped out into the open she slipped her hand into his.

CHAPTER XXXII

A HUFF

The Colonel was sitting in the shade of a wild grapevine rapping out a series of questions at Charley, but at sight of the young people coming back hand in hand, he paused and smiled understandingly.

"What now?" he said. "Is there a new earth and a new heaven? Ah, well; then Virginia's trip was worthwhile. But Charley here is so full of signs and wonders that my brain is fairly in a whirl. The Germans, it seems, have made a forty-two-centimeter gun that is blasting down cities in France; and the Allies, to beat them, are constructing still larger ones made out of tungsten that is mined from the Paymaster. Yes, yes, Charley, that's all right, I don't doubt your word, but we'll call on Wiley for the details."

He laughed indulgently and poured Charley out a drink which made his eyes blink and snap and then he waved him graciously away.

"Take your burros up the canyon," he suggested briefly, and when Charley was gone he smiled. "Now," he said, as Virginia sat down beside him, "what's all this about the Paymaster and Keno?"

"Well," began Virginia as Wiley sat silent, "there really was tungsten in the mine. Wiley discovered it first—he was just going through the town when he saw that specimen in my collection—and since then,—oh, everything has happened!"

"By the dog!" exclaimed the Colonel starting quickly to his feet. "Do you mean that Crazy Charley spoke the truth? Is the mine really open and the town full of people and—"

"You wouldn't know it!" cried Virginia, triumphantly. "All that heavy, white quartz was tungsten!"

"What? That waste on the dump? But how much is it worth? Old Charley says it's better than gold!"

"It is!" she answered. "Why, some of that rock ran five thousand dollars to the ton!"

"Five—thousand!" repeated the Colonel, and then he whirled on Wiley. "What's the reason, then," he demanded, "that you're hiding out here in the hills? Didn't you get possession of the mine?"

"Under a bond and lease," explained Wiley shortly. "I failed to meet the final payment."

"Why—how much was this payment?" inquired the Colonel cautiously, as he sensed the sudden constraint. "It seems to me the mine should have paid it at once."

"Fifty thousand," answered Wiley, gazing glumly at the ground and the Colonel opened his eyes!

"Fifty thousand!" he exclaimed. "Only fifty thousand dollars? Well! What were the circumstances, Wiley?"

He stood expectant and as Wiley boggled and hesitated Virginia rose up and stood beside him.

"He got the bond and lease from Blount," she began, talking rapidly, "and when Blount found that the white quartz was tungsten ore, he did all he could to block Wiley. When Wiley first came through the town and stopped at our house he knew that that white quartz was tungsten; but he couldn't do anything, then. And then, by-and-by, when he tried to bond the mine, Blount came up himself and tried to work it."

"He did, eh?" cried the Colonel. "Well, by what right, I'd like to know, did he dare to take possession of the Paymaster?"

"Oh, he'd bought up all the stock; and Mother, she took yours and—"

"What?" yelled the Colonel, and then he closed down his jaw and his blue eyes sparkled ominously. "Proceed," he said. "The information, first—but, by the gods, he shall answer for this!"

"But all the time," went on Virginia hastily, "the mine belonged to Wiley. It had been sold for taxes—and he bought it!"

"Ah!" observed the Colonel, and glanced at him shrewdly for he saw now where the tale was going.

"Well," continued Virginia, "when Blount saw

Wiley wanted it he came up and took it himself. And he hired Stiff Neck George to herd the mine and keep Wiley and everybody away. But when he was working it, why Wiley came back and claimed it under the tax sale; and he went right up to the mine and took away George's gun—and kicked him down the dump!"

"He did!" exclaimed the Colonel, but Wiley did not look up, for his mind was on the end of the tale.

"And then—oh, it's all mixed up, but Blount couldn't find any gold and so he leased the mine to Wiley. And the minute he found that the white quartz was tungsten, and worth three dollars a pound, he was mad as anything and did everything he could to keep him from meeting the payment. But Wiley went ahead and shipped a lot of ore and made a lot of money in spite of him. He cleaned out the mine and fixed up the mill and oh, Father, you wouldn't know the place!"

"Probably not!" returned the Colonel, "but proceed with your story. Who holds the Paymaster, now?"

"Why Blount, of course, and he's moved back to town and is simply shoveling out the ore!"

"The scoundrel!" burst out the Colonel. "Wiley, we will return to Keno immediately and bring this blackguard to book! I have a stake in this matter, myself!"

"Nope, not for me!" answered Wiley wearily. "You haven't heard all the story. I fell down on the final payment—it makes no difference how—and when I came back Blount had jumped the mine and Stiff Neck George was in charge. But instead of warning me off he hid behind a car and—well, I don't care to go back there, now."

"Why, certainly! You must!" declared the Colonel warmly. "You were acting in self-defense and I consider that your conduct was justified. In fact, my boy, I wish to congratulate you—Charley tells me he had the drop on you."

"Yes, sure," grumbled Wiley, "but you aren't the judge—and there's a whole lot more to the story. It happens that I took an option on Blount's Paymaster stock, but when I offered the payment he protested the contract and took the case to court. Now—he's got the town of Vegas in his inside vest pocket, the lawyers and judges and all; and do you think for a minute he's going to let me come back and take away those four hundred thousand shares?"

"Four hundred thousand?" repeated the Colonel incredulously, "do you mean to tell me—"

"Yes, you bet I do!" said Wiley, "and I'll tell you something else. According to the dates on the back of those certificates it was Blount that sold you out. He sold all his promotion stock before the panic; and then, when the price was down to nothing, he turned around and bought it back. I knew from the first that he'd lied about my father and I kept after him till I got my hands on that stock—and then, when I'd proved it, he tried to put the blame on you!"

"The devil!" exclaimed the Colonel, and paced up and down, snapping his fingers and muttering to himself. "The cowardly dastard!" he burst out at last. "He has poisoned ten years of my life. I must hurry back at once and go to John Holman and apologize to him publicly for this affront. After all the years that we were pardners in everything, and then to have me doubt his integrity! He was the soul of honor, one man in ten thousand; and yet I took the word of this lying Blount against the man I called My Friend! I remember, by gad, as if it were yesterday, the first time I really knew your father; and Blount was squeezing me, then. I owed him fifteen thousand dollars on a certain piece of property that was worth fifty thousand at least; and at the very last moment, when he was about to foreclose, John Holman loaned me the money. He mortgaged his cattle at the other bank and put the money in my hand, and Blount cursed him for an interfering fool! That was Blount, the Shylock, and Honest John Holman; and I turned against my friend."

"Yes, that's right," agreed Wiley, "but if you want to make up for it, make 'em quit calling him 'Honest John'!"

"No, indeed," cried the Colonel, his voice

tremulous with emotion. "He shall still be called Honest John; and if any man doubts it or speaks the name fleeringly he shall answer personally to me. And now, about this stock—what was that, Virginia, that you were saying about my holdings?"

"Why, Mother put them up as collateral on a loan, and Blount claimed them at the end of the first month."

"All my stock? Well, by the horn-spoon—how much did your mother borrow? Eight—hundred? Eight hundred dollars? Well, that is enough, on the face of it—but never mind, I will recover the stock. It is certainly a revelation of human nature. The moment I am reported dead, these vultures strip my family of their all."

"Well, I was one of them," spoke up Wiley bluntly, "but you don't need to blame my father. When I was having trouble with Mrs. Huff he wrote up and practically disowned me."

"So you were one of them," observed the Colonel mildly. "And you had trouble with Mrs. Huff? But no matter?" he went on. "We can discuss all that later—now to return to this lawsuit, with Blount. Do I understand that you had an option on his entire four hundred thousand shares?"

"For twenty thousand dollars," answered Wiley, "and he was glad to get it—but, of course, when I opened up that big body of tungsten, the stock was worth into millions. That is, if he could keep me from making both payments. He fought me from the start, but I put up the twenty thousand; and the clerk of the court is holding it yet, unless the case is decided. But Blount knew he could beat it, if he could keep me from buying the mine under the terms of my bond and lease; and now that he's in possession, taking out thirty or forty thousand every day, I'm licked before I begin. In fact, the case is called already and lost by default if I know that black-leg lawyer of mine."

"But hire a good lawyer!" protested the Colonel. "A man has a right to his day in court and you have never appeared."

"No, and I never will," spoke up Wiley despondently. "There's a whole lot to this case that you don't know. And the minute I appear they'll arrest me for murder and railroad me off to the Pen. No, I'm not going back, that's all."

"But Wiley," reasoned the Colonel, "you've got great interests at stake—and your father will help you, I'm sure."

"No, he won't," declared Wiley. "There isn't anybody that can help me, because Blount is in control of the courts. And I might as well add that I was run out of Vegas by a Committee appointed for the purpose." He rose up abruptly, rolling his sullen eyes on Virginia and the Colonel alike. "In fact," he burst out, "I haven't got a friend on the east side of Death Valley Sink."

"But on the west side," suggested the Colonel, drawing Virginia to his side, "you have two good friends that I know—"

"Wait till you hear it all," broke in Wiley, bitterly, "and you're likely to change your mind. No, I'm busted, I tell you, and the best thing I can do is drift and never come back."

"And Virginia?" inquired the Colonel. "Am I right in supposing—"

"No," he flared up. "Friend Virginia has quit me, along with—"

"Why, Wiley!" cried Virginia, and he started and fell silent as he met her reproachful gaze. For the sake of the Colonel they were supposed to be lovers, whose quarrel had been happily made up, but this was very un-loverlike.

"Well, I don't deserve it," he muttered at last, "but friend Virginia has promised to stay with me."

"Yes, I'm going to stay with him," spoke up Virginia quickly, "because it was all my fault. I'm going to go with him, Father, wherever he goes and—"

"God bless you, my daughter!" said the Colonel, smiling proudly, "and never forget you're a Huff!"

CHAPTER XXXIII
THE FIERY FURNACE

To be a Huff, of course, was to be brave and true and never go back on a friend; but as the Colonel that evening began to speak on the subject, Virginia crept off to bed. She was tired from her night trip across the Sink of Death Valley, with only Crazy Charley for a guide; but it was Wiley, the inexorable, who drove her off weeping, for he would not take her hand. His mind was still fixed on the Gethsemane of the soul that he had gone through in Blount's bank at Vegas, and strive as she would she could not bring him back to play his poor part as lover. Whether she loved him or not was not the question—not even if she was willing to throw away her life by following him in his wanderings. Three times he had trusted her and three times she had played him false—and was that the honor of the Huffs?

She was penitent now and, in the presence of her father, more gentle and womanly than seemed possible; but next week or next month or in the long years to come, was she the woman he could trust? They passed before his eyes in a swift series of images, the days when he had trusted her before; and always, behind her smile, there was something else, something cold and calculating and unkind. Her eyes were soft now, and gentle and imploring, but they had looked at him before with scorn and hateful laughter, when he had staked his soul on her word. He had trusted her—too far—and before Blount and all his sycophants she had made him a mock and a reviling.

The Colonel was talking, for his mood was expansive, but at last he fell silent and waited.

"Wiley, my boy," he said when Wiley looked up, "you must not let the past overmaster you. We all make mistakes, but if our hearts are right there is nothing that should cause vain regrets. I judged from what you said once that your present disaster is due to a misplaced trust—in fact, if I remember, to a woman. But do not let this treachery, this betrayal of a trust, turn your mind against all womankind. I have known many noble and high-minded women whom I would trust with my very life; and since Virginia, as I gather, has offered to bind up your wounds, I hope you will not remain embittered. She is my daughter, of course, and my love may have blinded me; but in all the long years she has been at my side, I can think of no instance in which she has played me false. Her nature is passionate, and she is sometimes quick to anger, but behind it all she is devotion itself and you can trust her absolutely."

He paused expectantly, but as Wiley made no response he rose up and knocked out his pipe.

"Well, good night," he said. "It is time we were retiring if we are to cross the Valley to-morrow. Have a drink? Well, all right; it's just as well. You're a good boy, Wiley; I'm proud of you."

He clapped him on the shoulder as he went off to bed, but Wiley sat brooding by the fire. Death Valley Charley took his blankets and rolled up in the creek bed, so that his burros could not sneak by him in the night, and Heine laid down beside him; but when all was quiet Wiley rose up silently and tiptoed about the camp. He strapped on his pistol and picked up his gun, but as he was groping in the darkness for his canteen Heine trotted up and flapped his ears. It was his sign of friendship, like wagging his tail, and Wiley patted him quietly; but when he was gone, he lifted the canteen and slung it over his shoulder. In the land where he was going there were more dangers than one, but lack of water was the greatest. He stepped out into the moonlight and then, from the cave, he heard a muffled sound. Virginia was there and he was running away from her. He listened again—she was crying! Not weeping aloud or in choking sobs but in stifled, heart-broken sighs. He lowered his gun and stood scowling and irresolute, then he turned back and went to bed.

In the morning they started late, resting in the shade of the Gateway until the sun had swung to the west; and then, as the shadow of the Panamints stretched out across the Valley, they repacked and started down the slope. In the lead went old Jinny, the mother of the bunch, and Jack and Johnny and Baby; and following behind his burros, paced Death Valley Charley with a long, willow club in his hand. The Colonel strode ahead, his mind on weighty matters; and behind him came Virginia on her free-footed burro with Wiley plodding silently in the rear. At irregular intervals Heine would drop back from the lead and sniff at them each in turn, but nothing was said, for the air was furnace dry and they were saving their strength for the sand.

At sundown they reached the edge of the first yielding sand-dune that presaged the long pull to come and Death Valley Charley stopped and opened up a water-can while the burros gathered eagerly around. Then he poured each of them a drink in his shapeless old hat and started them across the Sink.

"Now, you see?" he said, "you see where Jinny goes? She heads straight for Stove-Pipe Hole. She knows she gits water there and that makes her hurry—and the others they tag along behind."

He took another drink from the Colonel's private stock and smiled as he smacked his lips. "It's hot to-day," he observed, squinting down his eyes and gazing ahead through the haze; "yes, it's hot for this time of year. But Virginia, you ride; and when Tom won't go no further, git off and he'll lead you to camp."

He went on ahead, swinging his club and laughing, and Heine trotted soberly at his side; and as he followed the trough of sand-wave after sand-wave, the rest plodded along behind. A dry, baking heat seemed to rise up from the ground and the air was heavy and still; the burros began to groan as they toiled up the slope and their flanks turned wet with sweat; and then, as they topped a wave, they felt the scorching breath of the Sink. It came in puffs like the waves of some great sea upon whose shores they had set their feet; a seething, heaving sea of heat, breathing death along its lonely beach. It struck through their clothes like a blast of wind or the shimmering glow of a furnace and at each drink of water the sweat damped their brows and trickled in streams down their faces. A wearied burro halted and, as Charley chased him with his club, the rest rushed ahead to escape; and then, as they came to the crest of the wave, Virginia's burro stopped dead.

"I'll lead him," she said as Wiley came up, and started after the pack. Wiley walked along beside her, for he saw that she was spent; and as her slender feet sank deep in the yielding sand she lagged and slowed down, and stopped. Then as she turned to take her canteen from the saddle, she swayed and clutched at the horn.

"You'd better ride," he said and, taking her in his arms, he lifted her to the saddle like a child. Then he walked along behind, flogging the burro into action, but still they lagged to the rear. The moon rose up gleaming and cast black shadows along the sand-dunes, and in the lee of the wind-wracked mesquite trees; and from the darkness ahead of them they could hear crazy shoutings as Charley belabored his fleeing animals. They showed dim and ghostly, as they topped a distant ridge; and then Wiley and Virginia were alone. The pack-train, the Colonel and Death Valley Charley had vanished behind the crest of a wave; and as Wiley stopped to listen Virginia drooped in the saddle and fell, very gently, into his arms.

He held her a moment, overcome with sudden pity, and then in a rush of unexpected emotion, he crushed her to his breast and kissed her. She was his, after all, to cherish, and protect; a frail reed, broken by his hand; and as he gave her water and bathed her face he remembered her weeping in the night. Her tears had been for him, whom she had followed so far only to find him harsh and unforgiving; and now, weak from grief, she had fainted in his arms, which had never reached out to console her. He gathered her to his breast in a belated atonement and as he kissed her again she stirred. Then he put her down, but when she felt his hands slacken she reached up and caught him by the neck. So she held him a while, until something gave way within him and he pressed his lips to hers.

CHAPTER XXXIV
A CLEAN-UP

A cool breeze drew down through Emigrant Wash and soothed the fever heat of Death Valley, and as the morning star rose up like a blazing beacon, Wiley carried Virginia to Stove-Pipe. They had sat for hours on the crest of a sandhill, looking out over the sea of waves that seemed to ride on and mingle in the moonlight, and with no one to listen they had talked out their hearts and pledged the future in a kiss. Then they had gazed long and rested, looking up at the countless stars that obscured the Milky Way with their pin-points; and when the Colonel had found them Wiley was carrying her in his arms as if her weight were nothing.

They camped at Stove-Pipe that day while Virginia gained back her strength, and at last they came in sight of Keno. She was riding now and Wiley was walking, with his head bowed down in thought; but when he looked up she reached out, smiling wistfully, and touched him with her hand. But the Colonel strode ahead, his head held high, his eagle eyes searching the distance; and when people ran out to greet him he thrust them aside, for he had spied Samuel Blount in the crowd.

Blount was standing just outside the Widow's gate and a voice, unmistakable, was demanding in frantic haste the return of certain shares of stock. It was hardly the time for a business transaction, for her husband was returning as from the dead, but a sudden sense of her misused stewardship had driven the Widow to distraction.

"What now?" demanded the Colonel, as he appeared upon the scene and his wife made a rush to embrace him. "Is this the time for scolding? Why, certainly I was alive—why should anybody doubt it? You may await me in the house, Aurelia!"

"But Henry!" she wailed. "Oh, I thought you were dead—and this devil has robbed me of everything!"

She pointed a threatening finger at Blount, who stepped forward, his lower lip trembling.

"Why, how are you, Colonel!" he exclaimed with affected heartiness. "Well, well; we thought you were dead."

"So I hear!" observed the Colonel, and looked at him so coldly that Blount blushed and withdrew his outstretched hand. "So I hear, sir!" he repeated, "but you were misinformed—I have come back to protect my rights."

"He took all your stock," cried the Widow, vindictively, "on a loan of eight hundred dollars. And now he won't give it back."

"Never mind," returned the Colonel. "I will

attend to all that if you will go in and cook me some dinner. And next time I leave home I would recommend, Madam, that you leave my business affairs alone."

"But Henry," she began, but he gazed at her so sternly that she turned and slipped away.

"And you, sir," continued the Colonel, his words ringing out like pistol shots as he unloosed his wrath upon Blount, "I would like to inquire what excuse you have to offer for imposing on my wife and child? Is it true, as I hear, that you have taken my stock on a loan of eight hundred dollars?"

"Why—why, no! That is, Colonel Huff—"

"Have you the stock in your possession?" demanded the Colonel peremptorily. "Yes or no, now; and no 'buts' about it!"

"Why, yes; I have," admitted Blount in a scared voice, "but I came by it according to law!"

"You did not, sir!" retorted the Colonel, "because it was all in my name and my wife had no authority to transfer it. Do you deny the fact? Well, then give me back my stock or I shall hold you, sir, personally responsible!"

Blount started back, for he knew the import of those dread words, and then he heaved a great sigh.

"Very well," he said, "but I loaned her eight hundred dollars—"

"Wiley!" called the Colonel, beckoning him

quickly from the crowd. "Give me the loan of eight hundred dollars."

And at that Blount opened up his eyes.

"Oho!" he said, "so Wiley is with you? Well, just a moment, Mr. Huff." He turned to a man who stood beside him. "Arrest that man!" he said. "He killed my watchman, George Norcross."

"Not so fast!" rapped out the Colonel, fixing the officer with steely eyes. "Mr. Holman is under my protection. Ah, thank you, Wiley—here is your money, Mr. Blount, with fifty dollars more for interest. And now I will thank you for that stock."

"Do you set yourself up," demanded Blount with sudden bluster, "as being above the law?"

"No, sir, I do not," replied the Colonel tartly. "But before we go any further I must ask you to restore my stock. Your order is sufficient, if the certificates are elsewhere—"

"Well—all right!" sighed Blount, and wrote out an order which Colonel Huff gravely accepted. "And now," went on Blount, "I demand that you step aside and allow Wiley Holman to be taken."

The Colonel's eyes narrowed, and he motioned the officer aside as he laid his own hand on Wiley's shoulder.

"Every citizen of the state," he said with dignity, "has the authority to arrest a fugitive—and Mr. Holman is my prisoner. Is that satisfactory to you, Mr. Officer?"

"Why—why, yes," stammered the Constable and as the Colonel smiled Blount forgot his studied repose. He had been deprived in one minute of a block of stock that was worth a round million dollars and the sting of his great loss maddened him.

"You, may smile, sir," he burst out, "but as sure as there's a law I'll put Wiley Holman in the Pen. And if you knew the truth, if you knew what he has done; I wonder, now, if you would go to such lengths? You might ask your wife how she has fared in your absence—or ask Virginia there! Didn't he send her as his messenger, to make a fake payment that would have deprived her and her mother of their rights? If it hadn't been for me your two hundred thousand shares wouldn't be worth two hundred cents. I ask Virginia now—didn't he send you to my bank—"

"What?" demanded the Colonel, suddenly whirling upon his daughter, but Virginia avoided his eyes.

"Yes," she said, "he did send me down—and I betrayed my trust. But it's just because of that that we'll stand by him now—"

"Virginia!" said the Colonel, speaking with painful distinctness. "Do I understand that you were—that woman? And did Mr. Blount here, by any means whatever, persuade you to violate your trust?"

"Yes, he did!" cried out Virginia, "but it was all

my fault and I don't want Mr. Blount blamed for it. I did it out of meanness, but I was sorry for it afterwards and—oh, I wonder if I've got any mail." She broke away and dashed into the house and the Colonel brushed back his hair.

"A Huff!" he murmured. "My God, what a blow! And Wiley, how can we ever repay you?"

"Never mind," answered Wiley as he took the old man's hand. "I don't care about the money."

"No, but the wrong, the disgrace," protested the Colonel, brokenly, and then he flared up at Blount.

"You scoundrel, sir!" he cried. "How dared you induce my daughter to violate her sacred trust? By the gods, Sam Blount, I am greatly tempted—"

"It's come!" called Virginia, running gayly down the steps, but at sight of her father she stopped. "Well, there it is," she said, putting a paper in his hand. "It shows that I was sorry, anyway."

"What is this?" inquired the Colonel, fumbling feebly for his glasses, and Virginia snatched the paper away.

"It's a letter from my lawyers!" she said, smiling wickedly. "And we'll show it to Mr. Blount."

She took it over and put it in Blount's hands, and as he read the first line he turned pale.

"Why—Virginia!" he gasped and then he

clutched at his heart and reached out quickly for the fence. "Why—why, I thought that was all settled! I certainly understood it was—and what authority had you to interfere?"

"Wiley's power of attorney," she answered defiantly, "I fired that crooked lawyer, after you'd got him all fixed, and hired a good one with my stock."

"My Lord!" moaned Blount, "and after all I'd done for you!" And then he collapsed and was borne into the house. But Wiley, who had been so calm, suddenly leapt for the letter and read it through to the end.

"Holy—jumping—Judas!" he burst out, running over to the Colonel who was standing with lackluster eyes. "Look here what Virginia has done! She's bought all Blount's stock, under that option I had, and cleaned him—down to a cent. She's won back the mine, and we can all go in together—"

"Virginia!" spoke up the Colonel, beckoning her sternly to him. "Come down here, I wish to speak to you."

She came down slowly and as her father began to talk the tears rose quickly to her eyes, but when Wiley took her hand she smiled back wistfully and crept within the circle of his arm.

Center Point Large Print
600 Brooks Road / PO Box 1
Thorndike, ME 04986-0001 USA

(207) 568-3717

US & Canada:
1 800 929-9108
www.centerpointlargeprint.com